P9-CEF-390

"You can't run forever . . ."

The pages helped her disarm and put her horses away. The sun had set, and it was dim inside the pavilion. Suddenly something flashed across her field of vision, gleaming like a blade. It was the last thing she saw. She felt something slash at the back of her knees, and she fell.

"You can't run forever, you arrogant bitch," something whispered in her ear. "Give it up now, before I do *this* to you outside. Or *this*."

You couldn't be hurt in VR, not truly hurt; Mary felt only a slight tingle as one part after another was cut away. She set her teeth and endured. Blinded, hamstrung, and helpless, while the anonymous voice whispered curses in her ear, she could do nothing to stop him. But if she hung on long enough, rather than escaping outside, Nick or somebody might come along and see him. . . .

My thanks to Hilary of Serendip for checking the fighting scenes, Hal Ravn for computers and physics, Tristan av Ravnsborg for knowing all about games, Rachel Holmen for suggesting the title, and *ab initio* to Marianna of Silversea for saying, "Oh, write *that* one! I want to read it!" Most of what I know about global warming I got from James Burke's television production *After the Warming* (1990). The Kingdom of the West in the Society for Creative Anachronism is real.

A POINT OF HONOR

DOROTHY J. HEYDT

DAW BOOKS, INC.
DONALD A. WOLLHEIM, FOUNDER
375 Hudson Street, New York, NY 10014
ELIZABETH R. WOLLHEIM
SHEILA E. GILBERT
PUBLISHERS

Copyright © 1998 by Dorothy J. Heydt.

All Rights Reserved.

Cover art by Romas Kukalis.

DAW Book Collectors No. 1083.

DAW Books are distributed by Penguin Putnam Inc.

All characters and events in this book are fictitious.
Any resemblance to persons living or dead is
strictly coincidental.

If you purchase this book without a cover you should be aware that this book may have been stolen property and reported as "unsold and destroyed" to the publisher. In such case neither the author nor the publisher has received any payment for this "stripped book."

First Printing, April 1998

1 2 3 4 5 6 7 8 9

DAW TRADEMARK REGISTERED
U.S. PAT. OFF. AND FOREIGN COUNTRIES
—MARCA REGISTRADA
HECHO EN U.S.A.

PRINTED IN THE U.S.A.

Chapter 1

One Damn Thing After Another

The cross-shaped eyeslit framed the image of a knight in a glittering helm, his black surcote embroidered with silver crescents. His white destrier pawed the ground with an ivory forehoof and tossed its head. Sir Mary de Courcy licked her lips. The knight's long lance centered the cross as a tiny disk, for it was pointed straight at her head.

His first mistake.

Below the eyeslit a dozen small holes let in air, never enough and cleverly scented with dust and horse. Mary sucked in a deep breath and let it out again; from a long way away she could feel her heart pounding.

The Lists pages scurried out of the way as the two knights urged their horses into place, either side the barrier. Behind Mary's head the voices in the gallery fell silent as a trumpet sounded; it echoed from ear to ear inside her helm.

"Oyez, oyez!" the herald cried. "In these Winchester Lists in honor of St. Martin, upon the field of honor do meet Sir Dewi of Carlisle and Sir Mary de Courcy." And Mary settled her lance into its rest, pointed straight at Sir Dewi's heart. He was a renowned fighter and a crafty one, but he'd just let it slip that he tended to aim high.

For Mary also it was important to take careful aim. Sir Dewi couldn't be killed, but his horse might be. It was a beautiful creature, all silver-white and seafoam, with dangerous dark eyes, and Mary wanted it—or, at worst, to know where it came from.

"Well met, de Courcy!" Sir Dewi shouted, his deep voice booming across the field. "I shall knock you to the earth as gently as I can."

Sir Mary only raised her shield. *Sable, within an orle of lighted candles the sun in his splendor, all proper.* It was part of her fame that she never boasted aloud, only let her arms boast for her: a bright sun surrounded by a ring of envious candle flames.

(She had started out on the tourney circuit with a soft, maidenly voice and without the funds to get it augmented; but Sir Dewi didn't need to know that.)

"Laissez aller!" the herald cried, and Sir Dewi touched his spurs to his horse's sides and galloped toward the center of the field. Mary did the same. The little silver disk of his lancepoint swelled in the cross of her eyepiece—

CRASH

—and she had swayed aside to move her head out of line just at the right moment, while her own lance had taken Sir Dewi right in his well-armored heart. Her arms tingled with the lance's impact and her backside was numb against the saddle's high back, but that was the advantage of *Chivalry:* You never got really hurt. Her lance was in splinters, and Sir Dewi was on the ground. She brought her horse round and trotted up to the center of the field. "Do you yield?"

"Yuh—" Sir Dewi sucked in breath. "Yes, I yield, dammit. I can't move."

"Page," Mary said.

The page popped up beside her stirrup, wearing a green tabard marked with Winchester's arms and looking like a ten-year-old boy, fair haired and smooth skinned. They all looked like that; somebody ought to fix it. "Sir Dewi of Carlisle. His ransom, one thousand marks. His armor, five hundred. His sword Pride's Downfall, three hundred. His horse, six hundred. Total, two thousand four hundred marks.

"In addition, Sir Dewi has broken his left hip, and his chirurgery will cost him six hundred marks. Sir Dewi offers ransom."

"Page, Sir Dewi may ransom his person, his armor, and his sword. I'll keep his horse. And his chirurgeon's payment is on me. In the name of God and for the favor of good St. Martin."

The herald cried the terms aloud as Sir Mary rode from the field. "Page, let's see a tally," she said, and the darkness inside her helm lit up.

From Squire Cadwaladr of Powys	+ 700
From Sir Guy of Hastings	+ 1050
From Sir Andrew the Grey	+ 1100
To Sir Adam of Poitiers	- 1400
From Sir Bela of Pest	+ 950

From Sir Dewi of Carlisle	+	1800
To Chirurgeon's fees	-	600
Today's gains		3600

Not bad for a hard day's riding, even with the mark-to-dollar exchange dropping. She'd redeem her credits today before she went home. Some for savings, and some for maintenance, and a little for books and groceries. She wouldn't have to live off tuna fish sandwiches this week.

Four green-coated pages had lifted Sir Dewi onto a litter and were carrying him off the field. Mary raised her hand in salute. "Page, have I any jousts left?"

"Only one, Sir Mary. The Grey Knight of the Sea has laid a challenge against you, a joust of counted strokes, your choice of numbers. The Grey Knight also has a previous challenge against Sir Haakon of Jorvik. Do you wish to rest while Sir Haakon fights the Grey Knight?"

"Of course," Mary said. Even a few minutes' rest could go far toward mending the stamina of both horse and rider. "Let me see my stats and Bellefleur's." The dark lit up again:

Sir Mary de Courcy	81%
Cheval Bellefleur	78%

As she watched, the "78%" changed to "80%." Another ten minutes would have both of them back up to maximum. She dismounted and led Bellefleur to a water trough and waited patiently while she drank, and shook her head (water drops flew through the air, bright as diamonds), and drank again. The new horses were so realistic. Then she led her to the edge of the spectators' gallery, where there was some shade.

Without seeming to, she scanned the gallery with a slow turn of the head. Counting the house, so to speak. A percentage of the take went into the prize: tickets for the bleachers outside, login fees for the gallery inside. There was a sizable crowd, but she couldn't tell from here which of them were in full presence (and full fees). Some of them were mere ghosts, logged in on the narrow band from their PCs, able to see and hear but not to touch or speak. They paid a reduced fee; the idea was to let them save their nickels and dimes until they could afford the surgery that would bring them in as living citizens of this splendid world.

A shadow drifted past her helm, and a flower fell at her feet. She looked up and saw hands waving, sleeves bright as banners in the wind. Lady Gianetta, Lord Artos, Lord Peter: her partisans, and behind them Duke Kyle of Winchester himself. She waved back and tucked the rose into Bellefleur's braided mane. Lower down, hanging from the railing, a jester in black-and-white motley waved his staff of bells and looked at her with an exaggerated expression of unrequited passion. Him she ignored: he was only a Non-Player Character like the pages and the heralds, the work of the computer, and had no feelings to hurt.

Sir Haakon of Jorvik, a big man on a gigantic bay, rode up to the Lists. Across the way, the knight-bachelor who called himself the Grey Knight of the

Sea took his white shield and rode up to face him. His armor shone in the sun—new plate, so bright it almost cast sparks, and made by Hermann der Graue, if Mary's eyes didn't deceive her. A crest of gray ostrich feathers floated above his helm. The helm had a movable visor, but it was pulled down over the Grey Knight's eyes. She had never seen his face.

Nobody Mary knew had figured out who this youngster was. He had done fairly well in the Lists, but he'd been unhorsed and given ransom at least twice. He must have a new persona, or a private income, or both. She'd try not to hold that against him.

The page spoke. "Sir Mary, Sir Dewi asks if you will meet him outside for a drink."

"Oh. Do I have time? I suppose I do. Page, record this joust for me." She mounted, rode into her arming pavilion, dismounted again, and stepped outside.

She opened her eyes and blinked until the hall came into focus. Dim; immense; the internal lights had been turned off to save turning on the air conditioning, and the only light came through the west windows high above the bleachers and from the screen. The place served as a basketball stadium between tournaments. And there was enough air to breathe; it smelled faintly of coffee and popcorn, and sweat and beer, and dust.

On the huge projection screen on the far wall, bright pennants fluttered in the wind under a Delft-blue sky. The virtual camera panned across the spectators' gallery, full of lords and ladies as bright as tropical birds, their long dagged sleeves rustling like forests full of leaves, their coronets glittering. And behind the canvas roof of the gallery rose the towers of Castle Winchester, limestone-white, white pigeons fluttering around the conical blue roofs. Trumpets sounded to left and to right.

One missed most of that in the confines of a tilting helm. The one time Mary had watched a joust from the gallery, the sights and sounds of the world and its guests had been so spectacular she had been distracted from watching the Lists. She'd never done that again.

Sir Haakon and the Grey Knight were exchanging challenges. Haakon's voice was a booming bass—probably augmented—and the Grey Knight's a light baritone with a resonant quality Mary couldn't quite put a word to. Angelic? Fallen-angelic? or the Folk of the Air? Definitely augmented, expensively too. You got a software package when you first bought in that gave you a persona as like your real self as made no difference. Any changes or enhancements cost extra.

The bleachers were about three-quarters full: a bigger crowd than you usually saw, but then these were the Winchester Lists. On the floor of the court about sixty consoles had been set up. A silent man or woman sat at each, linked to the console by a pair of flat cables that plugged into his or her temples—like festival ribbons, for the latest style was to wear cables that went with your clothes, or your heraldry, or both.

On Mary's right was a woman wearing purple (cables, jumpsuit, earrings, and all), her mouth gaping.

To her left sat a copper-skinned man with curly dark hair and rainbow cables who had slid back into his chair so far that his vacant eyes were staring at the ceiling. Mary winced and thought of going to close his eyes for him, but as she watched he blinked; he'd be all right.

These were jousters who took the competition seriously enough to attend in person, and spectators who took it seriously enough to pay the fees for the gallery inside: A few bucks paid for software outside turned into a Très-Riches-Heures gown and fluttering veil inside.

Somewhere in the bleachers five or six voices were chanting "Mary! Mary! Mary!" and she raised her hand to them. Then she unplugged very carefully (once her hand had slipped, just once, and she'd had migraines for a week) and stood up.

Stiff as a board, as usual—well, she'd been in there four hours by the clock. (Time to take more of Dani's relaxation classes.) She stretched and bent over until her knuckles brushed the floor and her back went snap-crackle-pop. Then she straightened up and met Sir Dewi on his way to the bar.

There were more cheers from the bleachers—for both of them, probably. Dewi bowed and offered his arm, and Mary took it, and they walked down the dusty court between the consoles as if they were going in to a feast at the high table of a king. Mary did another quick house-count. Yes, nice and fat, and she and Dewi would each get about thirteen cents from each ticket. Many of them were as brightly dressed as those inside. She knew several of them: the local branch of the Society for Creative Anachronism mostly, those who couldn't afford surgery yet because they had to budget for armor and rattan swords and weatherproof pavilions and three weeks at the Pennsic War.

"Scotch and water—lots of water." Sir Dewi in persona was a big dark bull of a man; Dave Carlyle in the flesh was slender, and his eyes glittered behind old-fashioned wire-rimmed lenses.

"Gatorade, half-strength, very cold." Mary Craven, on the other hand, looked a lot like Sir Mary de Courcy. (Catch her paying extra for any enhancement she didn't need!) She was tall, blonde, and slightly bronzed from the sun, the type people had once called a "California girl" before even Hollywood had realized how ethnically mixed the state was. She took a long draft of her Gatorade and said, "Wow," and took another.

"Yeah. Well fought, Mary. Take good care of that horse."

"I will. He's a beauty. Where'd you get him? Who wrote him?"

"Benvenuto. Jerry Chu wrote him, and it's a better deal than you think. I bought the whole stud. Every year I get a new destrier just like this one. Cost me a bundle, and worth it." He reached into his shirt pocket and pulled out a memory card. "Here's his parameter file, if you ever need to reload him."

"Oh, Dave, thank you. That is true knightly largesse—"

"Sir Mary, you are called to single combat with numbered blows by the Grey Knight of the Sea," said a speaker above the bar.

"Already? Somebody must've died fast. Damn, I

should've been watching." Mary swallowed the last of her Gatorade in two gulps. On the screen the Grey Knight was climbing back into his saddle as Sir Haakon rode away. "I gotta get back inside. Have you fought this Grey Knight kid? What's he like?"

"Good, fast, overconfident. I got fifteen hundred off him. Try carrying your shield low till the last moment. Good luck."

"Thanks, Dave."

"You're welcome. Thank *you* for paying my leech's bills. Every little bit helps."

Mary shrugged. "Dave, your ransom doubled my winnings for today. I can afford to show largesse, and besides, it's period." She hurried back across the hall to her console. Dave might talk poor, but anybody who got that far in the Lists had made his expenses and then some. She plugged in and went back inside.

Sir Dewi's horse, the sleek snowy beauty with the ivory hooves, stood inside her pavilion, munching virtual oats; but she wouldn't field-test him in competition. Her dappled Bellefleur was rubbed-down and ready. She mounted and rode out to the Lists.

She had the herald call a combat of three blows: one to unhorse him, one to knock him down, one for a spare. (And hope that she could get to him before he could get to her.) The Grey Knight was mounted again, a new lance in his hand. He must have taken an interesting fall in his last bout; his shield was now Argent, semé of hoofmarks. The Lords of the Lists had a funny sense of humor sometimes. The Grey Knight sat low in his saddle, his shoulders slumped—tired, or frustrated, or wary. He spoke no challenge. Mary slumped a little too, and she let her shield drop as the herald called the *laissez aller*.

The Grey Knight rode toward her. Bellefleur started slowly at first, then accelerated as though her battery had been shorted to her motor, a burst of speed that might well take the Grey Knight unawares. He jerked up his lance toward Mary's breastplate, but her shield was already there and his lance brushed aside without breaking. Hers caught him amidships with a teeth-rattling jolt and knocked him to the sand.

She wheeled around at the far end of the Lists and watched him struggling to his feet. Tired—he hadn't bought enough stamina, or he had used it too lavishly. She had two blows left and he had three, since his lance hadn't broken. Nonetheless, she dismounted and gave Bellefleur's reins to a page. A gesture of chivalry at this stage increased her honor and magnified her name. She would make this short so they could all go outside and get a shower.

The Grey Knight waited until they were almost toe-to-toe before he moved. Then he raised his sword and struck swiftly, twice, high toward her head and low toward her hip. Mary blocked each blow with her shield, just in time; if he'd struck low and then high he might have gotten her. Again they stood together, an ell's distance or less between them. She could hear his breath whistling through the slots of his visor.

He struck again, lightning-quick to her head, but again her shield was there to prevent it. His sword swung low again, for a fourth blow to which he wasn't entitled, but she let the shield fall to guard her feet while her own sword caught him cleanly between helm and shoulder. In the real world the stroke would have crippled or killed him; here he fell rattling to the sand and lay still. Mary raised her sword in salute and returned it to the scabbard: she was still one stroke to the good.

"Page," Mary said.

"The Grey Knight of the Sea," the page said. "His ransom, two hundred marks. His armor, six hundred. His sword, two hundred. His horse, five hundred. Total, one thousand five hundred marks. The Grey Knight offers ransom."

"Accepted."

The page was silent for a moment. "Ransom cannot be paid," it said, its voice almost a monotone. The poor thing was only a computer, after all. "The Grey Knight of the Sea has insufficient funds to pay ransom."

Oh, drek, Mary thought in the darkness of her helm. *He's run over budget, he's out of credit, and now I get to shoulder his debt. Damn.* "Does he have enough to ransom just his person, if I keep his horse and armor?"

"No," the page said, and inside her helm where no one could see, Mary bared her teeth as if to bite.

She could, of course, set him free without taking ransom. "For the good of her soul, and for the sake of all poor prisoners and captives." It was a very medieval thing to do. It would be a further show of magnanimity; it would add glory to her name. She couldn't quite make herself do it. To return to Sir Dewi a third of what she'd won from him, that was one thing. To leave this bout with no gain at all—she stood with her mouth half open, unable to say Yes or No.

"Do you wish to take him prisoner?" the page said.

No, not that either. That would be, in effect, putting a lien on his credit rating, so that he couldn't joust again until he paid her off. He would probably resent this quite a lot, and in addition, she would be charged for his persona's virtual room and board till she set him free. It wasn't a large amount, but she wasn't willing to pay even small amounts to cover somebody else's inability to budget. She drew in a breath to say No.

"The Grey Knight of the Sea offers ransom," the page said again, "in the form of the manor of St. Chat's-on-Wye. Will you accept it?"

"A manor," Mary repeated. "Does he *have* it?"

"Yes, Sir Mary. Here is the deed, with a map." From nowhere in particular the page drew out a roll of parchment, full of Latin calligraphy, with a gaudy seal at the bottom and a map of the roads that led from here in Winchester to the manor of St. Chad's.

It had to be worth a lot—tens of thousands of virtual marks at the very least; she knew Sir Kyle of Dunbar had paid twenty-one thousand (but he had paid it in real money, of course) to be the Duke of Winchester. She could sell it to the highest bidder, if there were bidders. Failing that, she could sell it back to the computer for enough to prevent her from needing to eat tuna fish again for years. She could even—

"I accept the manor of St. Chad's as ransom for

the Grey Knight of the Sea and all his properties and for all his debts, and I count myself well rewarded. Take it to my pavilion, please. Oh, yes, and pay the chirurgeon." The page trotted off with the scroll. Mary loosened her chin strap and tugged off her helm, breathing deeply, and handed the helm to another page. (There were always enough pages around when you wanted them; it was a well-written system.)

The pages carried the Grey Knight to his arming pavilion. Inside, he would return his horse, his armor, and his virtual self to their electronic resting places on a handful of well-guarded memory cards, and step outside into the real world. The pages would take down his arming pavilion and vanish it back into memory until the next time it was wanted.

Trumpets sounded. Two pages beckoned Mary to the foot of the gallery. The Duke had descended to the lowest course and stood there with a wreath of laurels and daylilies in his hand. "Sir Mary de Courcy," he said as she approached. "This day you have earned both honor and glory. Earthly glory lasts but for a day; honor is eternal. Receive this wreath, and be named Champion of the Winchester Lists."

Cheers, waves of sound echoing to the furthest corners of the Lists. Flowers tossed from the highest courses of the gallery to land at her feet. Out-of-period wolf whistles—Lord Artos, probably. (He had been paying half-serious court to her for some months. Fortunately the rules permitted her to say No forever, if she chose. She had never met him in the flesh, and the system so far as she knew did not include what was coyly referred to as marital software.) She reached up to take the wreath from the Duke's hands and, at his gesture, set it on her head, light as feathers and smelling pungently of bay. There were more cheers, and she bowed and bowed and finally made a deep theatrical reverence onto one knee, her arms spread wide in gratitude, and then she got up and went straight to her pavilion.

Inside, the pages were packing for her. The glorious white stallion was already gone, and as she watched Bellefleur also disappeared. A page said, "Sir Mary, His Grace asks if you will join the revel tonight."

In the fourteenth century of the real Middle Ages, the end of the Lists would have led into several days of feasting and frolicking, with Mary as guest of honor at the Duke's right hand. VR still had too many limitations in that department: Food eaten inside, however tasty, provided no nourishment for the body, and though the Duke's palace at Winchester was as large and beautiful as the Duc de Berry's, you still had to go outside to go to the restroom. So the revel would only last the evening, a chance to talk shop and boast and flirt.

"I can't," she said. "I'm sorry." She meant it, for the Duke and his people were good company, and a virtual party was more fun than the real thing because people usually wore fantastic clothes and you couldn't get drunk, or hung over, on virtual wine. "I'm going home tonight, for I've promised to help train squires in London tomorrow. Salute His Grace for me."

The pages removed her armor (it came off more quickly than the real thing) and sent it away; one page remained, holding the scroll that held the deed and map to St. Chad's. "I'll take that with me," Mary said. That way it would be recorded on her own card and would be uploaded with her own backups onto the London system.

She stepped outside and unplugged gingerly; her temples were sore and she was just a little dizzy. She hadn't been inside *that* long; it must be the Champion's wreath and the sound of cheering. It was still going on, from the bleachers, and she got up carefully, holding on to the console's edge for balance, and bowed to left and right and sat down again.

One by one her memory cards slid from their slots. The primary card. The backup card. And another with the recordings of all her jousts that day as well as the one of Sir Haakon's that she'd missed. And last, her credit card. With her smallest fingernail she punched "Last Deposit."

Forty-six hundred marks, including a thousand in prize money—her share of the gate would be reckoned later. Not so shabby, even when translated into energy-poor dollars. The manor of St. Chad's was listed at a tentative value of twelve thousand—but that was what she could sell it to the system for today. If she kept it, invested in it, developed it, it could be worth a lot more.

A man was standing at her elbow, a technician waiting to take her console down. She stepped aside and let him do it. He detached the *trans* ends of her plugs, coiled the cables neatly, and gave them to her. It was four-thirty; she would have time for a shower before she caught her plane.

The water was only lukewarm—the best the solar showers could do since Philadelphia didn't get much sunlight that time of year—but it was wet and it washed the salt off her skin. She bundled her damp jumpsuit—black, with the sun in its splendor on the left breast—into the dirty-clothes end of her bag and put on a clean one. The memory cards went into the safety pocket inside her zippered bodice.

Dave Carlyle was still at the bar, or at the bar again, when she came out. A woman was with him, a woman with a shouldercam and throatmike and a perturbed expression. Dave gave interviews with his tongue in his cheek, and the media had to edit them down until there was nothing left.

As Mary approached, the woman said something that sent Dave into gales of helpless laughter, real or feigned. "All right, all right," Mary said. "What's so funny?"

"I'm Pamela Yee, of WCAU," the woman said, "and I asked him if it's true that *Chivalry* is primarily a rich person's sport, the way polo used to be," the woman said. "Between the surgery and the software—"

"Software's not that expensive," Mary said. "You win your first couple of jousts on good reflexes; after that your winnings will bootstrap your software expenses. You can travel cheap by bus, or just log in remote if you think you're fast enough. As for your surgery—"

The camera's red eye-light was on her, glinting and gloating. Oh, well, she might as well finish the paragraph. "Surgery does run in the low five figures—but back in the Gas Age people used to spend that much routinely on a car. They might have grumbled about it, but they paid it and considered it a necessity.

"I know of only one jouster who has *lots* of money, and he's one of the Lords of the Lists who wrote the *Chivalry* system and expanded his profits with good investments. A few of us are making a living, and the rest of us have an expensive hobby. It's like the guy who loves trains so much he saves all his nickels and dimes to buy a piece of a restored steam locomotive so he can ride it every weekend."

"Is that what you did? Saved your nickels and dimes?"

Mary laughed. "I didn't have any nickels to save; I was in graduate school. No, the VR center at the Student Union held a raffle: grand prize, one course of plug surgery at UCSF—and I won it. I assumed it would be an advantage in the mighty business career I was going to have—and then *Chivalry* came out, and now look at me. I worked like a dog on that MBA, and I've never used it yet."

"So you don't have to be rich to be a knight in shining armor?"

"You can be a knight in shining armor without ever getting near VR; join the Society for Creative Anachronism." She smiled at the camera. "But you don't have to be rich to play *Chivalry*. You just have to want it very badly." (There, she'd given them a sound bite they could use.) "And anyway, one of these years they'll make induction plugs work, and then you won't need surgery at all. Now, if you'll excuse me—"

"Oh." (Yee glanced sideways at Dave, who was

still snickering.) "I was hoping to ask you some more questions."

"I have a plane to catch," Mary said. "If you'd like to ride with me to the airport—"

"I'll *drive* you to the airport."

"Great. Can I have a minute with Dave first?" She drew him aside, out of the reporter's hearing. "Have you been here all along? Were you here when the Grey Knight came out?"

"I was here, but—"

"What's he look like?"

"*Sais pas.* He didn't come out here."

"He was remote?"

"He was remote."

"But Dave, that's bizarre. He was so fast."

"I know he was. But he was still remote. Maybe the techs are right, maybe it really doesn't make that much difference."

Mary shook her head. "I've always been able to feel the difference, even just into the next domain." She shrugged, and Dave shrugged, and Mary picked up her bag and followed Ms. Yee out of the arena.

The studio van wasn't the biggest thing in the parking lot (there were a couple of big hydrogen-burning freight trucks, hired to haul equipment for the Lists) but it must have massed five tons counting its own batteries, and it loomed above the minis and cycles like a stegosaurus among tiny furry animals. Mary rode to the airport in it, sitting on a battery box in the back, bouncing up and down over potholes in the street, with a dropcloth draped behind her. While the technician drove, Pamela Yee asked the usual dumb questions: "How does it feel to joust in virtual reality?" "Does it hurt when you get hit with a sword?" "What happens if the system goes down while you're in it?" And Mary smiled and smiled, and never lost her temper, because she knew the value of publicity as well as the next guy.

"Oh, I know what else I wanted to ask you about. Have you heard anything about somebody doing a VR based on *The Golden Road?*"

"That's impossible. Well, okay, maybe nothing is impossible, but I can't think of anything less likely." *The Golden Road* was a fantasy adventure set in Carolingian Europe, or something rather like it; it was this generation's *Lord of the Rings.* "You know Professor Markheim put his foot down long ago. No games, no VRs, over his dead body, he says—and he's still alive and kicking, and the copyright runs for life plus fifty years. I'm not going to hold my breath waiting."

A soft pink-faced man sat next to her on the plane; before her seat belt was fastened he began to tell her in short jerky sentences all about what he thought was wrong with the current administration. Mary opened her mouth and closed it again, because the man was plainly terrified of flying and a rude remark would go right through him like a neutrino, without noticeable effect. She kept her temper until they were airborne; then she said, "Excuse me, I have to get some sleep," and covered her face with an in-flight magazine, leaving him to the solace of airline courage in its expensive little bottles, one after another. He trailed off into silence somewhere over the Midwest, while the overhead screens played news and a movie and sports and more news.

The last surviving AIDS patient, frail but cheerful, had celebrated his eighty-first birthday. On the other hand, the weakened systems of TAV patients showed little resistance to the latest strain of flu; 143 had died since the first of the month and it was only November, just the start of the flu season. The Environmental Management Council was reporting a 3° global temperature rise and a sea-level rise of 60 centimeters; in the Mediterranean it was rising rather faster than that, and the Nile Delta was being evacuated by boat and helicopter. The U.S. government was offering another bonus for planting trees (hmm, she'd have to take another look at her water allotment, maybe plant another couple dozen almonds). Magazine still in place, she feigned sleep and went doggedly through the mantras and meditations that were supposed to keep you from tensing up inside the system. They worked better there than inside an airplane.

As they crossed over the Valley the sports news came on again, with a blare of trumpets and a shout of "*Laissez aller!*" Mary's eyes flew wide open behind her magazine. Sure enough, the Winchester Lists had made the in-flight sports news, and her interview with WCAU had been edited into it. She peered round the edge of the magazine.

In VR she had looked great; in the back of the van she looked tired and haggard and there was a great cowlick in the back of her hair. She put up a hand cautiously to feel it: It was still there. She retreated under her magazine again, hoping to God nobody on the plane would recognize her. Your basic layman, on learning that you did VR, always asked about marital software. Mary was in no position to answer, and the question always made her blush.

(There was something to be said for marital software. It was all there was for WarP survivors and Wither patients, who couldn't perform the act outside, and TAV patients, who didn't dare. For others, it provided a safe place for experiment—and if you declined to experiment, nobody thought you were insane, as in her mother's day.)

"No, you can't be killed, only disabled, and you can't be hurt. I lost an arm once in a melee and it didn't hurt at all; but it went numb and I couldn't see it. That's scary. The worst hurt you can get in the joust is stiff and tired and headachy when you come back outside."

The plane tilted, easing Mary further against the window as it banked for a spiral down to the airport. The cold windowpane felt good against her forehead.

"I've never been in a system crash. They tell me it's very unpleasant. First the world around you starts coming apart; then your body starts coming apart; then you sort of swirl down the drain and land outside with a rotten headache and dizziness and nausea. Nothing that really does you harm, but not much fun either."

At that moment the plane tilted further, almost wing-down, and went into free fall. Two seconds, three, while the pit of her stomach floated between a rock and a hard place and someone screamed in the forward cabin. Her magazine went flying, and the soft pink man beside her grabbed for his sick bag and barely got it open in time. Then weight returned, doubled and trebled, and the plane got its nose above its middle again and began to level out—

CRASH

And something went tumbling past the window, gone and vanished in an eyeblink, something smooth and fiery, like a wing. The plane shuddered and rocked, but it was still descending, not falling. Part of a wing, maybe, or somebody else's wing. Now the attendants were telling everyone to brace themselves against the seat in front, heads down, and a child was wailing and somebody else was screaming. The runway lights were coming up fast beneath them, and there was a thump and a terrible screech of abused metal against asphalt, and the plane came to a stop, tilted fifteen or twenty degrees off the horizontal. Every third window popped open and escape chutes inflated. Mary clambered out and slid, and landed and ran ten, twenty meters from the vulnerable plane. The pink-faced man was on her heels, and half a dozen others after him. The air was beginning to smell ominously of burning plastic.

The last down was a middle-aged woman who turned back toward the slide and began to scream. The pink-faced man ran back and spoke to her, and while she went on screaming he climbed the slide again, his feet braced against its slippery rims, his hands gripping the sides like a mountain climber's. He vanished inside. Mary had time to remember to breathe. The plastic smell was getting thicker, and she started to back away.

The pink man was back, sliding down the chute again with a white-haired man draped over his shoulder. He hit the ground and stumbled five or six meters across the asphalt before lowering the man to the ground. "My God," he said, and retched, and fell to his knees. Someone helped him to his feet and led him away.

The man's got guts after all, Mary thought, and winced. Fire crews had ringed the plane now, and medics and airline staff were shooing the milling passengers toward the terminal. "Please come along," somebody said to her. "If the plane doesn't catch fire, we can probably get your baggage out later on."

"All I've got is a duffel with a sweaty jumpsuit in it," Mary said. "It can wait; I'll check back tomorrow." She followed the crowd into the terminal, one hand delicately brushing the fabric over her safety pocket as a pregnant woman might touch her belly. The memory cards were still there; they were safe; everything was fine. She'd hit a ladies room and take a look to be sure, but it took more than a bumpy ride to crack those things.

The passengers were being herded into a waiting room, doubtless well-stocked with coffee and small bottles of courage and doughnuts and TV screens and busybodies. Mary slipped through the crowd and headed for the charging pods. The weather had been clear and cold in San José all weekend, and when she checked her mini out of its pod, its batteries were at full charge. She had only twenty miles to go, and it wasn't even ten o'clock yet. She pulled down the windscreens and guided the softly purring mini out of the pod yard.

A first-quarter moon shed a little light on the freeway, enough to see that they were tearing up its sides again, hauling away the concrete of the outermost lanes and preparing the land for bushes and trees. A wide lane for trucks and buses, a narrower one for private minis, another for bicycles; that was all anyone needed any more. Clear and cold. The stars glittered overhead, splintered into rainbows through the mini's clear plastic roof. It would be good to get home.

The mini's engine made no sound but a faint whine. She clearly heard the rumble behind her, a bus or truck pulling up to pass her on the left. She looked in the rearview mirror. It was right behind her, a big featureless bus-sized van, gaining on her swiftly—too swiftly. She jerked the steering bar to the right and swerved away just in time as the van scraped her side. Its airstream picked her up and tossed her into a crackling pile of dead oleanders that lay along the outer edge of the bike path. The van roared on into the night.

For a long moment she simply lay there and tried to breathe, waiting for her heart to stop pounding and the adrenaline to stop surging through her body. Then she shakily took stock of her own damages and the mini's: A bruised knee and a Safety Interlock light seemed to be the lot. She crawled out, set the mini back onto its wheels, and pushed Reset.

The Safety Interlock light stayed on. Well, she could push it off the freeway at least.

Son of a bitch, she thought. *Something really has it in for me tonight.* But it was only a hundred meters to her exit. Limping slightly, she wheeled the mini off the freeway and parked it in a brushy grove of half-grown trees. She'd call the repair service in the morning and hitch a ride into the city with them. It was twenty minutes by foot from the grove to her house; by the time she got there, her knee had loosened up and stopped hurting and she was so relieved to be home that she felt almost cheerful.

The security system recognized her code and let her in. The drapes had closed at sunset to keep the day's heat in, and the living room was pleasantly warm. The household system told her the animals and the garden had been adequately fed and watered in her absence, and the cats came up to purr and nuzzle at her feet and to tell her loudly that the system lied, nobody had fed them and they were starving to death.

It was now getting on toward midnight, but she took the time to upload her backups to her own datafiles and to make a quick eyeball survey in the barn. Rabbits and chickens all in place; there were even a few eggs. She shared a plate of scrambled eggs with the cats before they all crawled into bed.

It was (the system told her later) one-thirty in the morning when the panel by her bed buzzed softly and woke her up. She picked up the handset. "Intruder in the house," the system said. "One person, now in the kitchen, proceeding into the living room. Instructions?"

"Panic," Mary whispered.

All the lights in the house went on. All the wall speakers screamed with Red Alert sirens, except for the ones in the living room, which began to recite the criminal codes the intruder was violating and advising him/her to surrender at once or face additional charges. There was a clatter of feet and a slammed door.

The sirens stopped, and in the sudden silence Mary

could hear a siren go by on the road, moving quickly from west to east and dying away in the distance.

When the police arrived at the house, they found Sir Mary de Courcy in a shabby blue velour bathrobe, standing in her living room holding a rattan broadsword with a blackened steel basket hilt worn shiny in spots. "Good evening, gentlemen," she said mildly. "I've had an intruder."

"We know. He drove away just as we got here. We followed him as far as 101, but he lost us."

"I know. I heard you go by. You can see him on the monitor here—" she pointed to a blurred image frozen on her screen—"but he seems to have been wearing a mask."

"Looks like it. Can we have a copy of this tape?"

"I can make you one if you like. But the system's already sent the whole sequence to your headquarters. It's all part of the package, which has just paid for itself so far as I'm concerned. I wanted to ask you—look at his right hand. What's that he's holding?"

"That looks like a knife, ma'am. Maybe ten or twelve centimeters."

"I was afraid you might say that. And since there doesn't seem to be anything missing, I guess he broke in with violent intentions." Mary felt a chill despite the warmth of the house.

"Looks like it," the officer said again. "I wouldn't worry too much. You've got a good security system, and he had enough sense to run when it went on. I'd leave it on panic mode and go back to sleep. It'll go off again if he so much as looks through a window."

They made a quick survey of the buildings; they found the broken window where the man had gotten in and took some notes. She covered the broken pane with sticky plastic sheeting and reset the motion sensor to scream bloody murder if anything went through it.

The cats had all gone to ground under the furniture and wouldn't surface till morning. Mary put another blanket on her bed and curled up in a ball until she felt somewhat warm again. Then she stretched and turned over, but although she was dazed and exhausted, she couldn't drift off. Her feet were warm enough, but her back felt cold, and she squirmed and worked the blankets over the back of her neck; it didn't help much. What a weird, crazy, frightening day! After a while she forced herself into her most familiar fantasy: she was lying in someone's arms. His name and face were far from clear, but his arms were strong in her imagination, and she curled up against her pillow as if it were the shoulder of Hildebrandt or Widia or some other great hero. Eventually, she slept.

Chapter 2

Walk Before You Run

"You're late," Nick snapped.

"I sure am," Mary said, shifting her duffel further back onto her shoulder without breaking stride. Nick Carter was the senior programmer at the salle d'armes and a Lord of the Lists, but she was no butterfly-bellied young squire any more; she was a Knight of the West and the Champion of the Winchester Lists, and Nick could no longer scare her. Besides, he was three inches shorter than she was and beginning to pooch out over his belt. "Where is everybody? What time is it? Ten-thirty: They're in Dani's relaxation class, right?"

"Yes. You were supposed to be here for the introductory session at nine. What happened?"

"Car trouble," she said without breaking stride. Behind her she could hear Nick muttering something about, "Wish I'd arranged to pay you by the hour." Well, he hadn't: He'd contracted for a lump sum on the order of a consultant's fee, and she wasn't going to renegotiate it now. There was no point in his bitching anyhow: The salle was making money (she kept its books), and Nick was a rich man already.

She pushed open one leaf of the double door that led from the corridor to the Great Hall and kicked off her shoes before she stepped onto the mats. Dani in her thin beige leotard was pacing on delicate feet, like a tall heron, among the bodies that littered the floor. Mary did a quick count: twelve squires, or at least squire-aspirants, most of them so fresh from their surgery that their temples were still shaven. Seven women, five men. "Good morning, Mistress Dani," she said. "Do you mind if I sit in? Good morning, everyone, I'm Mary de Courcy and I'm wiped out." She dropped her duffel in the corner and lay down.

"You're welcome, of course, Sir Mary," Dani said. "What's up? Usually when you lie down both your shoulders touch the mat."

"Let me give you the condensed version." She took a deep breath and let it out again, slowly. "The plane I flew in on nearly crashed. Some jerk sideswiped me on the freeway, tried to push me off the road. He *did* push me off the road, rolled me into the oleanders. The mini wouldn't restart, so I walked home. That night my house was broken into by somebody carrying a knife. The house system scared the guy off. The Triple A came by this morning, and the mini's got a bent fork, so they gave me and it a lift into town."

"Good grief!" Dani shook her head in wonderment. "All right, you can be the demo dummy. Sit up, the rest of you, and watch. Mary really does know this already, but life seems to have caught her off guard and a short refresher won't hurt. Mary, relax your eyes. . . . Relax your forehead. . . . Relax your mouth. . . . Relax your jaw. . . ." Muscle by muscle she led her through the routine till Mary lay limp-fingered on the floor, a happy pancake, her shoulderblades sinking into the mat.

"This is what you need to learn before you spend very much time inside VR," Dani resumed. "Otherwise you'll come out after an hour or two, all tied up in knots. Lie down again, everybody. Relax your eyes. . . ."

Mary heard little rustles and grunts as the students settled in, and footsteps. "Nick, you forgot to take your shoes off."

"Damn," Nick said, and sat down heavily beside her. "How'd you know?"

"They squeak."

Nick unfastened the shoes with soft *rip-rips* and dropped them on the mat. "Did all that really happen last night?"

"Every word."

"Did the cops catch your burglar?"

"Not that I know of. I gave 'em the picture off my security system, but it wasn't very good. Maybe I'll break down and spend some prize money on an upgrade."

"Is that necessary, really? Surely he won't be such a damn fool as to come back."

"Yeah, but I'll sleep better. Nick, I'm sorry I missed the intro, but it really wasn't under my control. I'll do the riding lesson, though. I've got a spiffy new destrier."

The mats got stacked in the corner; they made a squashy divan that one could sit on. The consoles were wheeled in from the sidelines, and the soft chairs with the ergonomic headrests were brought in from the corridor. London had moved into a larger space twice since Mary had been jousting there, and the equipment had always expanded to fill the square footage. Nick went into his little cubicle, where the system console rubbed elbows with the sage-green cube that held London in the secret places of its memory, and shut the door.

Mary fed her memory cards into the console and plugged in.

She stood in her arming pavilion, just as she had left it, with Bellefleur and the white stallion side by side, munching oats from a wooden trough. But when she stepped outside, the walls surrounding the Lists were hung with her banner and the banners of her friends, and the six bezants of London fluttered overhead.

At the other end of the Lists was another pavilion, black like her own. A pennon floated from its peak, a long-bodied dragon glittering with gold thread. Sir Nicholas of Padua stepped out, a head taller than he was outside, wearing a black surcote and many golden rings. They exchanged courteous nods and walked together to the door held open by a page.

The place was a quasi-medieval cross between a locker room and a stable. Maybe there had been rooms like this in the real Middle Ages, changing rooms for young squires who didn't own an arming pavilion yet (or who didn't rate space for one on the field). Mary hadn't researched the question; maybe Nick had. He had certainly gotten the architecture right: a long room, rather low-ceilinged, supported by fluted pillars that curved just overhead into shallow arches, like the undercroft of a guildhall. All the wood fittings were young oak, pale as spring sunlight, and the lamps on the walls would never smoke or run out of oil.

Each stall had a name on the door, a bench and armor stand and shelves inside. (All they needed: They were not going to have to sleep in these stalls, not even shower in them.) One by one the twelve novices shimmered and took shape in their stalls, shouting or murmuring with excitement according to their natures.

No, not twelve, there were only eleven. Who was missing?

Mary stepped outside again and glanced around. It was the redhead at the console next to hers, a big muscular kid with agreeable light blue eyes, his shaven scalp patches no paler than his face. "Trouble?" she said.

"I—uh—can't do it, somehow."

"Never been inside before?"

"Five minutes in the doctor's office, when I got my stitches out. They had a little virtual garden. You just stepped inside . . . but now somehow I can't take that step."

"Ever see the old movie *The Andromeda Strain?* Remember how the doctor got into the isolation suit? He grabbed a bar and picked up his feet and slid into it? Close your eyes; that darkness in front of you is like an isolation tunnel. Just pick up and fall in feet-first—"

The kid's face went slack, and he was in. (Practically everybody looked so mindless when his mind was elsewhere that salles d'armes and exhibition halls had stringent rules about cameras on-site. It would be even better to put the spectators in an auditorium in front of their video screens and the jousters in another room, maybe in another building; but mostly the jousters hadn't managed to convince the exhibition autocrats, who wanted to sell lots of bleacher tickets.) Mary followed him in.

"Are we all met?" Sir Nicholas quoted. It was a rhetorical question; he had counted noses just as Mary had. "The first thing we'll do is to get you armored up.

"—No, the very first thing we do," he corrected himself, "is that I explain that this is the first time I've taught this course in VR, and, like you, I'm learning as I go along. We're going to try a lot of different techniques. Most of them have been proven outside, at SCA fighter practices. Some would only work in VR, so they're new. A lot of what we do will seem strange to you at first; but if we get to the end of a session and it still doesn't make sense, tell me. Maybe we'll find that some things don't transfer.

"Now, you've each got a pile of armor in there with you; some of it's good, some not-so-good. It's the luck of the draw from a random generator that took your body size into account. We'll help you arm, and then we'll go out to the Lists."

Five lords on one side of the aisle, seven ladies on the other. Mary wandered up and down the women's side, offering advice, occasionally going into a stall to help with a stubborn buckle.

The armor they were wearing, as Nick had said, was a mixed bag, reminiscent of the heap of loaner armor spread out on the pavement at any SCA fighter practice. Or the assortment of gear (handed down or bought cheap) that a young knight just starting out, without land or property, would have to make do with till he could win something better. William Marshall had started out that way, and so had Mary herself.

The novices didn't need much help. They had all been watching *Chivalry* demos on television, and most of them were SCA: They could tell a greave from a vambrace by looking at it. "Wups!" Mary said, peering into the next stall. "We're going to need some intervention here."

The lady was trying to buckle a battered breastplate over a green tunic that came halfway to her knees. She was tall and fair, and willow-slender in most places, but the breastplate hadn't a prayer of fastening around her upper body.

"Sir Nicholas! (Oh, don't be embarrassed, m'lady, we have a phrase for this kind of problem in the Society; we call it 'great tracts of land.') Sir Nicholas, this lady needs a new cuirass."

"Ah." Sir Nicholas leaned on the nearest railing, looking nowhere in particular—certainly not at the lady—but after a moment the dinged breastplate vanished and a shiny new cuirass appeared, about a century later in design and worth about a hundred marks on the open market. The lady had profited by the exchange. Mary fastened her buckles and glanced up and down the stalls. "Everyone's ready over here, Sir Nick."

They filed out to the Lists, clanking merrily and making excited noises, inadequately hushed. Maybe this was going to work after all.

The sky was bright overhead, mild as April in the middle of November. The twelve novices murmured and nudged one another, looking at Mary, and she realized she was still wearing Winchester's wreath. She took it off and tossed it like a quoit to hang from the peg that held her banner against the wall. The daylilies had already contracted into little rose-colored buttons, but the laurels would remain fresh forever.

"We'll start one element at a time," Sir Nicholas said. "You'll get the rudiments of fighting on foot before you transfer to horseback, and then learn to simply stay in the saddle before you try to fight from it.

"All right, move out, give yourselves some room. Stand with your feet a little farther apart than shoulder width—is anyone left-handed? No?—Then with your right foot in front and pointing forward, your left foot trailing and turned out almost 90 degrees." He demonstrated. "If you ever took ballet lessons, you might remember this as fourth position. If you've fought in the Society, it's the basic fighter's stance. Don't lock your knees, bend them just a little. Your weight should be evenly balanced, or just a little more on your left leg—that's right. Now take a step forward."

They did. "Ouch," he said. "Try a *little* step forward with the right, and a little step forward with the left. That's better. No one is asking you to lunge forward like d'Artagnan. Not yet, anyway."

Mary watched closely as they practiced. The theory was—the programmers claimed—that their virtual bodies were coded to learn the moves faster than their real ones could. If that was true, this class would work. Mary's own formal training had been outside, at the provincial fighter practice in the BART parking lot. She had learned to ride inside at odd moments and picked up jousting on the fly, like most of her generation.

But if the rumors were true that induction plugs were on the way, requiring no surgery but only a little tuning, then not only *Chivalry* but all the VRs were about to be swamped with newcomers, and Nick's short, intensive classes were about to become very necessary. If they worked.

Maybe they would; he had them moving adequately within forty-five minutes. Now he fell back and leaned against a wall while the novices gathered around Mary.

"All right," she said. "Each of you has a sword. This is the generic sword you got with your introductory package when you bought in. Later on you can buy or win better ones, but you don't need to yet. Has anyone fought broadsword in the SCA?" Several raised tentative hands. "But not a whole lot, right? Very well.

"Spread out a little more. Draw your swords—that's right, it's not going to bite you—and spread out till none of you can touch the tip of the other guy's sword with the tip of yours. These blades are dull, but they mass a virtual kilo and a half and you don't want to take somebody's hand off, even though it's fixable."

The circle took rough shape. The novices' swords were dull and had plain black hilts, all alike. "Now swing it around—no, no, edgewise, not like a tennis racket. Back and forth and around; and see how it moves." She swung her own sword over her head and then did an arm's-length windmill and a figure-eight in front of her. "There are things the sword isn't willing to do. We don't use Aristotelian physics in this system; it's going to move like a real sword. Swing it and let the sword talk to you. It'll tell you what it can and can't do." She paced slowly inside the circle, watching. When the first novice tried to switch his sword back and forth like a foil and wrenched his wrist, she said, "You see what I mean."

She gave them half an hour or so, while the swords swung in arcs and loops and the novices absorbed their first lessons in virtual mechanics. Nick paced around the outside of the circle. Occasionally he would step close to one of the kids and speak a word or two in private.

There was something else moving, just in the corner of her eye; eventually she noticed it enough to turn and look. It was a small brown bird, a sparrow maybe, hopping back and forth along the wooden railing of the Lists. It stayed all through the session, hopping back and forth, its beady eye always toward Mary and the novices. One would have thought it expected them to drop virtual popcorn and bread-crumbs, as real sparrows counted on humans to do in the world outside. Some Lord of the Lists, with an idle hour on his hands, had written a lot of verisimilitude into a little background subroutine. It was one of the things that made this reality so much fun.

"That's about enough," Sir Nicholas said presently. "Your arms and shoulders will be in knots when you get outside, and you'll find out what you took that relaxation class for. Sheathe your swords and follow me. Anyone have any experience riding horseback, outside?"

One youngster raised a tentative hand. "I went on trail rides sometimes when I was a kid." Mary hid a smile with her hand. The novice had by law to be at least eighteen, but he looked several years younger.

"Placid old horses that let you sit on them like rocking chairs, right?" Sir Nicholas said. "What you ride today won't be much different. This way."

"I'll join you on the green, Sir Nicholas," Mary called after him. She went into her pavilion and led out the white destrier.

The green was a long flat expanse of turf to the north of London, between the castle and the river. Nick had divided the novices into two groups; one was following him toward the Winchester road, and the others were waiting for Mary. They were staring at something, not Mary herself for once. She turned to see what it was: the castle, of course.

The White Tower of London, looking just as it had when Charles d'Orleans moved in in 1415, with a little Duc de Berry thrown in and just a hint of modern cartoons. Its white walls, its blue-tiled roofs, the Thames flowing beneath its shining turrets, bluer than ever in the real world. Somebody had even written salmon to swim in it, leaping upstream every spring. Inside, most of the doors off the Great Hall were sealed. Mary would mention later (if she had to) that a large part of the castle had no inside yet. Nick or one of his colleagues, the Lords of the Lists who were mostly working elsewhere now, would write it some day when they had time.

She rode up to the novices. "Now, did Sir Nicholas tell you what's to do here?"

"I don't think so, Sir Mary," said the tall woman in green. "He just said, 'Wait here.' "

"All right. I shall assume none of you has ridden before—I don't count those patient old nags from the trail rides. The horse you're riding today will have a little more spirit than they did, but not much. We call her Old Betsy. You're all riding the same horse—multiple copies of the same object; if you care to look, you'll find a unique process id on the saddleblanket. Betsy is thoroughly tested and reliable.

"I must point out, however, that's she's got one bug. If you take her down a slope of 30 degrees or more, she'll freeze up, skitter down the slope stiff-legged, and probably dump you off at the bottom. The only slope like that around here is by the river." She pointed to a line of trees. "Don't go near there and you'll be fine. Any questions?"

"Why 30 degrees?"

"My lady, the math is beyond me; but in essence, any time she is in motion and her hindquarters are higher than her head, she loses her sense of balance and goes rigid with fear. Anything else?"

"Do I have to get Sir Nicholas to lengthen my stirrups?" said the woman in the green tunic.

"No, no. They have buckles on them. Here, like this." She lengthened the straps till the woman's long legs were comfortable. "Now, let's be off."

They spent an hour or so in the saddle, walking and trotting across the green turf, learning to handle the reins and to stay on the horse's back. While they practiced, Mary got in a few good gallops on her new destrier, a ride like a cold wind coming in at the gallop to herald a thunderstorm. Jerry Chu had written him out of the stuff of legends, and he never seemed to tire. A matter of minutes from the green to the river and back, with the crushed grass underfoot sweet in her nostrils. She thought of names, and more names, none of them good enough.

There was a willow growing at the edge of the river, wetting its longest twigs in the slow-moving water. Here there was another little bird, green as leaves and no bigger than a bush-tit, that clung to the willow twigs with tiny feet and cocked its head to watch her ride by. She couldn't put a name to it, but since this was supposed to be an English countryside, she assumed it was an English bird. She'd ask Nick; if he didn't know, he could look it up.

Returning to the novices, she found them doing nicely. Old Betsy would let you fall off if you got too careless, but it didn't hurt and served to teach you better. Most of the novices were fans of Mary's, and each time she rode up, they broke off the exercise and clustered around her.

"Hey, Pete," she heard the murmur behind her back. "Why don't you lead these guys off somewhere? Challenge 'em to a race or something."

"When they're all on the same horse? Get real. It'd be an eleven-way tie, and anyway, why should I?"

"So I can talk to her alone, you fool."

"Fool, you."

Mary touched the destrier's sides and moved discreetly away, but hoofbeats followed her. "Sir Mary?"

He was a tall youngster, with a headful of tight blond curls like Persian lamb. "I assume we're going to break pretty soon; will you join me for lunch?"

"We'll probably go out in groups," she said. "Sir Nick likes Indian; I like Chinese. You're welcome to join whatever party suits your tastes."

"Oh. Okay. I was sort of thinking of Maria's—"

"We couldn't get there and back in time. Besides, if you've got lunch-at-Maria's money, save it and get yourself a new helm; yours is awfully borderline. A concussion in VR won't do you any permanent harm, but you'll stagger and throw up, and you'll feel *so* silly."

"Yes, m'lady," he said, and grinned. Unquenchable. When they held the revel at the end of the class, she would have to look out for this lad; he made her nervous.

Now she could see, far across the green, Sir Nicholas returning with his half of the class. The hour must be up; Nick always knew what time it was outside. But, then, as a Lord of the Lists he could see the code behind everything: the tightly coded subroutines that made up grass and trees and little birds and his own virtual body, and the system clock patiently ticking beneath it all.

She heard a thump and a burst of laughter and

turned around. The boy with the Persian-lamb curls had fallen from the saddle; he was sitting on the ground next to a fallen log three feet thick, rubbing his left hip. Above him—"Well, I'll be damned," Mary said. Above the fallen rider the horse hung in the air, Old Betsy frozen in mid-leap, her hindquarters higher than her head and her forefeet a yard off the ground. "However did you manage to do that?"

"I'm not sure." The boy had stopped rubbing his hip and started rubbing his head. "I was trying to get her to jump over this log—"

"And triggered the 30-degree bug on the way down and hung up the process. Interesting." She looked the motionless horse over from both sides. Not a muscle twitched, not a hair stirred in the breeze.

"Looks like you get to walk home, Scott," one of the other novices said.

"No, Sir Nicholas is here; he can kill the process and restart it. Look, Nick, we've found a new venue for the 30-degree bug."

"So I see." Nick raised heavy black eyebrows. "Jumping over a log, right." He made no visible motion, but the frozen horse winked out of sight. A second later she reappeared, hooves on the ground, as if nothing had happened.

"I think it may be time to fix that bug," Mary said.

"I didn't write her," Nick said. "That was one of Greg Hampton's. I'll e-mail him. He hasn't been around lately; he's got life (meaning, 'mundane chores are taking up all his time')." They got Scott remounted and rode back to the castle.

* * *

When they got outside, as predicted, some of the kids were stiff and sore about the neck and shoulders. Some of them pulled mats from the stack and lay down to reapply Dani's techniques. Mary yawned and stretched like a cat. Then they went out for lunch in bunches of three or four.

True to his word, Scott joined the Chinese-food faction, and when they settled at the big round table with the Lazy Susan, he snagged the seat to Mary's right. At her left was the redhead (Charlie Graham was his name), so Mary felt like a fan sandwich. They all asked questions, and she gave answers between bites.

"Well, but you all know how I got into *Chivalry,*" she said. "I found the SCA by getting lost in Dwinelle Hall and walking into a meeting, and then I won the ASUC contest. What about you guys? What persuaded you to spend five figures on the entrée into *Chivalry?*" That would keep them going for a while and let her catch up on the potstickers and the oyster-sauce eggplant.

Some of the answers were interesting. The tall woman, whose mundane name was Sophia, hadn't chosen a persona name yet, but she had been saving for nine years working as an administrative assistant. "I don't want to choose before I know who I am, what sort of fighter I'll make. Till then I'll fight with a blank shield and be 'the White Knight' or 'the Green Knight' or—" but that got her a chorus of "You can't be the Green Knight, he's a fictional character."

"And supernatural, too," Scott said. "Don't worry about it, just be Sophia till you think of something else. (Spareribs, anybody? I don't want to be a pig.)

It'll be a while till any of us are fighting in competition and have to worry about name recognition.

"Me? Oh, I always knew what I wanted, though I didn't know how I was going to get it. I had an old tape of *Ivanhoe* when I was a kid, played it to death and had to get a new one. I saw my first VR jousting when I was eleven, that show they ran on PBS. I found the SCA at twelve, but they wouldn't let me fight until I was eighteen and had my full growth. Meanwhile, my parents kept wondering when I would grow up and face reality and go into my father's paint business."

"Having a good day job is almost a given for playing this game," Mary said. "I managed to avoid it, but for heaven's sake don't take me as an example."

"So finally my father said, 'Oh, hell, let's let him do it and get it out of his system,' and he bought me my plugs. He's really a very nice guy. He's going to give me a year, and then we'll talk about the paint business some more. What about you, Charlie?"

"Huh? Me?" Charlie seemed startled out of deep thought. "About the same. TV, books; I heard about the Society when I was eight and made my mom write to SCA headquarters in Milpitas for me—to get information on my local branch, y'know?—because I couldn't spell so good yet. And I saw the same PBS program you did. God, I thought I would never make it. And then an uncle I had never even seen died and left me a little money. Just enough for a trip out here, and my plugs, and this class. I know what you said, Sir Mary, but I'm gonna *have* to make it fast or I'll never make it at all."

Then he seemed to realize how much he had said

and went silent. Others picked up the thread, talking of the ominous rises in sea level reported by the EMC, and how cholera was taking out most of what was left of Bangladesh, and the case, just coming to trial, of a supplier of illegal plugs.

"Why are they illegal? That's what I'd like to know," one of the students said. "Is it because of the mask laws? What harm do they do?"

"The mask laws have nothing to do with it," Mary said. "People have killed themselves using illegal plugs." And seeing the student's uncomprehending look, "Legal plugs have a timer or sensor or something that automatically logs you out if you get too fatigued. Otherwise you could go into kidney failure or something and never know it."

"Is that all?"

"Isn't that enough?"

"I thought it was because you could have a persona that looks nothing like you. Like, Sir Nicholas is a foot taller inside than outside—"

"Doesn't matter. Look, the mask laws assume that if you wear a mask, you're enabling yourself to commit anonymous crime. Restricting unlimited plugs is a health issue, like restricting tobacco products, in hopes that if you can't get any, you can't hurt yourself with them."

"Like doing Ultrajolt," Scott said.

"Like taking Ultrajolt," Mary agreed. "Take enough of that and even with legal plugs you could stay up till you dropped dead. Or at least dropped. Even the military doesn't use it much anymore.

"But you can have an anonymous persona, the way you can have an anonymous e-mail account. The computer knows where to send the bill, but nobody else needs to; because you can't hurt anybody with it, because it's all VR. I broke lances with one last weekend, and we're still wondering who he was."

"Well," Charlie said. "It's time we got back. Anyone else want the last potsticker?"

"I'll split it with you," Scott said, and they did.

Back inside after lunch, Sir Nick set the novices to work at the pells, thick poles as tall as they were and planted firmly in the ground. The youngsters swung at the pells with their blunted swords again and again, learning how they moved. Nick and Mary watched, making comments and giving advice.

Scott tried a blow he had probably seen on TV, a mighty circle in the air like a berserker, but his hand was at the wrong angle and he only clocked himself in the head. Nick let him say "ouch" and "damn" for about a minute and then healed the virtual bruise, saying, "Now you know why not to do that."

After an hour or so of this he and Mary went to their pavilions to arm. Mary leaped into the saddle—no one was watching, but it was a point of pride not to touch the pommel—and rode the great white destrier onto the Lists. The squires were lined up against the walls, murmuring and looking from one end to the other. (You couldn't make them work all the time, Nick had said: Give them some entertainment now and again.) At the far end of the Lists, astride his black Nightgaunt, Nick raised his shield and shouted, "If you're *quite* ready. . . ."

She had jousted so many times against Sir Nicholas that he held no surprises for her anymore. (If nobody ever won prize or ransom at a tournament, they would all attend anyway for the pleasure of meeting new opponents, fresh blood and new and different tactics on the field.)

Nick, as a Lord of the Lists—one of the half-dozen programmers who had written the original system software—was barred from competing for prizes. Theoretically, he could (if he thought he could get away with it) rewrite his horse, his armor, his lance—or his opponent's—or himself, or the laws of physics. It didn't matter, though, because he owned five-eighths of London and collected his share of royalties from the other systems, and lived in very fine style. And he visited and did exhibitions, and others visited the Lists in London, and every jouster in Santa Clara County dropped by to break lances with him.

The new destrier was a surprise for both of them, though, and Nick broke two lances on Mary while she was still learning the motions. After that she unhorsed him twice. The novices cheered them both impartially.

"Once more?" Nick suggested. "Then we'll have to dismount and teach sword practice."

"Best three out of five. So be it," Mary said, and set a fresh lance in its rest. But something was wrong; her right arm felt strange. She flexed it; it moved all right. Not an armor bite. She couldn't *see* anything wrong. She rode to the near end of the Lists and turned to face Sir Nicholas.

They were both at the gallop before she sorted out the sensations and realized: It was her *real* arm. She ducked outside and looked, saw something flat pasted to the inside of her wrist; she pulled it off and was inside again in time to knock Sir Nicholas from his saddle. "Outside!" she shouted, reining in. "There's something wrong."

Outside, thumb and fingernail were still clutching the thing, a powder-blue disk a couple of centimeters across. "Digiplaq" was written on it, and some numbers and a minuscule bar code.

Around her the novices opened their eyes and took notice, one by one. Nick came out of the system cubicle. "What the hell is that thing?"

"Let me see it," Sophia said. Here outside she was wearing faded sweats. She unplugged and came over to Mary's console. "That's a 48-hour digitalis patch. My father takes them—they're for heart trouble."

"My heart is as sound as a bell," Mary said, trying not to clench her teeth. "Or it used to be—after the last couple of days I make no guarantees. Somebody put this thing on my wrist while I was inside."

"But that's stupid," Sophia said. "That could make you really sick."

"The *door's* open," Scott said. They all looked through the open salle door, down the corridor to where the outside door stood ajar.

"In context, it's more than stupid," Mary said. "Somebody call the cops."

Chapter 3

The Kindness of Strangers

Somebody called the cops, while Nick protested and Mary unplugged very, very carefully, one-handed, one plug at a time. She was still holding the patch between thumb and fingernail when the police arrived.

"Hell," said the paramedic, after he had checked Mary's vital signs and examined the patch. "Look at this, sergeant. It's been cracked."

The sergeant took the patch and squinted at it. She was a heavy-set black woman with short graying hair and a mouth like a snapping turtle. "You mean this little crease? What would that do?"

"It means she would've gotten forty-eight hours' worth of digitalis in—mmm—a lot less than that. I don't guarantee it," he said to Mary, "but it *might* have killed you. It's just as well you picked it off when you did."

"And this happened while you were all inside and couldn't see. What about the surveillance system?"

The sergeant pointed to the camera that hung like a Russian icon in a corner between wall and ceiling. "That model's got a twelve-hour cycle time."

"Yes, but we didn't have it on," Nick explained. A lesser man might have shuffled or avoided the sergeant's eye. "It came with the building. I suppose it works."

"You didn't have it *on*." The sergeant turned a scandalized eye from Nick to Mary.

"We don't like being observed while we're inside," Mary said. "It's like being watched while you're asleep, all rumpled and open-mouthed."

"We'll turn it on now," Nick offered.

"Suit yourself. I'm not going back inside anyway."

"But I need you for sword practice! I can't watch a dozen people by myself, and watching tapes afterward isn't nearly as good as on-the-spot feedback."

"Sorry. I'm not going back till this is cleared up. You know what they say: Once is an accident, twice is a coincidence, three times is an enemy action. I'm not counting the plane crash."

"*Third* time?" the sergeant asked.

Mary explained about the truck on the freeway and the intruder in her house. "You can check with the Gilroy police about him; they've got copies of my tapes. Assuming they're good enough for an ID—somehow I think not." She began to shiver, suddenly, and clutched the edge of the console till the trembling stopped. "I'm going home, I guess. Perhaps you could give me a lift to the shop? If my mini isn't fixed, maybe I can rent something."

"Sounds wise to me," the sergeant said. "I think there's somebody after you, all right, but so far we've got no identification on him—if it's a *him.* We can't give you around-the-clock protection. Your best bet, probably, is to go home, where your security is good, and stay there."

"No, no, wait," Nick pleaded. "Mary, I think I've got an idea. Look, you can use the system console. You'll be all by yourself and you can lock the door. There's even a deadbolt."

"Right. That'll work till they shoot the door in."

"They can't. It's pickproof and burglarproof; look, it's even steel-clad on the inside."

It took him a while (during which time the police finished their note-taking, decided not to arrest Sophia on the grounds that her ailing father lived in West Virginia, turned on the camera and left), but eventually he persuaded her. She switched her plugs to Nick's console, fed in her disks, and locked the door and threw the bolt. She took a deep breath, made a couple of false starts, and went back inside.

After that it all seemed normal. The standard procedure at your local fighter practice was to pair the novice with an experienced fighter and let him learn by doing. Maybe Nick had intended that originally, before circumstances had left him so short of experienced fighters. Instead, he had written a dozen or so NPCs as sparring partners.

They stood in a row at one side of the Lists, shiny in their armor, all shapes, all sizes. Nick paired each of the kids with a trainer about his or her own size and mass; later they would switch around and work with the others. "Get your shield in front of you; that's what it's for," he reminded them.

The NPCs seemed to be working fine. Even for human trainers this was fairly mindless work. Swing at the lad's head and let him raise his shield to block it; swing at his thigh and let him drop his shield to block it; all in slow motion.

"Charlie! Hold!" Mary shouted, and the boy froze in his tracks. (It was the first word you learned in the Society.) "You're speeding up. This is slow work. Try not to get hit; but you lose points if you speed up to avoid getting hit."

"Sorry, m'lady," he said. "Are we collecting points? Is somebody keeping score?"

"No, no," Mary said. "Just a metaphor. Go on."

The NPCs, of course, were making all the right moves. Nick's theory was that this way the kids wouldn't pick up bad habits that would take long hours of work to unlearn—such as hitting at each other's shields instead of at each other. And Nick owned most of the salle, and Nick had set up the class; and the kids were bringing in money, and Nick was paying Mary some of it, and not for having opinions.

"Hold!" Nick bellowed, and Mary jumped. "I don't want you swinging at each other yet, I don't care how many times you've done it outside." The two novices backed away from one another, shamefaced. No wonder Nick had objected; one was a head taller than the other. "Stick with the NPCs until I say otherwise."

The virtual sun was setting behind the towers. It was November in both worlds; it would be getting dark outside too. Nick was suddenly nowhere in sight. The sparring partners disappeared; the novices were scattered all round the Lists and into the alleyways. "My lords and ladies!" she called to those in sight. "Time to make an end. Indeed,"—she glanced at the sun again—"we've gone past the time. You'll want to go home to your dinners. Tomorrow is another day." She pulled off her helm, sucking in breath, as she went into her pavilion.

The pages helped her disarm and put her horses away. The sun had set, and it was dim inside the pavilion. Suddenly something flashed across her field of vision, gleaming like a blade. It was the last thing she saw. She felt something slash at the back of her knees, and she fell.

"You can't run forever, you arrogant bitch," something whispered in her ear. "Give it up now, before I do *this* to you outside. Or *this.*"

You couldn't be hurt in VR, not truly hurt; Mary felt only a slight tingle as one part after another was cut away. She set her teeth and endured. Blinded, hamstrung, and helpless, while the anonymous voice whispered curses in her ear, she could do nothing to stop him. But if she hung on long enough, rather than escaping outside, Nick or somebody might come along and see him.

Thinking of that, and guessing by the sound that the owner of the voice was stooping near, she half-rose suddenly and struck her elbow where she thought his midsection might be. That got her some more curses, lost her the effective use of her left arm, and won her a little more time.

It wasn't all that long, probably, by the clock, though Mary had plenty of time to think things over. It ended suddenly, with the whisper breaking off in mid-sentence and then another voice saying, "Sir Mary, are you in here? Oh, sweet Jesus! Are you all right? My God, what a dumb question."

"I'm all right," Mary said. Fortunately, the guy hadn't gotten around to cutting out her tongue. "This is VR, remember? I can go outside and reboot my persona." *(If I ever want to.)* "Did you see him? Could you tell who it was?"

"I only got a glimpse. He vanished as soon as I opened the tent flap. Somebody in a tunic and trews; I couldn't see his face." She recognized the voice now; it was Scott with the curly hair. "I couldn't even tell if it was a man or a woman. Sir Mary, is there any way I can help?"

"No," she said, and went outside.

She opened her eyes and looked at her hands, counted all her fingers. Shuffled her feet. Remembered to breathe. There was a knock at the cubicle door. "Yes?"

"It's me, Scott," his voice muffled by the thickness of the door. "Are you all right?"

"I'm fine. Who's still out there besides you?" Though whoever had attacked her could've made a fast getaway while Scott was still inside.

"Nobody, Sir Mary. I'm the last one here. I hung around waiting—well, to see if I could take you to dinner. I finally went back inside looking for you. Uh, look, if you don't feel like dinner, maybe I could see you home?"

"No. Thank you." She clutched at *politesse* with both hands. "I appreciate the offer, and particularly your showing up when you did. But I'm going to stay in here a little longer. Good night, Scott. Go home."

"All right," he said after a moment. "Good night, Sir Mary. I'll see you in the morning."

Maybe, she thought as the sound of his footsteps died away in the distance, and the salle door closed with a soft *click.* There was no way of telling whether it hadn't been Scott himself; all whispers sound alike. Maybe she would dare to go inside again in the morning, and maybe not. She unplugged and slumped back into the chair, and thought about going job-hunting with a five-year-old MBA and minimal experience, in a soft economy. It looked like a lot of tuna fish sandwiches. She felt queasy, and wondered how long it would take her to muster the courage to leave that locked cubicle. For one thing, she needed to get to the ladies' room.

"Sir Mary." She looked at the door. Still locked and bolted. "Sir Mary." The voice was coming from the console.

She had forgotten, if she ever knew, that the thing had a speaker on it. It was a man's tenor voice, not Scott's and not a whisper. "Yes?"

"Sir Mary, my name is Brother Gregory of St. Alban's, and I have a problem."

"What's that?"

"I need to talk with you, and I'd rather do it inside. How can I legitimately persuade you to come back in, after the fright you've had?"

"Good question." She thought for a moment. "Well, start by telling me who you are besides Brother Gregory. Have I met you?" *(Would it matter?)*

"I don't think so. My mundane name is Greg Hampton, and I used to—"

"Oh! You wrote Old Betsy. Nick mentioned you this afternoon."

"That's right. Are they still using her for riding lessons?"

"Yes, and I need to give you a bug report. You know how she freezes going down slopes? She also freezes when you try to jump her over something."

"This afternoon you found this out? Let me look at the system log." A pause. "Oh, my gosh, yes: head over heels in midair. Definitely time for a bug fix. I'll try to get to it within a few days. First, though, I'd like to sort out this business of yours, and I need to do it inside where my tools are. I need to persuade you to trust me, and I realize it's no small task."

"Do you take your persona seriously?" Mary asked after a while. "Would you keep an oath?"

"Yes, I do. I swear by God almighty, Father, Son, and Holy Spirit, that I mean you no harm and would like to help. And—it's like falling off a horse, Sir Mary. If you don't get back on soon, you may never get back on at all."

"Well." Mary realized she had set in one plug while he had been speaking. "Oh, why not." She set in the other plug and went inside.

She stood in a round room that appeared to be in a tower. The walls were lined with wooden aumbries holding stacks of books. There was a table in the center with more books on it, and a long-legged stool drawn up to it. "Oh, here," said Brother Gregory, and a chair appeared, soft with dark red cushions.

Mary's refurbished persona felt fine, full of energy, but she sat down anyway.

Brother Gregory was a little man in a black Benedictine habit (perhaps a little shorter than Mary, but it was hard to tell while he was perched on that stool). He had a long cheerful face with a prominent chin and bright brown eyes. What hair the tonsure had left was chestnut colored and curly. He reached across the table to give her an earthenware cup full of a virtual wine as fragrant as spring. "I'd give you a real drink if I could," he said. "You could probably use it. But I'm remote. So, incidentally, was the guy who attacked you. If I'd come on the scene a little earlier, I could've traced him, but he was gone before I could touch him. I've set up the system now to trace every remote login, but a fat lot of good that does us tonight."

"Who *was* he?"

"I don't know. This is what the system log shows." A large mirror took shape on the wall, and in it a human figure appeared, bent over another that lay on the ground. The picture zoomed in to show only the attacker's face and upper body.

It was a perfect face, beautiful as an angel's, vaguely Eurasian in quality. It was certainly nobody she knew, but it looked vaguely familiar . . ."It's a composite, isn't it," she said. "You read in thousands of pictures and take an average."

"Almost certainly," Brother Gregory said. "Pretty, computer-generated, and anonymous."

"Nick turned on the surveillance system this afternoon," Mary said. "Can you access that, from where you are? See who was still out there when this happened?"

"Of course; how not?" The mirror flickered and blurred, and the image of the salle took shape. Scott sat there alone; as they watched, he turned back to his console and plugged in. "At that moment," Brother Gregory said, "Your attacker had already been in for, um, two minutes and thirteen seconds." The screen showed Scott appearing in the changing room, walking out into the Lists, approaching the curtain of Mary's pavilion, pushing it aside to catch a glimpse of a tall shape with a bright blade in its hand before it winked out like a quenched candle flame.

"So it couldn't have been Scott."

"It couldn't have been. As I said before, the attacker was remote. Anyone logging in from your salle wouldn't have been remote."

"You're a Lord of the Lists," Mary said. "Why have I never met you before?"

The little monk shrugged. "I haven't spent much time on the system since it was finished," he said. "Not much challenge. As you can see, I don't joust. I've been doing contract work mostly. But I lurk sometimes, wander around at night; that's what I was doing this evening. Sir Mary, I agree with you that what's been happening to you is no accident. I'm not even certain I'd rule out the plane crash, because I think I know what caused it. Some hacker got into the air traffic control VR last night and moved a lot of pointers—unintentionally, maybe. Your plane ducked to avoid a blip that wasn't there and clipped wings with that little private plane."

"What happened to the other plane?"

"Fell into the Bay. No survivors. So you see, Sir Mary, whoever it is that's trying to kill you, though he hasn't yet succeeded, may already have killed others. I say 'he,' having no clue to gender or number. But at least one attacker has access to this reality."

"All right; what do we do?"

"Well, I've taken the liberty of looking at your persona log over the last couple of days. I'd like to take a look at that map the Grey Knight gave you, the deed to St. Chad's-on-Wye."

"Uh. Where is it? Page?" Instead of the usual green-clad mannikin, a hand appeared out of the air to hand her the scroll. She gave it to Brother Gregory.

He held it for a minute without unrolling it, examining things Mary couldn't see. "I thought not," he said. "This manor does exist, on the upper waters of the Wye in the outskirts of the Winchester domain. But it's not supposed to be there. It wasn't part of the original system, and no one I know of wrote it. The system is spreading like the early Church, you know, outward from the cities. Out there between London and Winchester there ought to be nothing but grass and trees. Yet there is St. Chad's. I find that interesting. I want to take a look at it."

"Go ahead. You can go there, can't you?"

"Oh, yes, I could take the coordinates and appear there, in a puff of smoke *ad libitum.* But for various reasons I'd rather go overland. Sir Mary, would you like to spend a couple of days traveling through pleasant landscapes to St. Chad's-on-Wye? You own it, after all."

"I'm not sure—I don't know how long I can stay

here." She gestured back over one shoulder, indicating outside and Nick's console cubicle.

"I don't want you to stay there. Now I've really got to ask for your trust." He clasped his hands under his chin and leaned on them. "I'd like you to come to my place. I've got a lovely guest room and my own system, and the security's very good. Will you come?"

"Oh." Mary hesitated, but Gregory was the first person who seemed to have any knowledge about her situation. His eyes looked honest, and when she reluctantly agreed, his smile of relief seemed genuine. "Talking of security, can I access my home system from here?"

"Sure you can." He drew a circle in the air with his finger. A crystal ball appeared, with a keypad beneath it. Brother Gregory politely turned his head away while Mary keyed in her passwords. Everything appeared to be normal at home, and the animals had food and water, and the garden didn't need watering until Friday (if it didn't rain before then). "All right," she said, and logged out. The crystal ball vanished like a bubble bursting. "How do I get to your place?"

"It's the Kendall Building, between First and Second."

"I've been there. It's only about six blocks from where I am. No problem."

"I hope not. I'd go up First, where there're lights and people around. When you get there, tell the security box *'Aperite mihi portas justitiae.'* "

" *'Aperite mihi portas justitiae.'* Right. I'll see you

there." She put her cup down on the table and went outside.

She tidied up the console for Nick's use tomorrow, just in case. Her plugs went coiled up into the safety pocket with her disks.

The hardest part, probably, was opening the door. The salle was dark and empty. She closed the cubicle door and heard it lock behind her: Bridges burned now. She hit the ladies' room and zipped the bodice of her jumpsuit snugly to her neck. Her rib-soled shoes were good for walking or running, if she had to. If only she had a stick of rattan.

Out through the dark hallway to the outside door. It had been properly locked; maybe that kid, Scott, was on the level after all. Unless this was meant to put her off her guard. How many layers of deception could one set up? Could she trust *any*thing? She squared her shoulders and shut the door. This one she had a key to, but so did a lot of people.

She stepped down to the sidewalk. There was a sound overhead, a faint crunch like a foot shifting on gravel. She jumped and turned, and a chunk of concrete the size of her head fell with a crash to the sidewalk where she had been standing. Another attempt: But the sucker had missed.

There was a shape on the roof, the shape of a person silhouetted against the pale skyglow. She thought it was a man. He scuttled backward across the roof and vanished.

"*Missed!*" she shouted, and, "I saw you, you son-of-a-bitch! You can never hide now!" Heart pounding, she ran the two blocks to First Street. By the time she reached First, she felt wide-awake and ready to fight.

First was still enough of a major downtown street that it was lighted at night; she was just north of where it turned into a pedestrian mall. A bus went by, and a few minis. She set off at a brisk walk. It was only six blocks. She crossed the street at an intersection with a four-way stop. The few people she passed on the sidewalk didn't look like anyone she wanted to meet; but she was tall and walked quickly, and she had a fighter's stance and the body language of someone you didn't want to tangle with. Nobody bothered her.

She'd been in the Kendall Building once before, a big turn-of-the-century concrete block with an atrium inside and a forest of retrofitted solar panels on the roof. Within minutes she saw its windowless back overlooking a parking lot. You could still see where the stall lines had been blacked out, and the scars where the concrete blocks had been shifted to make spaces for minis.

It was very cold now, and quiet, but behind her she began to hear a sound out of her childhood. A muffled roar, the growl of an endangered monster, and the whisper of broad tires over the pavement. She half-turned. She could hear it a block away; she could see it a block away, shiny under the street lights, a car at least thirty years old, probably more. With a gasoline engine—you couldn't mistake that sound. The few that were left cost piles of money to operate. It was coming nearer, drifting across the center line, heading toward her. For a nightmarish instant she thought it was moving by itself—but no, the driver's head and shoulders showed backlit against the streetlight. He was wearing a dark mask of some kind. Hell! that was breaking the law right there. She turned and ran for all she was worth.

She pounded through the parking lot, dodging tree trunks and leaping concrete blocks. The car, if it tried to follow, might knock down the young trees, it *might*, but surely the blocks ought to slow it down. She heard it go past and turn (tires squealing), then accelerate again. It had found the bus lane.

The far end of the parking lot was marked by a head-high wall. She sprinted across the bus lane, got one foot atop a trash can, and vaulted the wall just as the car came into sight.

Head down, she scuttled along the building's site. As long as whoever was chasing her stayed in the car, he probably couldn't see over the wall. When she reached the Second Street side, she stood up, flattened against the building's chilly wall, and listened. No pursuing footsteps; good. She heard the car door slam and the engine start up again.

But he'd seen her going toward Second; not unlikely he'd drive round the block and try to pick up her trail again. There was a row of bushes planted along the building's Second Street front with just enough room to lie down behind them. Between that and her black jumpsuit she ought to be practically invisible.

She lay there, tried to relax, and tried to think. She didn't know anyone who collected antique cars. She didn't know anyone with that kind of money but Nick, and he drove a little green Stiletto; she'd seen it. But then, almost anyone could have stolen the thing who was old enough to remember when they were common. It might even be pre-electronic, its security system a mere mechanical lock and key, capable of being bypassed by anyone who knew which two wires to twist together. She didn't know which two wires they were, but plenty of people did.

And here it came, broad tires whispering over the pavement; she lay unmoving, hardly breathing, as it went past: rrrrrrRRRRRRrrrrrr and dying away into the distance. After a long time, when it hadn't come back, she raised her head and looked. There wasn't a living soul to see her, unless someone was peering from behind some blanked-out window.

She got up and went to the black grill at the door. "*Aperite mihi portas justitiae.*" The door clicked, and she pushed it open and went in.

A blank corridor, lined with numbered doors, the night lights barely enough to walk by. "Second floor," Brother Gregory's voice murmured from a hidden speaker. "Elevator to your right." She found the elevator and reached for the button, but the door slid open at her approach. Greg Hampton must have this whole building wired—or, more likely, he'd found his way into the wiring it already had.

The second floor was even darker than the first. "Right; then left at the T-intersection. The door isn't numbered; it's the second unnumbered door past Number 212. On your right again." This door also opened before she could touch it, exposing a bare little hallway with a Burne-Jones print on the wall. Then the inner door opened onto warmth and light, and Mozart playing in the background, and Gregory Hampton reaching out to take her hand.

Chapter 4

The Loathly Worm

A few minutes later—wrapped in a quilt, her feet up, and a steaming mug of tomato soup in her hand—Mary was saying, "But I'm supposed to help train a dozen new fighters. Nick was expecting George and Laura to be on hand when he set this up, but now they've gone to Europe. So now there's just him and me. Half an hour ago I was ready to tell him to forget it. Now it's beginning to come back to me that I promised and, more to the point, that I'm getting paid for it."

"Two good reasons," Greg agreed, and zipped into the kitchen to turn the chicken on the grill. Greg Hampton in the flesh looked a lot like Brother Gregory, except that instead of a tonsure he had a mop of curly hair that hadn't been trimmed recently, and instead of a black Benedictine habit he wore narrow faded blue jeans and a purple T-shirt, with gold lettering that said, "I'm Virtually Perfect." And the wheelchair, of course, which was an ultralight narrow-gauge job that darted between hall and kitchen with a flick of the wheels.

The apartment had clearly been designed to accommodate him, with wide doorframes and all the work surfaces at wheelchair height. What she couldn't figure out was how he'd persuaded the city authorities to let him install the apartment in the middle of an office building; the worksteading laws generally ran the other way, letting you establish your business (if reasonably quiet and nonpolluting) in your home. Maybe he had documented special need, or maybe he had hired a high-priced lawyer and pulled strings; or maybe he just knew where the right body was buried.

Or maybe he just hadn't told them.

She finished her soup and set the mug down on the tray. Greg had put her on a big three-way futon, its back up, its foot extended. The thing was so comfortable she thought she might never get up again. She stretched and arched her back. She was facing a wall-sized TV screen—turned off—and by stretching out an arm she could reach the console of Greg's very high-powered system. He could run a domain of his own on that thing and be the Duke of Normandy or something, but apparently he didn't care to; or if he did, she'd never heard of it. Over the console hung a copy of the old sign that began "Achtung! Alle Lookenspeepers!" and ended "Bitte relaxen und watchen das Blinkenlights."

Next to the TV screen an alcove full of potted plants provided a touch of nature and a whiff of oxygen. Among them stood a tall statue of an armored knight, carved of some kind of hardwood, thin as a broomstick. No, wait, it was not just any knight but Don Quixote with his barber's-basin helm. The patron saint of *Chivalry* players, or if not, he should be.

Greg had plugged in briefly while dinner was cooking and come outside to say, "I was right. The Duke of Winchester knows nothing about St. Chad's. Neither does his sysop. They're curious about where it came from too, and the Duke has given me *carte blanche* to run and find out."

Dinner was grilled chicken, rice pilaf with peas and fresh mint in it, and salad. At first Mary had thought she was too jittery to eat, but the hot soup had changed her mind for her. For several minutes neither of them spoke.

"The manor of St. Chad's is illegal, isn't it?" she asked presently. "I mean, besides that the Duke didn't authorize it in his domain. It's an illegal entry into the Winchester system."

"Oh, it's all of that," Greg said. "The rules are different inside and outside, which makes it difficult for me at least to focus on what's wrong. Certainly whoever it is shouldn't have set up without the Duke's permission. But in the real Middle Ages they didn't value open space the way we do, having so much more of it. To call a place 'a wilderness' was not to pay it a compliment. Anybody who wanted to set up a new settlement would've gotten the landowner's leave—if he'd asked for it. There's the rub.

"Incidentally, the Duke sends his greetings and says he'll be perfectly happy to let you keep St. Chad's on the Winchester domain and do some kind of homage for it—pay him a fee of a virtual peppercorn per year, something like that. Or, of course, you could pay a more substantial fee, wainloads of grain or horses or six NPC knights to fight in his wars. I'd be happy to write them for you. No. No." He tapped his forehead with his fingertip. "Stay on track, Greg. We have to figure out why it's there first."

"We haven't got enough people playing *Chivalry* to fight wars anyway."

He gestured nonchalantly with his fork. "Wait till they get the induction plugs on the market, which could be as early as year after next. Then you'll have people." He waved the fork again, took notice of it, and speared a piece of chicken and ate it.

"In outside terms, well, yes, it is an illegal entry into the Winchester system, an illegal addition to it. But whoever built it hasn't done any harm; in fact he's made improvements—in the realtor's sense—and one's first impulse is to say So what?

"But then you remember that either the same guy or a different one went blundering into Air Traffic Control and killed four people Sunday night, and you start thinking, 'Well, no, we'd better shut this guy down, fix the holes in our security, so it doesn't happen again.' Or I do, anyway."

"I should think you'd be involved in the intellectual property issue. This is your code the guy is hacking, or some of it."

"Oh, intellectual property." He forked up his last bite of salad and ate it. "I have the fuzziest feelings about intellectual property, you can't imagine. It's not a medieval concept. If this person has taken my code and written a good manor with it, it seems outrageous that I should be able to prosecute him for his creativity. Or that the law should do so on my behalf. If he did a sloppy job, that's another matter. I'll catch him inside and fry him.

"I don't know, though. How tolerant am I really? I've never been tried. It may be that when we get there I'll see some subroutine that I wrote, modified into something else, and I'll rise up crying, 'That's *mine,* you bastard!—' "

The microwave rang, and Greg brought out peach turnovers. "I do really cook sometimes," he said, "but this is faster."

The turnovers were still too hot to eat. "Well," Greg said, "I do want to go overland to St. Chad's, because there are things I want to look at on the way. And I would like to have you go with me, because you own the place. Your name is on the deed now. If there are only subroutines there, they'll accept you as the owner, accompanied by your faithful clerk. Or they ought to. And if there are people there—well, we'll take that as it comes.

"Just how much coaching did you promise Nick you'd do?"

She thought for a moment. "A couple of hours every afternoon. I've been helping out with sword practice and riding lessons because Nick's short-handed, but all I contracted to do was coaching in the Lists. I think it was part of Nick's advertising: Learn to joust with"—she waved a hand—"la-de-da, the Champion of the Winchester Lists. Though I wasn't Champion then, only—"

"Only a famous knight who makes a good living on the tourney circuit."

"Not that good. I hate to think of how many tunas have gone to a tinny death on my account."

"Then will you come with me? I can set up a door between wherever we are and the Lists at London. You can just step through, and even Sir Nicholas can't tell where you came from. Not that I suspect Nick particularly (I think these are cool enough to eat now), but what he doesn't know he can't accidentally let slip to somebody else."

"Why is this happening?" Mary burst out. "Why is it happening to *me?* Does it have something to do with St. Chad's?"

"That's what I want to find out. It's the only unusual thing that's happened to you recently. In VR, anyway. Has anything unusual happened outside?"

"God, no. Paid my bills, petted my cats, dug in my garden."

"And St. Chad's itself is unusual, to the extent that it shouldn't be there. That's one of the reasons I want to go overland, to see if anything else is strange and different in Winchester."

"Should we tell the police all this?"

"We haven't much to tell them—just my hunches and suspicions. I *think* that paramedic convinced the sergeant that something was fishy. But it's going to take the San José police a while to interface with the Gilroy police and put it all together. They're busy, and they get so many paranoids and conspiracy theorists, it's hard for them to tell when somebody's got real enemies. If I hint at industrial espionage, maybe they'll take an interest. I'll e-mail them in the morning—from an anonymous login."

"Why anonymous?"

He shrugged. "If I can get into the police system and read the reports, so could others. Maybe when this is all over, I'll send them a prospectus, offering to plug their holes for them."

"At a nice fat fee."

"Oh, the money doesn't matter. But I think it'd be fun."

"I'll have to call my neighbor," Mary said, "have her come in and tend to my cats. The food and water are automated, but the litter box isn't, and besides, they get lonely. The door knows her. I could call her in the morning."

She hadn't actually said she'd do it. But Greg smiled. "Let me get the dishes into the sink. Then we'd better get some rest. You need it, and I'm going to."

The guest room had a wide bed and a bathroom big enough to dance in, and the closet had rods at both sitting and standing heights. Greg was prepared for guests of all kinds and conditions. ("The money doesn't matter." Clearly this man came from a different side of the tracks.) There was nothing hanging in the closet but a terry bathrobe. The walls and furnishings were in soothing shades of green and brown. There were no pictures, no windows, but a single bookshelf by the side of the bed held *The Lord of the Rings, The Golden Road, Moonwise, Le Morte d'Arthur.* She put out a hand and drew it back. She was so tired her eyes wouldn't focus. She shucked off her jumpsuit, did a sketchy wash of hands and face, and crawled into bed. The air conditioning made a little sound like trickling water. The darkness felt like safety. She fell asleep before she could analyze it.

"Unfortunately," Greg said the next morning, "I don't have a washer here; I send the laundry out. His T-shirt this morning had visited the laundry many times. Its black had faded to a burnished gray, and the lettering was faint: *PhinisheD.* "And I don't think it would be a good idea to send out a muddy black jumpsuit with a sun in splendor on it and my address attached. I can order you some new ones, though. Park's can deliver them by mid-afternoon. They'd better not be black. What other colors do you like?"

"Doesn't matter. Green. Size 38, long." If she survived this, she'd pay him back later. If not—no, never mind that.

"I think we've covered everything," Greg said. He was already plugged in. "You've got your cables?" Mary uncoiled them, held the *cis* ends, and gave him the *trans* ends to plug into the console. After that, she plugged in—do it in reverse order and you'd live to regret it—and they went inside.

The room was small and cold and had huge heavy doors in at least three of its walls. The smells of outdoors, early morning with a hint of rain, leaked in from one of them. From the door opposite came a whiff of incense and the sound of Gregorian chant. "This way," said Greg, and opened the third door.

Dawn was breaking over London. The castle was a black silhouette, the trees were skeletal shadows, and the birds were just tuning up. "Birds!" she remembered suddenly. "Yesterday, there was some bird or other watching me everywhere I went."

"Was there, now. Yes, if I wanted an unobtrusive

bug, and I couldn't go invisible, there are plenty of good all-purpose birds in the library that would make a good mask." He looked thoughtful. "There are no birds around at present that are anything but birds. Just the same, I think it's going to be a very foggy morning in London. It's November, and the mist is rising from the Thames." And it did, and it poured over the ground and engulfed them until Mary could barely see Brother Gregory, an arm's length away. "By the time it burns off, we'll be out of sight. Let's go; the road is this way." He led the way, small in his black habit and cloak atop a sturdy mule.

There was nothing else to look at—if he could see the road, she couldn't—and she might as well take the opportunity to think. But her thoughts led nowhere of any use.

Somebody, or perhaps several people, had tried to kill her. Why? Because of the manor of St. Chad's? Granted it was worth a pile of virtual marks, but why couldn't the unknown hacker simply shrug, "Oh well, easy come, easy go," and hack another someplace else? Surely he had kept backups. If the manor was already written—and Brother Greg seemed convinced St. Chad's did exist out there—with a few changes it could become St. Cuthbert-on-the-Strand or St. Guthlac-in-the-Marsh. Or Sts. Peter and Paul on the Severn, if the Peters estate ever gave permission. Or if they didn't. Maybe that was the problem, there was something illegal about St. Chad's other than its having been hacked into the Winchester domain, that they'd find out about when they got there.

Was that why? Had somebody decided she had to be killed rather than let her get a look at St. Chad's? The thought should have scared her witless. Instead, it stiffened her resolve. Chase *her* through darkened parking lots, would they? She'd show 'em.

If only the Grey Knight had managed his finances better, not taken on jousts he couldn't afford to lose, none of this would have happened, blast him. He deserved to bear semé of hoofmarks for the rest of his career, going over budget like that.

The Grey Knight, now: He must be part of the mystery. The white-shield whom nobody knew. He was a decent fighter, though foolhardy. Who had trained him, and where? Had he written St. Chad's himself, which would explain his having it to give away, and had he thought better of it later? Or did he have partners who had put pressure on him to get it back? This led back to the question of why they couldn't change a few lines of code and generate another manor in a quiet backwater of another domain.

She was of the opinion that there were more than one of them. It didn't seem likely that the same person could have put the Digiplaq on her arm, there in the salle, and also logged in remote to bushwhack her in her pavilion. Though some hours had intervened.

She didn't know of any system closer than Tintagel, in San Francisco, several hours away by mini, bus, or BART. Well, that antique gasoline-powered monster could've done it in two. But it would've had to break some speed limits and then make it back again while she was inside talking to Brother Greg.

If he'd logged in from a PC, he'd have been a ghost, unable to touch her.

Wait—she did know of one other system nearby: Greg's. But she wasn't going to waste time suspecting him. He could have done her in by now: poison in the soup or another Digiplaq while she slept. The idea intrigued her: The result would've been a genuine death by heart failure, and then he could have taken her up to the roof (in the wheelchair? Of course: His arms must be strong as a wrestler's, and she could have rested in his lap, draped over his shoulder) and dumped her over the side. No, scratch Brother Greg.

She had thought the fog was thick already, but now they were riding down into a dip in the road where she couldn't see so much as the mule's tail in front of her, and the air was like a lungful of thick damp wool. You could carry VR verisimilitude too far. The tail reappeared slowly, like the visitation of a saint, as they climbed the hill.

And how had the Grey Knight managed to fight as well as he did, if he was remote? The farther away you were from the system your brain was connected to, the longer the impulses took to travel over wire/cable/satellite link. It might be only fractions of a second, but that kind of lag in your reflexes was enough to make you lose. The technicians and engineers kept saying the lag was too small to make a difference, but the fighters could *feel* it. Had the Grey Knight been remote only as far as another part of Philadelphia? Or did he know something they didn't, new technology or mental discipline? Was *that* what they'd find at St. Chad's?

She opened her mouth and closed it again. She'd ask questions later, when the mist cleared and she could see. Right now any number of birds, beasts, or banshees could be eavesdropping. At some point or other the mist would burn off, or they'd climb out of the valley of the Thames and leave it behind.

They were passing through woods now, cold, wet, naked trees whose leaves had all fallen to carpet the wood with muddy beige. The sky was growing brighter; the wet fog smell was yielding to the sweet smell of grass in the sun.

Then they rose over the shoulder of one more little hill, and on the other side it was clear. The land here was full of gentle dips and rises but flat on the grand scale. The wood was breaking up into little scattered groves, and the green grass was bright under the early sun. From time to time they heard birdsong; no other sign of life.

"These birds are just birds?" Mary asked.

"Oh, yes. The system, you understand, generates these sub-objects in idle time, and disperses them via a random-number generator coded to resemble the real English ecology. The life forms are spreading out. In a couple of years you'll see rabbits and squirrels in the woods, maybe an occasional fox. Someday, sheep, plowed fields, peasants' cottages."

"Peasants, too?"

"Ummm." Greg rubbed his chin and threw back his cowl. "You wouldn't believe the arguments we've had, and are still having, about NPCs. Not so much whether they'd chew up too much cycle time as whether to have NPCs at all is politically correct. It's the Little- and Big-Endians all over again."

"Do you ever get people wanting to come in and be peasants?"

"Not very often. You don't go through tedious and expensive surgery so you can plow all day. There was one couple who wanted *us* to pay for their surgery so they could do the peasant act they do at the Ren Faire. But they weren't peasants, they were clowns, and when they learned we hadn't any marital software, they gave up the whole idea—"

"Shhh! What's that?" It was a bird, she supposed, but a bird in the grip of some ecstatic vision, whose voice played through the still air like a fountain that rose and fell and rose again.

"That's a skylark. They always start tuning up this time of day." They reined in the horses and listened for a minute, while Greg looked around him and overhead. "There he is. See him? That little dot? They nest on the ground, fly straight up and straight down again."

From time to time one of the local radio stations play a piece called "The Lark Ascending." This sounded just like it, but much faster, a cascade of notes almost too quick to follow. The composer must have slowed the melody down so that the violinist could keep up with it. They listened until the tiny speck descended at last and was silent. "Now it's morning," Greg said, and touched his mule's sides with his sandaled heels and rode on.

"Who wrote him?"

"Nobody. We fed in all the recordings we could get and told the computer to write its own algorithm. Sounds like it worked."

"Up above the world you fly, like a dust mote in the sky."

"Ah. I like that. I've got a garden in St. Alban's. I'd like to have a whole monastery, but so far no one else has been interested in a Benedictine persona. But I have an herber, and an orchard. And I've got nightingales. Come and visit sometime, when all this is over."

They rode for some hours through the pleasant, empty landscape. Up and down the little hills and valleys, and from the crest of each hill they could see a little stream, like a silver thread, sparkling in the distance. The hills on the far side were marked here and there with patches of white. At first, Mary thought it was more mist.

"Well, well," Greg said at last, when they had reached the river bank and could see clearly. "Sheep."

They were fine-looking sheep, rather cleaner than the real thing, gleaming white against the green hillsides. The wool curled on their backs, having grown in since their last shearing, if they had been there that long. No peasants, Greg had said. Who or what came out to shear them, and what happened to the wool? Or did they simply change into shorn state when the system clock said so?

"You said sheep weren't due to appear yet."

"So I did."

"So what are they doing here now?"

"Good question," Greg said. He was staring ahead of him, intent on something she couldn't see. "Let's get a closer look."

The stream was shallow; clumps of yellow iris

grew in it. They forded it easily where it ran over the road. Something darted away through the shallows: small fish, or tadpoles.

Seen closer up, the sheep were still unremarkable. (Except that they were there at all.) They raised flat white faces to watch the horses ride by and lowered their heads again to their grazing. Sheep weren't very bright even in the real world. She wondered how much code it took to write one, and if you could roast it, and how it would taste.

Now, *there* would be a market for virtual food and drink: reconstructing lavish banquets nobody could afford any more. Why, they could serve beef! You'd have a sandwich or something outside and a multi-course feast inside: subleties, venison, roasted swan and all complete. No heartburn, no cholesterol, no heterocyclic amines. She opened her mouth and shut it again. She'd talk to Greg about this outside where it was secure.

"Sussex Downs sheep," Greg said. "Close enough to what you would've found in reality."

They turned a bend in the road: a different view of more green hills, clotted with white sheep. There was a blackened patch on one of the hills: There had been a grass fire. What was that in the road ahead—? Mary couldn't help but remember the old linguistics joke from one of her English classes: "What's that in the road—a head?" For it *was* a head, a sheep's head, or part of one. Yuck. One of her cats had left her a present the other day, the remnants of a mouse he'd caught. He'd bitten neatly through the braincase and eaten the rest, leaving her the facial bones, ears, and frontal lobes in a tiny, nasty lump. Something had done the same with this sheep.

"It's a neat job," Greg commented. "I don't mean the segmentation, I mean the coding."

"Coding of what?"

"What would you think?"

"Lion?" Mary guessed, thinking of her tomcat. "Were there still lions in England in the Middle Ages? There certainly were in legends. . . ."Her voice trailed off as she looked at him. His expression was that of one saying "Come on, come on, you're getting warmer. . . ." In a small voice she said, "Dragons?"

"Only one dragon at a time, actually. They're very territorial, and their territories are the size of a county. In this case, a domain."

"Oh, come on, Greg—"

"When Nick and George and Chandra and I first started putting this system together, we drafted up some dragons. They were pretty low-res, but they worked okay. But we finally decided we wanted to do a realistic medieval setting, not a fantastic one. I wonder who took the time to write a dragon realistic enough to drop stray morsels out of the corner of his mouth. This explains the sheep, you see. Somebody put them out to multiply and be dragon food. They could have made it run on magic, of course, and never have to eat at all. But it's so much more effective for you to come upon it, squatting among the scattered flock, its prey still bleating in agony as it munches on the hindquarters; it makes you feel justified in killing it. Would you like to kill it?"

"Moi?"

"I don't see anybody else. Oh, I could kill it if I

had to, get the process ID and kill that. It would look a lot like magic. But some programmer wrote that dragon so some knight could have the fun of slaying it. Wouldn't you like to give it a try? We can solve the problem of where it came from later."

"Where is this dragon?"

"Up the road a piece. We'll find it, or maybe it'll find us."

"I'll need a lance. I didn't bring one."

"You wouldn't want one of those hollow tournament numbers anyway; they're made to break easily. Here." It lay in her lance rest, a long wooden pole tipped with steel, its handle leather-wrapped. "That'll weigh a little more than you're used to; it's ash." Mary lifted it, tested how it moved. Not too bad. She set it in the rest again and rode on. Brother Gregory on his mule fell in behind her.

They rode on for several minutes. Once the road forked and Greg said, "To the right." And when she had taken that road, "St. Chad's is in this direction anyway."

They came upon it more suddenly than she expected. They rounded another turn in the road, and there it sat. She almost missed seeing it at first; it was as green as the hills and almost blended in. Its skin was matte and soft-looking—if it had scales, they were too small to see at this distance. It looked more like a worm than a snake. A faint whiff of sulfur blew in on the breeze. *Oh, good, the wind's in our face; it won't catch our scent.* But no doubt it would see them.

Its body was coiled up like a rattlesnake's, its front paws tucked under like a cat's. Its wings were folded against its body. Even if she could sneak up to it, even if its skin was permeable, not much of it was exposed. They'd have to stir it up.

The horse and mule had stopped in their tracks when they saw the dragon, but they made no move to flee. Probably Greg wouldn't let them. He seemed determined to have her fight this thing. Wanted to see how well the program worked, no doubt; and the exercise would add a dollop of blood-guts-and-gore to what so far had been a fairly intellectual pursuit. Well, she'd show 'em. She took her helm from the saddlebow and put it on.

That did it: Its eye had caught the movement. The dragon raised its sleek head from among its coils and gave her its attention.

The head on its long neck was as smooth as a swan's—was it covered with feathers? she thought not—and had a hooked beak and brilliant eyes, large, round, and golden, blinking only seldom; it turned its head this way and that to look at her from both sides. She had to move her own head to keep seeing it through the eyeslit.

Somebody had reasoned dragon:dinosaur:bird. Not a bad choice. "Can it see only when its head is still? Does it have to bob its head like a pigeon when it moves?"

"Ummm," Greg said. "No, that was a good guess, but its vision seems to be continuous."

"What about its skin? It looks soft. Is it armored?"

"Oh, yes, a two-phase material of skin and bone. You'll never get through the dorsal side; go for the soft underbelly."

"Which it hasn't shown me yet. Do I have to attack it?" But as she spoke, it began to uncoil.

Somebody had written it to be killed; it had to be killable. But was she going to survive it, or would she die in the process like Beowulf, dying for the people? But there were no people, only sheep. The dragon raised its head high, like a cobra, and spread its wings.

Small wings, webs of skin stretched across long fingers, proper to a dragon and gracefully shaped but small in proportion to its body. "Can it fly?"

"Yes," Greg said. "Its nature tends to seek its own element, which is fire. So it's lighter than it looks, and those wings don't so much lift it as propel it. There's earth mingled with its fire, or it wouldn't be visiting here at all."

He must have that right; the dragon was rearing into the air, higher than a real snake could have gone. Its taloned forelegs were outstretched. It seemed to have no hindlegs at all. Real snakes—or their ancestors, crawling through the duff on the forest floor—had lost the forelegs first; but what the hell, this was a dragon. And it was displaying acres of pale green underside, ready for her to strike. She'd hope that meant it was stupid. She spurred her horse and leveled her lance as they began to charge.

"Fortuna audaces adjuvat!"

But she should have charged earlier; the worm's vital parts were rising out of her reach. She galloped over scorched, flattened grass and plunged her spear into the soft hide.

It was like connecting with a sandbag stuffed with meat. The lance went home, the stallion set his hooves to the ground and came to a stop. Mary's feet, braced in the stirrups, and her high saddleback kept her from a flying fall.

Her lance was rising, still stuck into the tail; she gripped the handle and pulled it free. The blood on its shaft was red and glossy, and it steamed like a washed hand in winter.

The last five or six meters of tail left the ground with a lashing motion that nearly sent horse and rider flying. (Perhaps it had only now realized it'd been wounded. That was a long body for the nerve impulses, or whatever it used instead, to travel.) It moved faster than she had expected. Low mass, a skin that shed turbulence like a dolphin's—? She'd ask Greg. Later.

The sulfur smell was stronger here, where it had been lying. The dragon turned in the air, preparing to attack. Thin plumes of smoke rose from its nostrils, like a hardboiled detective in an old movie—"Greg!" she shouted. "This thing breathes fire, right?"

"Yes!" he shouted back. "But don't worry, your shield's enchanted."

My shield's what? Mary spared a moment's glance at her shield, the same one she'd carried ever since she'd been knighted. It looked no different. The dragon was close now, headed directly toward her, claws tucked in, smoke escaping its mouth in puffs as it pumped its lungs. She raised the shield to cover her face—

The dragon's breath was no more than pleasantly warm, but it stank. The shadow went by overhead. When it had passed, she turned stiffly in the saddle to see where it had gone. There it was, off in the south, turning for another run. It seemed not to notice Brother Greg and his mule; perhaps they were invisible to it. She looked at the ground beneath her, fire-blackened except where a bow-wave of green curved round the stallion and herself and trailed off behind them. The shield at any rate was performing as advertised.

The dragon was coming her way again, not head-on this time but circling toward the east. It was bleeding, she noticed. Too much to hope that puncture in the tail had hit any vital organ, but it must have opened the wound in lashing its tail about. Great gouts of blood fell like bombs, drifting slowly to earth after the shadow had passed.

Wait a minute—

But here it came again. She turned the horse to face it and raised her shield to guard. Last time that spell had protected not just the shield itself but the entire area of horse and rider, two meters wide and more than that in height. So shieldwork was going to be different from what worked in the Lists. She could peer out from behind it and still be safe. Logic said so, and this was a very logical dragon.

It was upon her now, mouth open in a silent roar, sparkling yellow-white plasma pouring forth like the blast from a rocket engine. It was growing darker overhead. She raised her lance—just an armslength short—she stood up in the stirrups and thrust the lance as high as she could.

The spearpoint slit the worm's belly and opened it up, neat and nasty as a paper cut, as it went by. It wasn't very deep, though, blast it. Once again she hadn't pierced its heart, or whatever it used as symbolic equivalent. It hissed like a boiler bursting, fiery blood oozing out all through its underside. It was rising now, gaining altitude until it seemed no longer than Mary's forearm, high above. It turned, flipping its tail aloft like a dolphin, and fell headlong. She raised shield and spear overhead and took a couple of deep breaths.

Again the cloud of glittering fire that would have made cinders of her, if not for the shield. The spear struck home—and was jerked from her hand as the dragon pulled out of its dive and skimmed low over the ground. Blast! Her sword hadn't nearly enough reach—

But perhaps it wouldn't be needed. The spear had hit something important, and the dragon's wings were beating slower and slower, neck and tail lashing about in pain and turning the creature this way and that in the air. The wings gave one final beat and fell limp, and the dragon came to a stop in midair. Slowly it settled to the ground, leaking fire like an elderly balloon losing helium. Mary lowered her shield and made the sign of the Cross: It seemed appropriate.

"Well done, Sir Mary," Brother Gregory called to her. "You didn't need my rain after all." Overhead, black-bellied clouds had gathered; now they were beginning to break up. If you dismount, you can finish it off. Its heart is right behind its forelegs."

She slid to the ground and drew her sword. Her shield she held close to her breastplate: The thing might be dying but it wasn't yet dead, and she didn't want to catch its last breath in her face. There behind the foreleg was a slight depression, as if to say "Insert Here." She plunged in the sword: It slid through soft tissues and encountered something solid. She pushed harder and felt it penetrate, and warmth crept up the blade into her hand. In fact, the fingersbreadth of visible blade was shining white as moonlight. She hastily withdrew the sword and watched it cool again. The dragon's mouth puffed forth a little smoke and it lay still. The eagle eyes glazed over. Mary wiped her swordblade on some surviving grass—it was still brighter than real steel—and sheathed it.

"Don't forget your spear." Greg had ridden up on his mule. "There it is, under the abdomen."

"Broken, I should think."

"Oh, no. Pull it loose, and you'll see a sight."

She grasped the leather-wrapped grip and pulled it free. The blood had stained the shaft: It looked more like polished mahogany now than white ash. If the blood didn't rot it, it would probably increase its strength. An extra zillion spell points.

The body moved, and Mary jumped back by reflex. No, it was dead; it might be reptilian enough to go on twitching till sundown—

The head began to rise on its long neck, and she hastily fell back several steps. "It's all right," Greg said. "Watch. The weight of your lance was all that was holding it down."

First the head and tail, then the trunk, the body of the dragon rose into the air like a long-drowned man rising through water. Twisting aimlessly with every breeze, it rose into the scattering storm clouds, hissing and sputtering like a bonfire in the rain. There was a flash of light, as if some fiery organ had finally shorted out. Then it was gone, leaving a large open patch in the cloud cover. The sun poured through it, a long shaft of light that pointed north, further along the road.

"Greg! That was an Aristotelian dragon, right?"

"Well, yes."

"It uses non-Newtonian physics. It's a *really* medieval dragon. I knew when I saw its blood falling behind it, not under it. And then it stopped dead in midair and fell straight down. Tartaglia hasn't been born yet and nobody knows about trajectories. How long have *you* known? How did you find out?"

Greg shrugged. "I looked at the code. The source code isn't on this system, which I find very interesting, but I found the comments in hypertext. It's one o'clock; let's go outside and get some lunch."

Neither of them cared to cook; Greg heated soup and piroshki in the microwave while Mary took a badly needed shower. She emerged wrapped in the terry robe. "That jumpsuit is getting strong enough to get up and walk around on its own."

"Oh, don't stand on formality on my account. Anyway, Park's will be delivering sometime this afternoon." He looked at his watch. "As soon as we've eaten, we'd better get off to London."

"We?"

"Oh, I'm going along. To observe. Nobody will notice me; I've been doing invisible personae for years. You might see a shadow or something; nobody else will."

* * *

When they went inside again they were still on the road, where black patches on the green marked where the dragon died. The sheep were beginning to drift back in. "Now what? Will the sheep overrun the place without a predator to keep them down?"

"Oh, no problem," Greg said. "The system will generate another dragon in about another week. Now, then." A door appeared in the air, a solid-looking pair of wooden doors big enough for a horse and rider to go through, with two standard green-coated Lists pages standing by to open it. "Go on through," Greg said. "It opens directly onto the London Lists; you won't need your arming pavilion. Though I can set it up out here if you want it."

The pages swung the doors open, and Mary rode through. The novices on their Old Betsys and Nick on black Nightgaunt were just assembling, ready to tilt at the Saracen. She looked behind her: no sight of the road or of Brother Greg, only a sparkling mist. Good. The doors swung to.

But she still had the reddened spear, not the sort of thing to use on the Saracen. "Page! Put this somewhere safe and bring me a tilting lance."

She got cheers from the squires and a polite greeting from Nick, who kept watching her out of the corner of his eye. "All right," she said, grasping the lance. "This is how it's done."

The Saracen was an effigy mounted on a pole, a red crescent painted on its chest like a target, an arm holding a wooden sword extended from its side. It took less energy to make it spin on its axis than to knock it pole and all out of its socket, and the idea was that if you hit it dead center with your lance, you'd knock it down. If you hit it off-center, it would spin like a weathervane and spank you with its sword as you rode past. For the rest, it had a turban on its wooden head, a beard and a scowl on its painted face, and Persian slippers on the canvas feet that dangled below the target. From where Mary sat the red crescent looked no bigger than a fingernail paring. She spurred her horse to the gallop and lowered her lance.

The lance-tip struck the Saracen dead-center, between the horns of the crescent, and the effigy fell to the ground with a muffled thump. The novices cheered as Mary wheeled back toward them, and pages scurried forth to set up the Saracen again. "That's how it's *supposed* to look," she said. "Now you try it."

They formed a long line, a dozen iterations of Old Betsy nose to tail, and took their turns riding full tilt at the Saracen, hitting it somewhere off-center and getting spanked as the wooden sword swung around. Charlie actually hit the thing amidships and knocked it down.

"Well struck!" Mary called as he joined the end of the line.

"Beginner's luck, m'lady," he called back. "Watch me blow it next time." And she watched, and he did blow it, and got clouted, and rode away trying to rub his back through his armor.

Nightgaunt edged up, and Nick leaned aslant to speak into her ear. "Where was that door you came out of?"

"Elsewhere. Look, Nick, somebody's been trying to kill me."

"Again?"

"Again, or still. So I've found a place to hide out, and I'll come in to train these youngsters, because I said I would. But I'm not telling anyone where I am."

"My God, woman, do you suspect me?"

"Not particularly; but what you don't know, you can't accidentally let slip. Wups!" One of the novices had overbalanced and fallen over the Lists barrier. Mary rode off to right him and offer advice.

"So how's it feel to you, working remote?" Nick again, taking advantage of a moment's lull.

"Not bad. Not nearly as severe as I'd expected." In fact, she hadn't noticed any lag in her reactions at all. This didn't surprise her, really, since she was logged in only six blocks away, a mere sidestep for photons traveling through cable. But Nick wasn't to know that.

Her glance slid sideways and she went tense. There was a little bird hopping along the gallery railing, turning its head this way and that, watching her. She helped another squire rise from the sawdust and, while Nick took on the next one, rode up to the railing. How did you confront a sparrow? Or tell it, "Cut it out, I know what you're up to"? Particularly when you didn't?

But the bird didn't flee as she approached. Instead, it hopped closer. It was a pretty little thing, with smooth breast feathers and an ivory beak tinged with rose. But rather bedraggled; it was missing most of the russet feathers from the top of its head—

A bird with a tonsure. Right. It cocked its head at her, and she raised one hand in unobtrusive salute.

By the end of the afternoon the trainees were shaping up nicely; this idea of Nick's might actually work. Tomorrow they would tilt at the Saracen some more and try a few bouts against the NPC sparring partners. By Friday, if Nick's timetable didn't go belly up, they would be jousting against Nick and Mary and each other. Some of the youngsters were showing signs of real talent; one or two seemed destined for the spectators' gallery, but she didn't tell them that. It was time to go anyway. "Page, my sp—"

And something screamed like a banshee, and her stallion reared and turned in midair. (Jerry had pulled out all the stops on this horse.) Mary kept her seat, just.

Bearing down on her was a knight in scale, on a scale-armored horse. Or was that its hide? All the scale was a dull burnished gold. The lance in the rider's hand looked solid. She waited a moment, until he was close enough, and touched the reins. The stallion stepped aside and the golden knight plunged on past.

"Page! My *spear!*" But the pages had scattered across the arena. This made sense if they had been real, but they were only subroutines; how had the golden knight frightened them? He was turning for another pass. "Brother—!" but she mustn't mention Greg's name, and where was he, anyway? Mary drew her sword.

As the golden knight went past again, she struck at the lance and sliced it in two. He threw the useless fragment to the ground *(Ah! Temper, temper!)* and drew his sword.

Now he approached more slowly, looking for an opening. Would he find one? Would the enchanted software of her shield repel sword-strokes all about her as it did fire? If so, she could ignore all his blows, ride up to him and cut his helmet-straps. (And if so, it would be unfair advantage and she'd have to retire it from the Lists.) She wouldn't put it to the test just now. She raised her shield to guard and drew her arm back to strike.

The golden knight struck first, a good head blow that rebounded noisily from her shield. She struck in return, and caught his shield slantways across its top edge.

But the moonbright sword cut through the shield like cheese, hissing slightly like a drop on a griddle, and cut through the knight as well. A furrow as deep as a hand opened up in his chest; fragments of scale went flying. Mary had never seen so much blood, not even in real life. The golden knight screamed again—Christ! what a sound!—and toppled slowly from his saddle. For a moment he writhed on the ground, changing shape, his arms and legs contracting to mere flippers. Then horse and man winked out together.

"Page!" Mary bellowed, at the top of the augmented voice she'd never needed to use before. "My spear and my door. *Now!*" And she had them. She sheathed her sword and rode between the doors, through a curtain of mist, onto the dusty road between green hills. The blackened pastures were still there, with a few brave grassblades beginning to poke through. The sheep were moving in. There was no sign of Greg.

She looked from one hillside to the next. There was no sign of anybody. But a moment later Brother

Gregory winked in, mule and all. "I'm sorry, Sir Mary, I wasn't there during that fight. There was a person from Park's at the door. I just looked at the system log. Your opponent was remote again, like the other one."

"Remote from where? Could you tell?"

"No, not in the physical sense. My trap did capture his netaddress, but that doesn't tell me where he is on the planet. Sir Mary, I'd like to ride on another mile or two before we stop for the night. Get us out of this marked area, which might draw the interest of whoever wrote that dragon." So they rode on for another few miles, through quiet hillscapes empty but for sheep.

"I still need a name for this horse," she said after a while.

"You haven't chosen one yet? If I may suggest one: Virtue."

"Oh. Because he's virtually perfect? Well, but the original meaning is 'manhood', isn't it. Yes, I like that. Does your mule have a name?"

"Ignatius. It's an obscure joke—St. Ignatius of Antioch preferred being a martyr to having his friends rescue him—but it fits this mule. Twelfth Night present from George, a couple of years ago."

It was becoming too quiet to suit Mary. It was almost as if she, like Greg, could look through empty hills and sky into the subroutines, automatic and unchanging, that generated them. Oh, someday all this landscape would be filled with moving things, birds and rabbits and people. As the last dregs of fossil fuel trickled out, unless solar cells improved by orders of magnitude or somebody discovered the One True

Storage Battery, people would have to abandon travel altogether, except by foot or fiber-optic cable.

"So how did it feel, fighting remote?" Greg said after a while.

"Nick wanted to know that too. Truth to tell, I couldn't feel any difference. But we're only six real blocks from London."

"Well," Greg said, "I've been wondering when was the best time to tell you this."

Mary sat straight up in the saddle. "Tell me *what?*"

"Well," Greg said again. "You haven't been out having tea somewhere all the time the electronics folk and the jousters have been feuding over lag time. The one lot insist that with optical switching there's no appreciable lag between London inside and London outside, and the others insist they can feel the difference, and the first lot say it's all in their minds—"

"And?"

"We're remote *here,*" Greg said simply. "We're plugged in in San José, but this is the Winchester domain. Feel any different? Wait, there's more. That brook we forded is the domain boundary. You were remote when you fought the dragon. Did you feel any difference?"

"No!" She could feel her mouth hanging open, and closed it.

"Sir Mary, I hate like anything to tell you it's all in your mind, which is a fine one. But these signals are traveling at nine-tenths of *c*. Neural impulses travel at a hundred meters per second, plus or minus. There is just no way you can tell the difference."

Mary raised her hand and looked at it, stripped

off the gauntlet and looked again, rubbing her fingers together. "Well, I'll be." A moment's pause. "Whatever works."

They were riding downhill now, toward where the road ran into a grove of trees. "We'll stop here for the night," Greg said. "And since we can vanish under the trees, no one will notice when we go out or when we return."

The living room looked small and cozy, and it was cluttered with packages from Park's; this was no mere couple of jumpsuits. Suddenly uneasy, Mary lifted one slat of the blinds and looked out the window. It looked onto the atrium in the center of the building, a humdrum collection of shrubs and walkways, quite empty of human life.

"It's all right," Greg said, rolling up beside her. "We're on the second floor and the windows only open a few inches, top and bottom."

"Good," Mary said. "Lord, what a day. Brother Gregory, you make me think of the lady in *Glory Road,* leading the hero through all sorts of battles to toughen him up for something really nasty at the end. What are you toughening me up for?"

"I haven't the slightest idea."

After dinner Greg went back inside (for the Office of Compline, he said). Mary went to bed early, on the grounds that she was bound to need the extra rest before she was done, and took *The Golden Road* with her.

"No, over there," said Hildebrandt. "I'm sure I saw some kind of light." They followed him between the mossy trunks till they reached the place where a single shaft of

sunlight pointed like a finger out of the treetops at a patch of golden pavement showing through the fallen leaves.

"It is the road," said Widia. "Thank God. Now we can find our way out."

"Can we?" Theodoric looked to right and left: The road stretched empty between the trees till its ends vanished in shadows. "I can't tell east from west in this gloom. If we wait till sunset, we might see a flash of light to mark the way, or we might not. But if we wait that long, they'll be upon us in any case. If they can't set foot here, they can still stand back and shoot at us. Now what are you doing?"

Kneeling, Hildebrandt made the Cross. "St. Michael, God's thane, make haste to help us. Show us a sign, to lead us back into the lands of men. In Christ our Lord's name."

"Amen," said Widia, kneeling beside him. After a moment Theodoric joined them, glowering from under his dark brows. All nature seemed to be holding its breath.

Then a gust of air blew along the road and was gone, brown leaves trailing in its wake. The men looked at one another, and rose and followed.

In mid-afternoon the road began to climb, and they came to a hill that rose out of the trees into a light that had grown pale under thin clouds. When they came to the top, where nothing moved but rabbits and the wind in the grasses, they saw the sun falling silver into the West ahead of them.

But somewhere on the hilltop the book had slipped from Mary's hand, and she slept.

Chapter 5

A Passage at Arms

She was dreaming of dragons, little fat ones the size of kittens, that floated like polka dots in a purple sky. Then something rattled, the sky went dark, and she woke.

Somebody was outside the car, fishing for the lock with a wire coat hanger, trying to get into the car. There was a flashlight by her side; maybe if she shone the flashlight in his face, the man would go away. But she wasn't really awake yet—she couldn't move, she couldn't scream. *Rattle, scrape.* The end of the wire hooked round the lock button, pulled, slipped loose. Patiently he tried again.

And she woke shivering, and knew she had dreamed of waking. She rubbed her thumb against her fingertip and flexed her fingers, and the rest of her went into waking mode and she could move again. She stretched, curled into a ball, and stretched again. *God.* She hadn't had that dream in years. She sat up and turned on the light.

She looked around the room. It had no windows—what a great idea that was. She looked at the door, and thought warm, soothing thoughts of Greg's hyped-up security system, and his airlock or portcullis or whatever you chose to call it, bristling with spy-lenses and passwords. Eventually, she found she could even turn off the light again, lie down, and try to sleep.

On Wednesday morning it rained in San José and all over the Bay Area, with long silver drops crawling down Greg's windows, and bicycles and minis skidded across the slippery streets.

It rained even harder in the Winchester domain; the rain turned the road to gravelly mud and beat the long grass down to the ground and beaded on the oily fleece of the sheep. Robins went wild over worms half their weight and twice their length. Greg covered himself and Mary with dark hooded cloaks that shed water like ducks' backs. It was nearly noon before the storm blew on over them into the east and the sun shone again.

"That's better," Mary said, taking off her cloak. She handed it to Greg, and he made it go away. The grass and the sheep began to dry in the sun, steam rising thinly from turf and fleece and turning into mist. Greg and Mary went outside and ate lunch while waiting for it to clear.

"So," Mary said when they returned to the road. "We've covered maybe fifty kilometers and we've met a dragon. Is that what you were looking for? What *are* you looking for?"

"Anything that doesn't fit," he said. "The dragon counts, though I wasn't expecting him. But the sheep, too. Oh, I admit my motives weren't entirely pure. I wanted to get you across that domain boundary and see if you noticed anything. But mostly I'm looking for things that are wrong."

"Can't get much wronger than that dragon."

"By St. Michael, I hope not. But you understand, even if I hadn't known there aren't supposed to be sheep and a dragon in the Winchester domain, I'd know it by their code. The Aristotelian physics is the most blatant example. But all the code—

"Well, look. There's a tree." He pointed, and they pulled up to look at it, a young oak already bending to leeward under the force of verisimilitude and lots of English weather. "I look at that tree and if I choose, here's what I see." A large scroll unrolled in the air, and lines of text began to scroll upward, endlessly unrolling at the bottom. Mary could tell it was written in C, but she had never studied graphics (let alone VR) software and most of the logic was beyond her. The scrolling slowed and stopped, displaying a pair of lines surrounded by asterisks: "Following 1175 lines make the tree growth respond to the wind direction. G.H."

"All the code we wrote is annotated," Greg said. "Good code should be. There is one comment in the dragon, about the non-Newtonian physics. There are no comments in the sheep. Did you notice, by the way, they're all the same sheep?"

"Like Old Betsy."

"Yes, except I put my name on Old Betsy, and I

initialed all the modifications, and when I fix the 30-degree bug I'll initial that too."

"Whereas these sheep are all running around full of anonymous code. What about *that?*"

"What about what?" The scroll rolled itself up and disappeared, giving Brother Greg a better view of the road ahead. There was a little dark shape, no, a pair of shapes. "That's Sir Dewi of Carlisle and his squire Peter of Whitford."

"Oh, I know Sir Dewi. Broke lances with him last Sunday at Winchester. Shall we go meet them?" She glanced at Greg. "Or should we hide?"

"We'll go meet them. I want to find out what's wrong."

"Something else is wrong? Oh, great." They rode on until they descended the east slope and could see the others plainly. Something was definitely wrong. There were brown stains on Sir Dewi's armor, his left arm was resting in a crude sling, and his squire's hand was on the hilt of his sword.

"Well met, Sir Dewi. What's befallen you?"

"Sir Mary. Right glad am I to see it's you and not somebody else. Pete, relax. She's a friend." The squire let his hand fall from his sword. "What's befallen us is an Adventure with an illuminated A, and though later on it's going to make a great no-shit-there-I-was story, just now I'm hobbling to London to find a leech. If you were thinking of heading west along this road, I'd advise against it."

"Dewi, stop making brave-fighter noises. What's *happened?*"

"There's a Black Knight at the ford who challenges all comers. And his blade's enchanted. This gash I've got in my shoulder won't heal. We tried nineteen different bug fixes; no luck. I can't use my left arm at all, and there's a sort of dull ache in it. I think it's psychosomatic."

"Log out and back in and restore from backups," Mary suggested.

"We tried that. When I log back in, the wound's still there. Somehow the enchantment has messed with the system—"

"A small-scale virus," Greg said. "It remembers you've been wounded and overrides any backup that says different."

"Whatever. So we're on our way to London, in hopes that it can be healed in another domain, by Sir Nicholas's hand."

"That may not be necessary." Greg rubbed his temple with a fingertip and looked at Dewi for a long moment. "Sir Mary, of your courtesy, will you lay your hand upon Sir Dewi's wound?"

Mary caught her breath. No doubt that Greg could do his will with her hand or his own or a willow twig, but why—? She touched Virtue's flanks and urged him forward. The gash in Sir Dewi's pauldron was a span long, and the shoulder beneath oozed dark blood. Mary glanced at Greg, whose lips were moving silently. He raised his hand to make the sign of the Cross, and Mary laid her hand on the wound.

It closed like a zipper, the blood drying to powder and drifting away. The metal grew together like a spaceboat in the special-effects lab. Mary let her hand fall and felt a pair of tears trickle down her cheeks. Dewi let out a long sigh. "Fairest of ladies, my thanks. I didn't know you were a programmer."

"I'm not—" she began, and cut herself off, seeing Greg's eyes narrowing. If he wanted to be anonymous, she'd let him. "It was a gift from a friend."

"Then God bless your friend. Is he going to put this out on the market?"

But Greg cut in, "Amen. Give glory to God, who made all the ones and zeroes. Sir Mary, we should be on our way."

Sir Dewi gave Brother Gregory a long, awed look, as one who has met a saint in humble guise and witnessed a miracle. He asked no more questions, but reached out to take the hand that had healed him, kissed it and let it go. "Good luck, Mary. Watch out for his sword. If it weren't against all the rules, I'd say it was cursed."

"He'll be cursing by the time I'm done with him," Mary said (for, after all, boasting was period, and real medieval knights always did it), and they rode away.

"Why did you use my hand and not your own?" she asked when they were out of earshot.

"It seemed appropriate," he said. "Also, those two don't know me, and I'd rather keep it that way. Oh, there's no harm in them; but what they don't know they can't repeat. And you're the closest thing to Sir Lancelot that I've got." After that Mary was silent for a long time.

The road crested and fell into a valley. "Greg," Mary said at last, "surely ones and zeroes are out of period?"

"A subtle paynim device," he said. "Look there." Where the road ran down to ford a river, there stood a dark horse tethered to a tree, a shield hanging from the tree, and beside them a pavilion as black as ink.

"Pity about the rain," Mary said. "If it'd been hot today, he would've steamed his brains out in that pavilion and nobody'd have to fight him."

"Maybe," Greg said. "As it is, I can't read this fellow's code at all. His horse, his weaponry, himself and his pavilion are all execute-only object code."

"Nothing but zillions of Our Lord's ones and zeroes?"

"Right. So I'd be obliged if you'd take him apart and let me see what he's made of."

So Mary rode down to the ford, reminding herself that her sword and lance were proven dragonsbanes and her shield possessed a bow wave tough enough for a small planet. And behind her waited a Lord of the Lists who could, by definition, fix anything. And her heart beat louder and louder and faster and faster, all in the name of verisimilitude.

She came down to the ford and raised her lance to strike the shield hanging from the tree, as token of challenge. Only at this close range could she see that the shield was not pure black, but spangled with a semé of dim stars. It rang like a bell when she struck it, a deep humming note that lingered for a long time in the echoing air.

But just as she had raised the lance to strike, a mailed hand had drawn aside the starry curtain of the pavilion, and the Black Knight had stepped out, so that it seemed the touch of his foot to ground had set the whole earth ringing.

He was tall, slender but for broad shoulders, and one might have said a sufficient blow would drive him into the ground like a peg—if one had muscle enough and a mallet worthy of Archimedes. He wore full plate, unornamented, and a closed helm through which she could not see even the glint of an eye. Every surface was enameled as black and shiny as tar.

(The original Black Knight had been a wandering knight-errant who, traveling without a squire to polish his gear, had treated his armor with burnt-on linseed oil to prevent rust. It would have been sable-brown in color and not quite so shiny. This was something else.) She couldn't imagine that Dewi had failed to land a single blow on him—but if it had been enamel it would have cracked. Magic, she decided with a mental shrug.

"Demoiselle," said the Black Knight, in a light tenor voice surprising of one of his size, "go home to thy bower, for I would not raise arms against thee. I have sworn to joust with any that might assay to pass this ford, and little would it add to mine honor to defeat in battle a tender maiden."

"Proud, false knight," Mary answered, "dost thou dare to speak of honor, and to make thy challenge at this ford, on land that longeth to the Duke of Winchester and not to thee?" (He wanted Malory, she'd give him Malory.)

"Demoiselle," said the Black Knight again, "I go whither it liketh me, and I hold any place I choose; and but thou yield thee, thou shalt die."

"Better deeds than words," said Mary. "Get thee to horse."

Without answering, the Black Knight turned his back on her and went to his horse, mounting in the proper fashion in a single leap, without touching a hand to the pommel. (Give him a point for style.) Mary turned Virtue away from the ford, backing up to allow room for a good charge. She found Greg at her elbow.

"It's almost two o'clock," he said. "You don't have a whole lot of time if you don't want the wrath of Nick on your neck. If you can't take him in three passages, I'll give you something extra."

They faced off, some hundred yards apart, the Black Knight just this side of the ford and Mary on the slope above. The height would give her a little extra momentum as she charged downhill: a fair trade-off against his size.

They came together with a clash, spears against shields. Both lances shattered and splinters flew. The Black Knight's shield rang again, and Mary's a few notes higher. The horses, rushing past each other, slowed to a walk and turned again. Virtue's hooves stirred the shallows of the ford, and muddy ripples ran downstream. Before Mary could reach for her sword, the lance reappeared unbroken in her hand. (It was only software. You could restore it as often as you liked.) So did the Black Knight's. (When Arthur fought Pellinore, squires kept appearing and disappearing like mere grammatical constructions to replenish broken spears; Malory had taken them for granted, as modern knights did subroutines.)

On the next pass it was Mary who was moving uphill, and the Black Knight who had the advantage of momentum. It was different from tilting on a level ground, with more factors to figure in. They ought to set up contentious knights at fords more often—

leaving out the part about wounds that wouldn't heal. Because he was descending the slope, the Black Knight rose and fell in the saddle a little higher than usual; Mary caught him hard across the shield at the top of his rise and sent him flying.

"Do you yield?" she asked politely, and the Black Knight muttered something that was probably blasphemous and certainly meant "no." In recalling his horse and mounting again, he gave Mary a moment to think. Twice now, her lance had struck his shield like an ordinary lance. She glanced at it, restored again to her hand: the dragonblooded lance, stained a subtle red and smooth as well-polished furniture. Instead of breaking or merely unhorsing him, it should have cooked the Black Knight's goose. Which meant his own arms and armor were enhanced. Or, as one would have said in period, enchanted. She glanced toward Greg, not far off on the hilltop, and raised the lance as if in salute.

On this third pass, Mary had the advantage and disadvantage of momentum again. She watched for an opening as the Black Knight approached; she found none but kept looking. His lance struck her shield, pushing it against her with such force that she thought her heart would stop, and she fell to the ground with a loud thump and a jangle of plate. Virtue's hoofbeats clattered into the distance. Mary put a hand to the ground, trying to get her feet under her. The Black Knight rode up to her and drew his sword: The steel was dark, and a blue radiance flickered along its edges. "Foolish, vainglorious knight," he said, "now art thou in my danger; here will I spill thy soul," and raised his sword to strike.

But before Mary could think, she blurted, "That's not Malory, that's Bunyan." The Black Knight's helm lifted a bit and his sword faltered; in that moment of incongruity Mary rolled away, and the sword-stroke fell on empty air. Then Virtue came trotting in again, and she leaped into the saddle and backed him away for another pass.

The lance that appeared in her hand was different, lighter in color and lighter in weight, with a subtly blunted tip: the "something extra" Greg had promised her if she couldn't take the Black Knight in three passes. No time to ask Greg what its qualities were; here came the Black Knight, sword still drawn, and she must gather what speed she could.

The lancetip struck his shield gently and did not break. It bent. It bent like a strand of half-cooked spaghetti, like the tales still told of that legendary Pennsic War when somebody had substituted a fiberglass war arrow for the usual wood: No one could break it in token of defiance, and they had had to redefine the terms of the war. So the lance bent, and bent, and the tip slipped downward across the shield to catch the Black Knight in the groin. Now it straightened with an audible twang and tossed the Black Knight high into the air—impossibly high—above the treetops.

He fell on his head, and Mary heard a snap that ought to mean a broken neck. As she rode up to take a look, he vanished; and his fallen sword vanished, and horse and pavilion and all faded into the air like wisps of shade, leaving only the tree.

"Here's a nice standard tournament lance," Greg said as he rode up. "I'll be along in a few minutes;

I want to fix this ford at least, maybe the surrounding countryside, so that if he comes back, he's still got a broken neck."

"Like what he did to Dewi."

"Yes, only I want to encrypt it so he can't undo it, and that will take me some time. He's good."

"He's very good," Mary agreed. "What he lacks in chivalry he makes up for in skill." And her door opened and she rode through into London.

She found Nick and the trainees all a-horseback, riding around in a circle and slashing with their swords at something that took her eyes a moment to take in. A pipe had been rigged from the nearest rooftop, and from it a stream of water fell into a catchbasin that seemed never to overflow.

The riders, each passing by in turn, were slashing at the falling water with their swords. A clean stroke, edge-on, scarcely disturbed the smooth-sided column; a stroke with the flat splashed bright drops in all directions. It was an old Sikh training technique she'd read of but never seen in action before.

Sir Nicholas caught sight of her and left the circle. "Neat," she said as he approached.

He bowed in the saddle to acknowledge the compliment. "Though I wouldn't call it *neat*," he said. "It's jury-rigged, and I'm going to have to erase it in a minute. I'll build it its own courtyard, I think. Got any suggestions for concealing that damned pipe?"

"Make it a fountain," Mary said. "You know, gravity-fed. The water's flowing from way up there somewhere, so when it's released, it leaps umpteen feet in the air. It'll look prettier too."

"Mmmm. That might work. Yes, Charles, what is it?"

"My lord, if we're finished with the water exercise, I would like—"

"You're not. Give it another fifteen minutes and then we'll bring out the sparring partners again."

"But I thought—"

"You let *me* speak; this is my class. Another fifteen minutes at the fountain and then back to the sparring partners; Sir Mary and I will observe."

"Yes, m'lord." The crestfallen student turned away to rejoin the circle around the falling water.

"Gosh, Nick. Can't you even let him finish a sentence?"

"I know what he wants. He wants to joust against you. He's ahead of the rest of the class, and he's getting bored with the NPCs. I'd joust with him myself if it were only the two of us and we had more time for it. Anyway, today they get a mixed bag, NPCs of different body types from their own. He's not ready to go up against you yet; or anyway, I don't think he is, and that's what counts."

"It's a compliment, though. Tell him I'll joust with him on Friday afternoon; I'll take on all comers."

"If you like." They watched the novices circle the fountain, cutting and slashing at the water, until Scott overbalanced and fell into the catchbasin. Then Charlie fell in trying to pull Scott out, and the exercise broke up in silly jokes. "Enough!" Nick said, and made the water go away.

From a side gate the sparring partners emerged. Nick had added more sizes and body types, including one larger and heavier than any of the students and one small, delicate-looking NPC that moved like lightning and was very hard to beat. Their differences were less apparent when they all rode copies of the same horse. They were now wearing tabards representing their serial numbers, with one or two or many ermine spots against simple fields of white or gold. The effect was only a little like the playing cards in *Alice.*

A herald announced the first joust. As promised, Nick was putting the students up against physical types unlike their own. Tall Sophia broke lances with the smallest NPC and, to everyone's surprise, knocked it to the sand. "Luck," Nick said.

"Or leverage, maybe," Mary said, thinking of the Black Knight. "Or just the advantage of mass. Why don't you have the computer run a vector analysis this evening?"

They watched the next joust, and the next. Presently Charlie came up against the biggest NPC; they broke lances three times, neither unseating the other, and Sir Nicholas called it a draw. "I would have thought he could take that one," Nick said. "Maybe Number Three's size scared him. He was fighting very conservatively, did you notice?"

"All defense and no attack," Mary agreed. "Well, he'll get over that or he'll never get anywhere."

Next Nick had to ride forth to explain to an indignant student that the NPCs never "cheated," didn't have the intelligence to cheat, and that what had unseated her was the laws of physics, which never cheated either. *(Not in this domain anyway,* Mary commented to herself, *not unless someone's been messing with it.)*

Charlie took the opportunity to leave the line and ride up to her. "Sir Mary? Sir Nicholas says you're in some kind of trouble and that's why you haven't been here most of the time. Is there anything I can do to help?"

"Uh—no. Thank you for asking."

He reached out as if to take her hand but thought better of it. "Please tell me what's the matter. If there's anything—"

"Somebody's been attacking me in the outside world," she said. "I don't know who it is; neither do the police. So I've gone to ground like any fox. Nobody know where I am, so I'm quite safe for the present."

"Oh, damn," said Charlie, and was silent for a moment. "I suppose it's the game. Here in *Chivalry* it seems that I ought to be able to save you just by throwing down my gauntlet and issuing the right challenge. It's very frustrating."

"If the opportunity comes up, I'll let you know," Mary said. "I think the herald just called you," and Charlie rode away.

Mary watched him during the course of the afternoon, along with the others, and Nick was right. The kid was jousting conservatively, his motions deliberate and thought-out beforehand, and the NPCs were unhorsing him too often. And he kept turning his head at the wrong time to watch Mary.

She decided after a while that there were two things she could do. She could call it a day and go back to Winchester and meet Greg beside the ford. Or she could take the kid and shake him up. "Sir Nicholas!"

"My lady?"

"I wish to beg a boon." She spoke so that everyone could hear, thus putting Nick on the spot.

"Name it; if it's in my power, I'll grant it."

"I wish to joust with—(Charlie, what's your other name?)—with Charles of Greyfalls." And in a lower tone, "Because if that doesn't shake him loose, you're going to have to send him back to the Saracen."

"You may be right," he said, and aloud, "Granted." The herald broke off in mid-sentence, and the other students backed off a little farther.

On the first pass Charlie spurred his horse to an enthusiastic gallop, but he checked at the last moment, and Mary struck him so hard that horse and man fell to the ground. The second time he came forward at a moderate pace, barely cracking his lance against Mary's shield. She wheeled Virtue around and caught him in the center of the arena.

"Don't play the craven with me, Charles. It isn't worthy of you. Get over there and come at me, dammit!"

Charlie galloped away, turning his horse in a tight circle and a shower of sand, and got another lance. This time they came together like a thunderclap, and at the last moment Charlie raised his lance and caught Mary in the dead center of her shield. Splinters flew in every direction, and both of them were knocked from the saddle. Virtue reared high above them to avoid Old Betsy as she stumbled and fell, and he leaped clear over the heads of the fallen riders.

"Well!" Mary got to her feet and slapped Charlie on the pauldron with a loud clang. "That's more like it. Do that a few more times and you can call yourself a jouster. Now back to the sparring partners; I'm going home." Her door opened, thick with mist, in a wall where there had never been a door before; she rode through, the tonsured sparrow fluttering overhead.

She and Greg crossed the ford and rode through sleepy, empty landscapes until they could no longer see the road in the dark.

That night she dreamed only that she was back in college, unprepared for finals and trying to remember where her classes were.

Chapter 6

The Road Through the Woods

On Thursday afternoon they crossed for the third or fourth time a little brook that had been interlacing the road for the past several miles, rode to the crest of a hill, and came upon St. Chad's. It was just after lunch in San José, but the Winchester domain kept Philadelphia time so it was mid-afternoon there. The sky was overcast, the veiled sun well into the west, and St. Chad's lay beneath them in a narrow valley. To Mary it looked very straightforward: manor house, barn, cluster of outbuildings, plowed fields lying fallow or sown to winter grain. But Greg stared at it without speaking.

"What's wrong?"

"Good question," he said. "The source code is either not on this system or very cleverly concealed—like the dragon's. The hypertext comments, which ought to explain things, are cryptic. See the church, the little cross-shaped building east of the house? The comment should tell me the names of the source and object files, a literature source for the design, an author's name, and probably a pointer to an architectural plan. All it says is, 'Beware St. Chad's cracked chimes.' And everything seems to have a shadow behind it that doesn't follow the sun." He set Ignatius in motion, and they rode down into the valley.

Whatever shadows Greg saw were not apparent to Mary. The fields around the manor were neatly plowed, well-hedged against foraging cattle. (She hadn't seen any cattle yet, but the principle still applied.) The buildings—barns, sheds and cottages—were squat blocky things with thatched roofs that reached nearly to the ground, with few or no windows. Most of them had chimneys.

She was going to have to revise her plans for developing the place—two-and-a-half days' ride from London was too damn far—unless she could fill the countryside along the way with interesting sights. Dragons, for instance; knights-errant; a white hound or a white hart that sprang across your path and led you off to adventure. Most of which would violate the no-fantasy rule, of course. Maybe she'd think of something.

On the valley floor the road joined another, coming in from the south, probably from Winchester. That might be a shorter ride. She might have to get leave from the Duke to use it—

Not far from the manor house they saw the first sign of life: a man of about forty, digging trenches in a kitchen garden. He glanced up as they rode by and bent to his work again. "What does his comment say?" Mary murmured as they passed out of earshot.

"It says, 'This is old Buckman the gardener,' and his age and who he's married to. But he has a shadow," Greg half-chanted in the voice Mary had come to associate with speculation and growing distrust, "and his comment has a shadow too, and I can't read it. . . ."

They were almost at the front door. "Do you want me to stick around?"

"No. But I'm going to stick here, if you don't mind. Since things were so quiet there yesterday. Go teach your class, and if . . . um. A magic ring wouldn't do under your gauntlets, would it. Here." Two golden wristbands flashed, settled in, became part of her gauntlets. They showed a faint tracery of acanthus leaves, and over the pulse of each wrist there was a cross. "If anything awkward shows up, put your hands together as if in prayer, and say "Help." You don't have to say it very loud."

The manor house appeared to be about thirteenth century, from a time somewhere between King Stephen and the Wars of the Roses, when every house didn't have to be a fortress. There was no moat, no curtain walls. But the windows were mere arrowslits, and the door had a portcullis above it, ready to drop. The manor and the small church near it were the only buildings of stone.

A face at the window vanished as they looked at it, and a moment later the door swung open.

"Welcome, sir knight, good brother," said the man at the door, with only the faintest undertone of *and who might you be?* He was evidently the steward, a man of about thirty, big and burly with brown hair and beard, wearing dark hosen and a wine-colored tunic, a little worn at the elbows.

"I am Sir Mary de Courcy, the new owner of this manor," Mary said, talking the deed from Greg, who had pulled it as if by magic from his sleeve. The man glanced at it and bowed low.

"Welcome, Sir Mary, to the least of your houses. I am your steward, Peter fitzUrse. Will it please you to dismount? *Ranulf!*" he called over his shoulder. A youngster with tousled blond hair appeared, tugging into place a tunic that should have been laundered and mended long ago. (Perhaps he was an orphan? She'd ask Greg. In any case, fitzUrse needed to run a tighter ship around here). "Take the mistress's horse and the Brother's mule to the stable and see Wulfric feeds and grooms them well; they've come a long way." They dismounted, and he led them into the great hall, a room with a high timbered vault overhead and a fireplace in one long wall. On the other hung a large tapestry, a scene of fresh-faced young men hunting deer from horseback. Two chairs and a bench by the fireplace were all the furniture in sight.

"By your leave, Sir Mary," Greg said as they crossed the hall, "I think you should get some rest." (This was from their prearranged script.) "They'll be singing Nones soon, and after I say the Office, I can look at the place and report to you later on."

"Very well," said Mary, also by the script. The steward led them up a flight of narrow stairs to a solar, a room meant for luxury, with four real windows in it. There was a wooden settle with a footrest that sat two, a cushion to kneel on, and a canopied bed with curtains. The western window let in the light of the sun. "Ah," Mary said, and laid her helmet gently on the floor. "I'm going to need an armor rack."

"I shall procure one, my lady," the steward said, and bowed and went away.

Mary stretched and arched her back. She felt genuinely stiff and tired; if she was going to do much of this daylong travel overland, she'd have to have her stamina augmented. She bent double, her knuckles almost brushing the floor, to stretch her back and hoped all those creaking sounds were her armor straps and not herself.

"Allow me," said Greg, and from the nearest bit of thin air he drew out a tiny cup made of horn. The rose-colored drop inside tasted like a single wild strawberry and washed away all her fatigue in an instant.

"Mmmm. Thank you. Is this stuff available commercially?"

Greg looked thoughtful. "I don't think I could market it for *Chivalry*. Because it's magic. But it would be my pleasure to give you a bottle of it for Christmas. Don't tell George.

"All right," he went on, looking around the room. "This is perfect. We'll draw the curtains, and anyone who glances in here will think you're in the bed. Anyone who actually comes in to look at you will activate alarms that will teleport me up here in a jiffy, puff of smoke and all. I'd rather have them think I'm a mage than have them know you're taking shortcuts between domains."

He frowned. "That's another thing. It feels like

there's another domain boundary somewhere near here, but the closest boundary is Oxford, forty miles north of us." A bell began to ring, a sour note with little reverberation. "Cracked," Greg confirmed. "Hmph. You go to London, and I'll go to Nones, and then we'll see."

The door appeared between two windows, and Mary picked up her helm and stepped through. The saddle materialized beneath her, and on Virtue's back she trotted into the arena.

The squires were already at practice, taking turns at the Lists or doing slow work with sword and shield around the perimeter. Nick stood under the gallery, looking as if they were eating a feast he'd just cooked. Well, he had some cause to be smug. This venture was working out, and he was going to make a bundle out of it. Not that he needed it.

There was someone sitting in the gallery, wearing what looked like a black academic cap and gown. Not the standard American-college style, not with those starched white bands falling from the collar. But it looked familiar—*Merchant of Venice,* that was it, Portia done up as a lawyer. A woman in Renaissance lawyer's garb—and she caught Mary's eye and beckoned.

As Mary rode up to the gallery, Nick gave her a slight bow and a sketchy salute and rode away. He hadn't had much to say to her the last couple of days. She assumed he was pissed because she'd cut back to her agreed-on afternoon training sessions and wouldn't come to the salle in person. But the man had grown moody of late, and she didn't really know why. "M'lady?"

"Good afternoon, Ms. Craven," the woman said. "I'm Lt. Rosa Fernandez of the San José police. Ordinarily I handle computer crime, but Sgt. Cooper asked me to sit in; no one in her division is equipped for VR. I'd like to ask you a couple of questions."

The "couple of questions" took half an hour; the lieutenant took her over everything she had told Sgt. Cooper on Monday, everything Greg had mailed in on Tuesday morning. Mary told her also about the golden-scaled knight on Tuesday afternoon. (The lieutenant was beginning to look perplexed; whatever kind of VR she was used to working with, it wasn't this kind.) "And did they ever trace the vintage car that tried to run me down?"

"Oh, yes. Stolen from an antique dealer five miles north of you and abandoned a few miles to the south."

"How'd they get in? I should think a place like that would have tough security."

"They did, but somebody cracked the system. A very nice job, that, left almost no traces. Maybe, instead of trying to figure who would want to kill you, we should ask who you know that's good with computers."

"*Everybody* I know is good with computers. I don't call myself a programmer, but I've spent enough time fine-tuning my home security that I could probably crack a medium-level system myself. Are you done for now? Because I think I'm wanted." Nick, from the opposite end of the Lists, was glaring at them. "I'll be here again tomorrow afternoon."

"You are getting paid to train these louts," Nick muttered as she rode up, "*not* to hang around chatting with spectators. I don't care what you do if there's nothing else to do."

"Sorry, Nick, but she's police."

Nick's mouth framed an "Oh," but no sound came out. He turned Nightgaunt with a jerk on the reins and rode back into the Lists. When Mary next looked up into the gallery, the black-robed lieutenant was gone.

Mary rode back through the door and landed lightly on her feet. The last of a winter twilight was pale in the windows. "Welcome back," Greg said. "Things are getting interesting."

"Oh?"

"About an hour ago a party of men rode in from the Winchester road. A rough lot. Some armed as knights but none with any knightly qualities. The rest are ruffians—brigands, sneak thieves. One or two of them I'm not sure are human. Pointy ears, that sort of thing. It's a standard dungeon-crawling party, and I'd like to know what it's doing in the Winchester domain, which is supposed to be straight medieval."

"Maybe that's why somebody doesn't want us to see St. Chad's, because it's an outcrop of fantasy and they're afraid we'll blow the whistle. When you went to Nones, was anybody else there? What were they like?"

"A chaplain and two acolytes. Software of mine, in fact, cut down and simplified to run in less memory space. Their comments say only that they are decent Christian men who stay indoors in night. I think that means they disappear at night, when things change."

"And the dungeoncrawlers come out. Is there a dungeon here for them to crawl?"

"A few hours ago I would've said no. There's a perfectly good wine-cellar: dry, whitewashed, no rats. But you remember I told you everything had a shadow? Well, it's all keyed to the system clock. At some time this evening, things in this manor are going to change to some other state, and God knows what that cellar is going to turn into. I think that's what those men have come for."

"Where are they now?"

"Down in the great hall, drinking ale and swapping No-shit-there-I-was stories. A real human steward might've thought better than to carry on, business as usual, with the new owner taking a nap upstairs. But Peter's only an NPC. He's down there seeing the ale poured as if nothing were any different.

"I'd like to propose the following strategy. You and I will sneak down the stairs—I'll cloak us, that'll be no problem—and go to the stables. That's where this odd domain boundary is."

The stairs seemed narrower and steeper than when she had climbed them. Being invisible was strange, almost like walking in the dark. She couldn't see her arms or legs, and she had only a sketchy idea of where they were in relation to the stairs. No, she decided, it was like carrying a box so large you couldn't see your feet. Feel with a toe for the edge of the step, ease your foot down onto it; repeat, let your vision keep you upright at least. And hope you're not treading on Greg, who is just as invisible as you are.

Once they got to the floor, Greg took her arm. The men sitting in the hall drinking ale were about as Greg had described them. Three of them were dressed very richly, with shiny armor and long unwieldy swords that stank of fantasy movies. If any of them went up against the dragon, she knew what would win. "So it came up on my left side, see, so I bashed it with my shield—" Dungeoncrawlers all. She let Greg lead her away to a side door that opened onto the yard.

The stable was a timber, with low walls and a high-pitched thatch roof, like most of the other buildings on the manor lands. A man, probably Wulfric, sat slumped against the stable wall, paring his nails with his belt knife. He had a long pale face and sullen pale eyes, and his clothes were shabby, with random snags and rips here and there and very dirty knees to his hosen.

The last of the twilight was fading from the sky. To Mary's unaugmented eyes it all looked normal—a depressing English November evening, but neither Cold Comfort Farm nor H. P. Lovecraft. "Oh, I remember!" she said as the stable door closed behind them.

Inside, the stable was comfortably ordinary and several degrees warmer than the hall. Horses (and Ignatius the mule) stood in neatly spaced stalls between the tall poles that held the roof up. The air was rich with the smell of well-dried hay and sweat and other smells, evocative but not too intense. A horn-paneled lantern hanging by the door provided enough light to stumble around by.

"You just passed through another domain boundary," Greg said as he reappeared. "Feel anything? What do you remember?"

"No, and I was waiting for it. I remember where the cracked chimes came from: It's Lovecraft. 'Beware St. Toad's cracked chimes' is how he put it. I don't remember the context."

"It fits, I guess." As if on cue, the bell began to ring. "That's Vespers. I have a feeling that's the signal." He opened the stable door just a crack and peered through. "Yes," he whispered. "Everything's reading the system clock and preparing to switch state." Mary peered over his head.

Peter fitzUrse stood at the door, listening to the chimes, taking his tunic off. Then he stripped off his hosen and hung them on a nail just inside the door. Mary's eyes were not offended; the man was so hairy he looked as though he were wearing furry thermal underwear. The candlelight from the hall shone behind him; he raised his head to sniff the air. His face was beginning to change shape—Mary pulled Greg back and firmly shut the door. "Right."

"What's right?"

"The steward's name is Peter fitzUrse. How's your French?"

"Son of—"

"Son of the bear. That's why he was taking his clothes off, so they won't get torn. Guess what he's turning into right now?"

"Got it. Let's get moving."

"And Wulfric and Ranulf both have 'wolf' in their names. And if they don't think ahead to strip first, that's why their clothes are so dirty and torn. Should we bar the door?"

"No need. This stable is a little domain all by itself, and I *think* the haunts and monsters can't come here." He led her between ranks of stalled horses, some sleek, some shabby, whatever the gamers could afford. "It's a safe place in case any of the dungeon crawlers wants to take a breather, maybe step outside and hit the plumbing, and it means their horses will still be here in the morning." He found Ignatius and began to saddle him.

"When will that be?"

"Dawn, or Prime, I don't know which. Long hours from now, anyway; remember it's November in a high latitude. Let's go." He took Ignatius' bridle and led him to another door at the stable's far end. "Another domain boundary," he remarked.

"What's on the other side?"

"I don't know; I waited for you. Oh, not just to be polite—I don't know *what's* on the other side of that door, and I wanted you, and Virtue, and your sword and spear, on my side when I went through. Ready?"

Out in the stable yard, something howled. "Ready as I'll ever be."

Greg pushed open the door, letting in a blaze of light, and they groped their way through.

"Well," said Mary once her eyes had adjusted. "It's very pleasant, wherever it is."

They were standing in a clearing in the woods whose trees had probably been felled to build the stable they had just stepped out of. It looked much the same on this side as it had in St. Chad's. The planks that covered the low walls were rough-hewn now and overgrown with moss, and the steeply pitched roof (designed to shed heavy snowfalls) was shingled, not thatched. It was the kind of North-European general-purpose building that could serve as house, barn, or workshop according to its furnishings. Or all of them together, family at one end, stock at the other, fodder stored amidships. The style had survived, practically unchanged, from the late Iron Age to the Thirty Years' War, so the building gave no clue as to when this domain was supposed to be.

The sun was just rising above the treetops. "I guess we're not in Pennsylvania anymore? I don't even think we're in the Middle Ages any more; the trees are too old and thick."

"You're used to the New Forest hunting preserve, right? The one Chandra wrote for Winchester? But that was planted at the order of William the Conqueror. It was still relatively young during the Middle Ages. This is old-growth forest, untouched since the last glaciers retreated. Up at York, for instance, the forest began as soon as you stepped out of Bootham Bar. In fact,"—he gave the woods a hard look—"this looks very like the forest I wrote for York. A slightly higher proportion of hardwoods; we're in a lower latitude. Either great minds run in the same ruts, or somebody's borrowed it. I'm not sure I mind; he's done a nice job. Let's go." Brother Greg hopped into the saddle and pointed to the east, where the forest darkness seemed just a trifle lighter. "There's a road over here, I think."

The road was a narrow path, one tree's-width wide; if one tree at a time had been felled to make it, there was no sign of the stumps. The trunks of ancient oaks rose high on either side. It was not impossible that the road was older than the forest, going back to an animal trail at the end of the Ice Age, deer and aurochs and men steadily treading down the path while the brush and the pinewoods died away and the great oaks grew up on either side. At some time—in the Neolithic, maybe, when people had time for such projects—the path had been inlaid with hard-packed yellow earth that gleamed through the leaf litter wherever a shaft of light made its way between the trees.

"Should we mark this place before we ride off?"

"Mmm, yes." A cluster of mushrooms popped up at the foot of the nearest tree, bright crayon red with white spots.

"Isn't that a little obvious?"

"Not really. Those are real mushrooms—or I mean of course representations of real ones. Poisonous as all-get-out. I think you should lead; it looks better."

There was room for two horses abreast on the path—if, as the joke went, they were very friendly. Mary consented to lead the way, splendid in her armor, her faithful monk following behind, all in the name of verisimilitude. The faithful monk would have to tell her which way to turn if they came to a fork in the road, but so far there was no sign of any: only trees and more trees and the bright-floored path. The brief song of a sparrow pointed up the great silence of the wood. Mary took a deep pleasurable breath, sweet with leafmold and moisture and growing things.

Ten minutes' ride brought them to a larger clearing with a cluster of buildings, a farmstead hacked out of the wilderness. People working in the fields (it appeared to be late spring here) looked up and stared as they went by. Women stepped out of their houses to watch and call small children away from underhoof.

"These people seem to be all right."

"I think so. They're all NPCs, of course. Nice simple subroutines, no shadows. Pious, too; there's a belief table in the church module, solid Christianity plus a zillion little old superstitions, and they all read from it. I would put us sometime between 700 and 1000 AD. Here's the church." It was a little boxy structure, the only stone building in sight, with a cross on its roof. The priest came out as they approached, and Greg dismounted and began a lively Latin conversation.

Mary sat and looked around. The peasants were beginning to gather round, curious but shy. Visitors must be rare in these parts. A young woman in a worn linen tunic came up to offer Virtue a handful of long grass, plucked from the verge of the road. Virtue took it politely and snorted. The young woman giggled. Then she looked up from horse to rider, and her eyes went wide. "Are you a holy paladin?"

Well, no. "No, my sister, I am only a sinful human like any other. But God in His mercy has given me the grace to be a knight." That was how you talked to pious peasants. She glanced at Brother Greg, who was probably telling the priest the same sort of thing but at greater length. He spoke beautiful Latin, rhythmic and fluid as a babbling brook, and as meaningful to those who hadn't studied Latin.

"But you go to fight evil and to right wrongs?"

"If I find them."

"Oh, you're going to the east, you'll find them all right. Evil things come out of the east. Be careful."

"I will." Greg was finally finishing up his tête-à-tête with the parish priest— "Pray for us." —kneeling for his blessing, the whole nine yards. He blessed Mary too, and she crossed herself without dismounting. Greg clambered into the saddle, and they rode away into the forest.

"So what is the evil that comes out of the east?" Mary asked once they were out of earshot.

"Dunno. Your friend wasn't speaking out of her own experience; it's in the belief table. 'Evil things come out of the east.' The priest, who is very nicely written by the way, warned me too, but he didn't seem to know any details—and I couldn't come out and ask him, we're supposed to know it already."

The road opened out into another clearing, a water meadow running down to a little stream, bright under the sun.

"Incidentally, I'm going to modify your armor, if you don't mind. You're dressed for—what, late fourteenth, early fifteenth century? It seems to be early period technology here, Carolingian or a little earlier. I'll give you a nice hauberk and an iron hat. Just slightly enchanted, so the protection'll be the same."

"All right." The armor on her back slumped, became a little heavier, became a hauberk of linked mail. The thousands of tiny rings shone brightly in the sun. Did she—yes, her feet were still planted in her stirrups, which had been invented in the last century or so. There wasn't much point in trying to fight on horseback without them.

The shield hanging at her knee blunted its corners

and became a roundshield with a handgrip inside the central boss. She picked it up and tested its weight: massive enough to help stop a sword blow, light enough not to sprain her wrist—she hoped.

Her face felt naked in the iron helm with its iron nasal inadequately guarding the bridge of her nose, but she could see much better and breathe more freely. She could smell sun-warmed young grass, the dust in the road, the damp sweetness of the tender plants on the edge of the stream as they forded it. It was a very pleasant place, evil out of the east or not. Greg's enchantments had better work as advertised, that was all.

"Any idea where we are yet?"

"Northern Europe somewhere. I can't be precise; the specifications on this place are immense, and my random searches haven't found anything of use. That farmstead hadn't any name, just 'here' or 'Lord Gerbert's land.' There's a monastery several miles east of here, St. Felix, which I don't know."

"What kind of evil out of the east would they have?"

"Teutonic or Slavic pagans, I should think, who would be quite nasty enough for anyone's purposes. But then why didn't the priest say so?"

They crossed another brook, where bright green frogs sat croaking, and leaped for the deeper waters as they splashed through. A pair of birds chirped in a tree overhanging the brook. Except for the hints of evil elsewhere, one might have thought the whole system had been merely for relaxation and pleasure. "Those brooks aren't domain boundaries, are they?"

"Oh, no. No boundaries in any direction that I can

sense. This is a big domain. I'd like to see the machine it's running on."

Now they came out of the forest altogether; a good many acres had been cleared and the land planted to grain and vegetables, an apple orchard, even a vineyard, its tendrils waving cheerfully among the tree stumps. A little further on a wooden stockade reared sharpened palings around two tall towers and other buildings they couldn't see much of.

In a field by the road a dozen peasants were weeding rows of beans or peas, newly staked out with tall poles to climb. The plants were just beginning to flower, and their scent was faint and sweet as a whiff out of Paradise. The peasants moved slowly between the rows, pulling up young dandelions and purslane and dropping them in rough twig baskets; most of the weeds were edible and would probably wind up on the table. A black-robed monk, his hood pulled up against the sun, paced beside them. He carried a long, thin rod, taller than the beanpoles.

The monk looked up as Greg and Mary rode up to him. The peasants stayed bent to their weeding. "God go with you, brother, knight."

"God be with you, brother," Greg said. "Is this the Abbey of St. Felix?"

"That's right. Will you be our guests?"

"Thank you, brother, but it's only morning. We'll ride on to the next house."

"That will be St. Paulinus. Twenty miles to the east. Excuse me a moment." The peasants had worked to the end of their rows and stopped. Slowly they straightened their backs, showing no curiosity at the sight of the strangers. Their faces were fair enough, but blank, with wide empty eyes. Retarded people, perhaps, barely able to tell little-weed-for-pulling from big-pea-plant-for-leaving-alone? Perhaps St. Felix's had taken them in out of charity, letting them earn their keep with such simple work as they could do. The monk was using his long rod now, not to strike but to herd them gently into the next rows as a goosegirl might herd her geese to the meadow to graze.

"Oh, sweet Christ," Greg murmured. He had never sworn before and Mary suspected he was not swearing now.

The monk had set his charges to work, each bending obediently to the row at a tap on the shoulder. As he returned, Greg said something in Latin, a question. The monk said "*Ita,*" and something else. Greg sighed. "We must ride on. God be with you, brother, and have mercy on those you tend."

"And go with you," the monk said, and turned back to the beanfield.

"What was that all about?" Mary demanded.

"Shh," Greg said, and in a near-whisper, "I know where we are."

"Well, where are we?"

"Shh," for they were still riding through St. Felix's lands, and monks and laymen with all their wits about them looked up to exchange greetings. Most of the buildings looked like the stable in the forest, varying in size and in the height of their walls, from man-height to a mere handsbreath. None of them had a chimney except for one that appeared to be a smithy. The tall-towered church was once again the only building of stone. Most of it had come fairly directly from the *Plan of St. Gall* CD-ROM.

They had passed the last open field; the dense forest loomed up on either side, and the road was dwindling again to a narrow way on which they rode single file. Now they heard ahead of them the hoofbeats of more than one horse, perhaps two or three, and Greg said, "Uh-oh."

"Trouble?"

"Yes. Ride forward, where it narrows up by that silver birch. Try to take them one at a time."

Mary spurred Virtue into a trot. "An 'encounter,' right? Are they as tough as the Black Knight?"

"I doubt it, but there are three of them. No, not that spear; use this one." As she reached for the dragon-blooded lance, another took shape in her hand, so white it shone in the sun but blunt tipped, almost padded like a pike for SCA use. Ultraviolet-sensitive dyes hadn't been invented yet, so she assumed it was magic. Virtue had just accelerated into a gallop as he rounded a bend in the path and she saw them.

At first she thought there must be some mistake. These were three beautiful young men, armored in shining mail and helms, little pennons atop their lances with images of flowers, a fox's head—the beginning of heraldry. But Greg must know what he was about; and besides, there was a look in those blue eyes she didn't like. Rather like the fanatical eyes of beautiful blond Nazis in old movies. She cried a challenge and lowered her lance.

She unhorsed the first man before he could defend himself; he hit the ground with a good hard thump.

His horse reared and came down again almost nose-to-nose with Virtue. The stallion bared his teeth and snapped, and the other horse shied away, edged along the path and trotted away behind him. Mary let them go; the next rider was almost upon her, his sharp lance lowered to the attack, crying out in some language she didn't recognize.

His spear, as it happened, was rather longer than hers, so she took its shock against her shield a moment before her lancetip struck. It slid upwards off his shield, caught him under the chin and sent him flying, possibly unhurt if this lance was magical enough. The horse trotted past; Mary let it go.

The third man had backed off, almost to the next turn in the road, and sat watching her. All right, they couldn't all be easy. She took a moment to look behind her. Greg, without dismounting from Ignatius, had somehow wrestled the first man onto his horse's back; he lay crosswise, inert as a sack of laundry. The second horse stood meekly beside Ignatius while Greg pointed with one stern finger to where the second horseman—No time to gawk now, she'd ask him later. She turned back to size up the third knight.

He was coming forward now, slowly; he had left his lance in its rest (the fox's head fluttered in the breeze) and drawn his sword. "Watch out!" Greg cried behind her. "Don't let him meet you sword-to-sword; he'll try to kill you!"

"Will you, now, my fine fellow?" Mary said. (The man was still too far away to hear.) "Not if I know it; I've had enough of that already." She spurred Virtue to the gallop. The knight tilted his shield at the last moment, deflecting her lance, and hacked at it and at her as he went by. He did no damage; perhaps the shield spell was active again. She reined Virtue in, and he reared, turned on two feet, and came down to the path again headed back the way he had come. At the other end of the stretch Greg was putting the second knight aboard his horse—

(Her eyes hadn't tricked her. He had lifted him without touching him, wrapped in a filmy cloud of light the color of her spear.)

—and behind him a monk and two venturesome peasants had appeared, the vanguard of a whole crowd of spectators. Fox's Head was approaching again, slowly, looking for an opening. She didn't intend to give him one. She charged again, the lance aimed at his throat; he raised his shield to guard. At the last moment she dropped her lancepoint and caught him in his mail-covered gut. He fell with a thud and a jangle as Mary reined in.

Greg, a broad grin on his face, pointed his finger again and began to lift the fallen man; but one of the peasants ran up shouting, "Wait, brother! Wait, please!" Greg obligingly held the man at knee level, while the peasant ran to him and anxiously looked into his face. "Oh, it is, it is," he murmured, and looking up toward Greg, "It's Bodo! It's my little brother!" He fell to his knees and clasped his arms round the man's neck, covered the unconscious face with kisses. Then he jumped up and ran back the way he had come, shouting, "Mother, Mother! It's Bodo!"

Now the monk of St. Felix was standing beside them. "Thanks be to God and to you, good knight, for the work you've done this day."

"They'll sleep for an hour or so," Greg told him. "Plenty of time for you to get them into the church. Now we must be off."

"Can't you stay for at least an hour or two? We would like to thank you properly—"

"We're needed elsewhere," Greg said firmly. "God be with you, brother. Move!" he muttered under his breath, and Mary took off down the road, with Greg close behind. The peasants were shouting and weeping and cheering, and two or three voices had started a shaky *Te Deum laudamus.* "Before the whole settlement tries to thank us," Greg finished.

They turned the bend in the path. "I gather we done good."

"You bet."

Mary turned a second corner. The woods were empty and the sounds of cheering almost inaudible. She reined in.

"Are we alone and unobserved? We are," she said. "*Where are we?*"

"You don't recognize it? You must be the only person in the English-speaking world who wouldn't. Didn't you see those wretched people in the beanfield?"

"Simpletons?"

"They're changelings," he said. "We're in *The Golden Road.*"

Chapter 7

Curiouser and Curiouser

"Good Lord!" Mary said. "So the reason that guy recognized his brother—"

"Was that their mother had tended Bodo's changeling all these years and knew what he would grow up to look like. Look, if I'm right, we've got a long day ahead of us—or rather, a long night. Let's find somewhere to turn off." He rode between two massive ash-trees into a small clearing, well-screened from the road, and disappeared.

Mary came outside on his heels. Greg had unplugged and was rubbing his eyes. "It's just after six, here," he said, "and I'm afraid I'm going to be up all night. We'd better get some dinner and some rest. Take a nap, if you like. I've got some thinking to do."

"I've been doing some of my own," she said. "There was a reporter in Philadelphia who asked me if I'd heard rumors about a *Golden Road* VR. And I said, 'Impossible, Professor Markheim would never give permission.' Yet here it is. It's an illegal system, isn't it?"

"Unless a seventy-five-year-old professor emeritus of history has suddenly changed his mind. I find it easier to believe in an illegal system."

"An illegal system that must be making big bucks for somebody, in spite of the fact that all the advertising's got to be done by word of mouth. And St. Chad's is the gateway into it. Have we solved the mystery, then? The Grey Knight bought himself off with the deed to St. Chad's because he hadn't anything else of value on him, and now he's trying to get it back. Possibly, before his partners find out."

"Maybe. Oh, I think you're right as far as you've gone, though St. Chad's may not be the only gateway into the Golden Road, and it's possible the Grey Knight went out and enlisted his partners to help do you in. But we still don't know who they are. Nor what other connections they've got."

He punched numbers into the microwave and turned away from it. "You remember when we were talking about intellectual property a couple of days ago, and I said I didn't care about it that much? But Markheim cares. His characters are his creations and he doesn't want anyone else playing around with them.

"Well, his characters *are* his creations. His Theodoric isn't much like the Theodoric of medieval legend and still less like the historical one. He built him up from very little into a coherent character"—Greg's hands moved as if shaping something rounded and solid—"and Hildebrandt and Widia out of even less.

If he wishes to keep other people from manipulating his work, as I see it, he's got the right.

"Now, copyright law doesn't care whether the violator made any money off his infringement or not. If he's published it, that's enough. But the law, which is built up of precedents, is still fuzzy about what constitutes 'publishing' a VR. The more documented access to this thing we can find, the better Dr. Markheim's case will be when he goes after these guys for copyright infringement."

"All right, I can see that. And to find the other gateways, assuming there are any, you've got to go back inside and search. Cripes, Greg, that could take months."

"No, it won't. I've searched the descriptor tables and found all the segments that contain pointers to other systems; I just have to find out what systems they lead to. There's the one connected to St. Chad's that comes out in that longhouse in the woods. There's one west of there—I'm not sure where it is geographically. And there's one segment in the east that has, all by itself, nine pointers outside. Nine."

"Where?"

"Somewhere east of the Rhine. But once I knew what world I was in, I could also search for names. I found the name for that segment right off. What do you suppose it is?"

"East of the Rhine? Alfheim?"

"Of course it is. Home of elf-warriors, source of changelings. Terminus for I don't know how many networks, but I intend to find out."

"Were those elves I fought this morning?"

"Oh, no. Those were elf-karls: men stolen in infancy, with changelings left behind, trained in the arts of war in Alfheim, then sent back like janissaries to ravage their own people. They were Player Characters, though, if that's what you're asking." Greg smiled. "Somewhere back there, three players—if they haven't logged out—are riding in their unconscious characters, being dragged through forest and field to St. Felix's Church to be baptized. When they wake up, they'll be on the side of Law."

"Which was not what they intended. Will they say 'the hell with it' and start all over again with new characters?"

"Well, they could, probably, by paying more money. On the other hand, a former elf-karl, now baptized and with the power of the Church behind him, would be a very powerful character. They may keep them."

"So they might. May I use the console? I want to look something up myself."

"Sure. Dinner will be ready in, um, twenty minutes."

Mary washed her face and phoned her cat-sitting neighbor. "Hi, Betty. Everything okay?"

"Everything's okay here," Betty said, sounding dubious. "Only your chickens seem to've stopped laying altogether and the cats are complaining 'cause I won't feed 'em nineteen times a day."

"They do the same to me. You know how much they're supposed to get; don't let 'em con you. Betty, I really appreciate this; I *hope* in a couple more days things will settle down and I can come home. As for the chickens, I'm not surprised; it's November and the days are getting short."

"You could put grow lights in the barn and fool them."

"I've thought of that, but I'd rather be a net producer of energy than a consumer. Let the poor things rest up for spring. Just keep the hoppers filled; the computer knows how much to feed 'em."

"Okay. Mary, are *you* all right?" Betty burst out. "Do you think it's the Mafia getting involved? I read an article—"

"*I* read an article that said the Mafia didn't exist any more. If it did, don't you think it'd be more efficient? I'm fine, Betty, no one has laid a finger on me and they're not going to because *they don't know where I am.*"

Dinner turned out to be more chicken, lots of it, and salad and french fries and chocolate mousse. "Fill ourselves with protein and carbohydrates and we may last out the night. I do have a couple of beefsteaks in the freezer, but I thought we'd wait till this is over, make it a celebration."

"I'm impressed."

"Oh, I know the guy that runs the cattle museum up in Altamont Pass. Every now and then he has to cull the herd. Everything all right at your place?"

"Everything's fine, except my neighbor's starting at shadows; she thinks the Mafia's in on it."

"I think any real *condottiere* would dismiss everything that's been attempted on you as the work of bumbling amateurs."

"That's about what I told Betty."

Mary ate with most of her attention on the console screen, busy playing back scenes from the system log and from her disks. "Yeah," she said presently, and Greg obligingly said, "Yeah, what?"

"I'll show you two clips," she said. "This one is me versus the Grey Knight of the Sea on Monday. The other is the guy in the golden scale."

Greg watched. Again the Grey Knight of the Sea charged toward Mary de Courcy—good, fast, overconfident—and was unhorsed and fell to the sand. Again the golden knight attacked on his strange steed, and was struck down and shriveled into simulated death. "Are you telling me they're the same person?"

"You can't tell? Well, you don't joust. I can tell. Couldn't put words to it though, not more than Dave's 'fast, overconfident'—cocky. I'd love to know where this guy trained. 'Cause he's not used to losing, and he should've been; he's good but not that good." She ate the last bite of her dessert and pondered while she let the last traces of chocolate dissolve on her tongue. "Maybe he trained in *Golden Road.*"

"Maybe. What about the Black Knight?"

"No. Nobody I've ever fought before. Greg, you heard his challenge. Would you say that he was a tenor—or that she was a contralto?"

"Dear me." Greg considered for a moment. "So narrow are my preconceptions, I assumed he was a he; shame on me. Now that you ask, I can't guess what gender that was. It'll have to wait till we meet again, if we do. Are we ready to go back inside?"

"Just about." She drank the last drop of her coffee—a lot stronger than she'd have chosen ordinarily, but she appreciated the principle of more caffeine and less water. It might be a long time before either of them had a chance to go outside for a pit stop. Coming back from the bathroom, she saw that Greg had changed T-shirts again, to a martial scarlet with a fierce-looking Viking ("Erik Bloodaxe wants YOU!"). He plugged in, and she followed.

It took her a moment to realize they weren't in the same place. It was later in the morning, of course, just as it was later in the evening outside, and Greg had placed them somewhere farther down the road. The underbrush had been thinned out here, making it easier to go from tree to tree. "Where are we?"

"Further east, a few segments away from Alfheim. Not far from the Elfwater—I can't tell what river it'd be on a real map, but it flows west into the Rhine."

They rode out of the clearing and saw plowed fields, flat and green between the clearing and the river. Elf-karls still had to eat; probably elves did too, though you wouldn't want one to invite you to dine. "All right," Greg said, "I'm going to disguise us."

Mary saw no change in herself, but Ignatius's ears shortened and Greg grew about six inches in the saddle and put on the shiny armor of an elf-karl. A white flower on a violet banner floated chastely from his lance. She turned in her saddle and saw that her own device had been changed again to a solitary sun-in-splendor. "That should do," Greg said. "None of these devices is in use—I checked the PC table—but nobody else is going to check them unless we arouse suspicion first."

They rode along the road to the river, through fields that seemed empty of elves or humans. No, there was somebody, a woman picking bugs off bean leaves and squashing them between thumb and finger. Her rust-colored tunic was shabby, and her unbrushed hair was bundled under a grayish kerchief. Her eyes were dull. What did you call a changeling that hadn't been exchanged? Had she been generated to match some baby girl somewhere in the west who had been made safe by baptism before the switch could be made?

The next field they passed wasn't grain, not quite; it grew a darker green than any field crop Mary knew of, and it seemed already to have headed. The stalks bobbed up and down, more energetically than the little breeze would warrant, as if the round heads were trying to break loose and fly away.

Now they were close enough to the river to look upstream to where the fortress stood. Alfheim was nothing Carolingian, not even Roman; still less was it anything that real migration-period Germanic tribes could have come up with. If the guy who built the Mausoleum of Theodoric—who was going to build it, fifty years from now—had just seen *Fantasia* and could build in reinforced concrete, he might have built this, grim and tall and foreboding. A fortress of tall towers, topped with rounded domes, arrow slits spangled up and down their sides, colored a dark brooding gray. It looked like the illustration in the hardback *Golden Road*. It looked, among other things, damnably hard to get into or out of.

Ahead of them the road ran into a patch of woodland, ten acres perhaps. It didn't seem big enough to keep a population of large beasts going, but now they heard the blast of a horn. Ta ra, ta ra. Somebody was hunting something, and they reined in to wait and see.

Three men on foot burst out of the wood at a run. No, not men: They were covered with hair from head to foot, shaggy and dingy green like a sloth's. Woodwoses. Wild men of the forest, terrible to meet on their own territory, but they were on the run.

They came to a crossroads and broke up: two toward the river, one westward toward Greg and Mary. It took no notice of them as it ran; perhaps they didn't look like a threat, or perhaps its eyes were blind with sweat or terror. Coral-colored eyes, small and truculent like a pig's. Its fur hung over its mouth in a walrus moustache, stringy with sweat and quivering as it panted for breath. Then it was past. It dove for cover into the field of knotgrain and disappeared, almost; it left a subtle trace, like a burrowing mole, as it crept through the stalks.

Ta-ra, ta-ra. Two elf-karls rode out of the wood at a gallop, checking to a trot as they looked about for their prey. The other woodwoses were still running toward the river, and the men took off in pursuit. They were nearly out of sight when they caught up, and Greg and Mary could only see the spearshafts rise and fall. Something cried out, a thick clotted bubbling sound, and fell silent. Ta-a-a, the horn sang. A kill, a kill.

Mary was reaching for her lance. Greg reached out to hold her hand in its place. "They're not people," he reminded her. "Not even real animals, not even real subroutines: just targets. They don't *live* in that wood, they're merely generated in it to serve as dangers for travelers and sport for hunters. They—"

Another scream tore through the air, inarticulate but recognizably human. It took them a moment to realize that the third woodwose had made its way through the field of knotgrain into the beanfield. Now it was hoisting the changeling onto its back, and she was screaming. Mary said, "Oh, hell," and took her lance again. This time Greg didn't try to stop her.

The changeling was no lightweight. The woodwose was bent almost double as it clutched her to its back in a half-assed fireman's carry, and its teeth were sunk into her arm to help it hold her on. It was moving slowly enough that Mary could pause a moment to take careful aim. The fiery spearpoint slid under the wose's right arm and pierced it through. The wose's mouth opened soundlessly and it toppled, its heart and liver (or equivalents) spit-roasted. The changeling fell off and scrambled away.

A clattering of hooves: the elf-karls, each with a dripping head on his saddlebow, piggy eyes glazed over, moustaches forlornly drooping. "You son of a bitch!" the leading elf-karl cried.

"Moi?"

Greg had risen up behind them. "What are you complaining about?" he said now, in a voice twice as large as Mary was used to hearing from him. "We left you one each. If you hadn't let this one get away, we wouldn't have had to intervene." He glanced at the dead woodwose, now shriveled almost past recognition, like an ugly green teddybear. Its blood had burned to powder on the spearshaft and was falling away. "If you don't take good care of your toys, you can't keep them; didn't your mother ever tell you that?"

Both men glared at him: An elf-karl's unknown mother was always a rich source of insult. But they looked at Mary's lance and put two and two together, and they galloped away without a word, back into the forest.

"I know, I know," Mary said. "I just blew our cover killing a subroutine to save another subroutine."

"Not a bit of it," Greg said. "Your motives were good, it's true, but they don't know that. For an elf-karl to be meek and obliging would have been way out of character. No, the harm that's done here," he continued as they rode into the forest, "is to the spirits of men like that, who have deliberately chosen to side with the bad guys and ride armed and armored, hunting naked things that look like men."

They kept a sharp eye out in the forest, which was only about a mile wide, but no one attacked them. The forest had run out of woses for the moment and the elf-karls, as Greg pointed out, had probably gone outside to bitch and have a few beers.

On the other side of the wood the town began. Peasant huts and larger houses huddled together apparently at random, each in its own little yard where a pig lived, or a goat (or—what *was* that thing? Pig-sized, black, and shaped like a frog!). Some higher authority had kept clear the road they were riding on, which led to the castle; elsewhere were mere footpaths the width of a horse between walls and wattle fences. Anywhere a house had burned or been torn down, its successor had been built to take up every inch of space it could, and the houses stood crammed up together around the little yards. To build the town would have taken several iterations on the computer, Greg said, but the software itself was as simple as could be. It was a medieval building pattern. *The Plan of St. Gall* showed how the classic North European house plan had mutated under crowded city conditions into something narrow, unaisled, more ingeniously braced by its timbers, and several stories high. All this was several centuries later than this place was supposed to be—but *The Golden Road* itself was deliberately anachronistic, a tale of fifth-century heroes told in eighth-century Europe, ignoring the fall and rise of empires in between.

A troop of a dozen elf-karls was riding before them toward the castle. They seemed tired, their horses walking slowly, and Greg and Mary caught up with them and fell in behind. The knights' lances were broken, their knees spattered with blood, and up ahead a riderless horse was being led, limping. Somewhere to the west, somebody had given as good as he got.

They passed through a gate in a stone wall that ringed the inner wards of the city. The gate guards had foxy faces, and it wasn't clear whether they were human or not. Within the walls there were fewer huts, more large houses, their roof beams rising high overhead. None of them seemed to have any windows; the doors were all shut and barred. In fact, there were no inhabitants in sight at all. Maybe they took to cover whenever the elf-karls went by; or maybe they only came out at night. If they were elves, or any of several sorts of elf allies, sunlight would kill them quickly and nastily.

And these were the doors of the fortress itself. Heavy slabs of—wood? Well, of something, bronze-bound, swinging on noiseless hinges that must be magical. Here the troop dismounted and let their horses be led away by little servitors who were certainly not human. Mary caught Greg's eye. "Yes, it's all right," he murmured. "Not real horses; they wouldn't hurt them in any case; and I can magic them out of the stables at a moment's notice if we need them. Quick, look to your left." Between the fortress and the nearest house a path ran, paved with smooth irregular flagstones, to a patch of uneven light that was surely water and probably the river. Then they stepped inside and there was no light at all.

Dark as the inside of a black cat in a coal cellar at midnight. Mary took a step forward and stopped. "Oh, here," came the murmur out of the darkness, and a hand took hers; Mary nearly jumped out of her skin, though she knew it was Greg. His other hand touched her eyelids, and suddenly she could see again, in a pale monochromatic blue light that came from no obvious source. "Elf-sight," Greg explained. "They've all got it anyway; we'd attract more notice if we *couldn't* see in the dark." They stood for a moment, hands clasped, while the troop filed across the floor and vanished under an archway. Greg's hands were trembling too. "Impressive, isn't it?" he said. They were now standing in a great hall, the base of one huge tower, whose roof vanished overhead in shadows. "Well written. I *know* it isn't real, and yet it makes my skin crawl. Well, let's see; we want to go this way."

A different archway led them into a tunnel vault with patches of fungus on the stone walls. Just ahead the tunnel branched into a Y-shape of approximately equal angles. To extend an arch into a tunnel vault and to make a cross-shaped intersection of two tunnel vaults were engineering problems the Romans had solved. For the elves of Alfheim, to whom a cross in any form was an abomination, it posed a problem both spiritually and architecturally. The three half-arches met overhead in a round boss carved with oak leaves, like those done centuries later in cathedrals of the High Middle Ages. She would have to ask somebody, later on, if this Y-shape would work in the real world, or if the boss was magical and held up the vault rather than merely ornamenting it.

While Greg paused to get his bearings, Mary turned and noticed that a patch of fungus the size of a cow had followed them, creeping along the wall. But it stopped moving when she looked at it and made no move to attack. When they went on, she glanced back again and saw the fungus, apparently unable to cross the floor, clinging disconsolately to the corner where two walls joined. Sadly it watched them out of sight, edges rippling in the blue air. Perhaps it was just bored.

The walls of the next tunnel vault were smooth, almost slick, as if the masons had done much more polishing here or the programmer much less. There was a single patch of fungus ahead, a huge one, several meters wide and reaching from vault to floor—no. No, thank goodness, it was only a tapestry hung against the wall, four meters wide and at least as high, clean out of period. It seemed to be a representation of the night sky, semé of stars, with a thin crescent moon in one corner and a few bats in flight. The nearest bat opened a toothy mouth in a soundless shriek, its large ears and wrinkled face all shaped to catch the echoes. Greg paid no attention to the artwork; he slipped between the tapestry and the wall, and Mary followed.

Here it was dark even with elf-sight, and Mary could just make out the shape of a door in the wall, man-sized, with iron hinges and some kind of inscription carved at eye level. Greg was fumbling with the latch. It opened with the softest of clicks, like a well-lubricated modern lock, and the door swung open into light.

They stepped through, and again Mary waited for her eyes to adjust, but they didn't. The light was pure white, bright but not painfully so, and filled with abstract shapes outlined in a chaste gray. Greg was nowhere to be seen. Neither was she: They had become invisible again. When she tried to look down at herself, her gaze floated effortlessly downward, and circled back around. She was a point of view with no body at all, suspended in a sphere of pale-gray abstract images.

Well, Greg had been right: The door was a pointer into a very different system indeed. She might have panicked if she'd had a body to do it with: no heart to race, no breath to catch; and besides, she could always go outside again. If she remembered how. The images were still moving past her, and she couldn't tell if she'd made one revolution or several.

But when she focused her attention on one of the shapes, it obligingly stopped and began to drift toward her—or she toward it.

It had a label on it—ILQ Module 4206—and a lot of little segments beneath that seemed to have labels of their own. But she didn't get a chance to read them; as she approached, the structure split open and expanded, an explosion in slow motion, and fragments flew past her bearing incomprehensible names. The only one she focused on read "junk." The fragments passed her and surrounded her, and in moments she was floating inside another sphere, full of chaste gray images ready to come close and explode if one looked at them. Frantically she tried to look nowhere at all.

<<Get out of there.>> The voice came from nowhere and wasn't really a voice. <<Oh, I'm sorry, you're not used to this kind of interface, are you? Just a second while I bring up Tulgey Wood.>>

It took more than a second, but no more than several. All of a sudden there was a floor, a dark blue-green surface with a broad path running through it, and as she watched trees sprouted up everywhere, great writhen trunks with an occasional cluster of leaves below and a dark featureless canopy above. It was like being inside a cartoon. She found she was sitting on a branch of one of the trees, three or four feet off the ground. She slid off and floated to the ground like a feather, but when she reached the path it felt solid under her feet. And twitching her toes didn't send her flying off again. The virtual gravity was funny here, but at least she had a body again—her own, or what looked like it, wearing her usual black jumpsuit with the sun on its breast. Her real-life persona, so to speak.

There was a flicker of motion in the corner of her eye, and she turned back to the tree she had just left. There was a bird in it—no, not a bird, damn it, a cartoon character: a pair of eyeglasses with little eye-dots in the lenses, with a long beak and a pair of bird legs. Birdlike, it hopped along the branch toward her and said, "Hello."

"Hello," she said.

"Hello," it said. This wasn't getting either of them anywhere. As she stared at the creature she felt her feet leave the ground again; hastily she dropped her eyes.

"Ah, there you are." She looked up: A little sparkling ball of light hung at eye level, speaking with Greg's voice. "Is that better? A little easier to cope, once you know which way is up?"

"Yes, thanks. Not to mention having hands and feet. Greg, what is this place?"

"This is just about the latest thing in VR CAD-CAM. Prometheus, it's called. It's a design system; the designer can get right into the data without either a physical or a virtual body to get in the way. What you're seeing now, though, is called Tulgey Wood; it's an interface designed for people who have to get into the system occasionally—managers and administrators and so on—but who aren't used to its normal appearance and don't want to be. The trees are directories. The paths are . . . well, paths. The spectacle bird is a prompt. This is a UNIX-based system, as you've probably figured out by now. If you'd asked the spectacle bird for a file, he would have led you to it. Shoo, bird." The spectacle bird bent its knees and hopped straight up and out of sight.

"The only problem we have right now," Greg's light went on (it was like Dante talking to Charles Martel in Paradise), "is that the door *in* isn't in the same place as the door *out*. I'll do a search. In the meantime, why don't you sit here and watch the world go by; this interface is really pretty cute. If anything passes you on the path, just watch and don't speak to it. Except the Cheshire Cat; you can talk to him, he's just a screensaver." The light took off along the path and disappeared among the trees. Mary sat down to watch.

For a while everything was quiet, but that was all right; in the context of everything else she had been doing lately, a little quiet was good for the nerves. After a while an owl flew by, an owl with the body of an accordion. This place was starting to look familiar. She was just putting her finger on it when a dozen little mollusks ran by on tiny legs, followed by the Walrus and the Carpenter. *Alice in Wonderland,* of course: not the Victorian Alice but one of the cartoon versions. Yes, and that shape in the branches over there wasn't the moon—it was the grin of the Cheshire Cat.

"We're all mad here," the Cat remarked, as its stripes coiled rapidly around emptiness and solidified into a body and a fat, plumy tail.

"I believe you," Mary said. The Cat's eyes were spinning round in their sockets like pinwheels. No matter; the original Cheshire Cat grinned because it was a vampire. She was happy to settle for this one. Tweedledum and Tweedledee did a fast two-step up and down the path and disappeared. The Cat was unwinding; the grin faded out and in again.

"If you go that way," the grin said, "you'll meet the Mad Hatter. If you go *this* way, you'll meet the March Hare. He's mad too." The head reappeared on the branch, with the body dancing a slow can-can above it. "And if you go on long enough, you could get to almost anywhere."

"Thanks. I think Greg is taking care of that for me."

"Of course, if you don't care where you're going, it doesn't matter where you go. Does it?"

"I'll pass on that one, Cat," Mary said. "I spend most of my time just keeping my head above water, which is like running the Red Queen's race."

"Oooh," the Cat said. "Do you know the Queen?"

"Only too well. But you've got a point, Cat. If I ever get to the stage where I'm self-sufficient—energy, food and water, money—what do I do then? Sit down on my pile like Smaug and grow old? Take up backgammon? Exhibition jousts? What's your advice, Cat?"

"Don't step on the mome raths," the Cat said earnestly. They were gathering on the paths, tiny things like Technicolor mushroom brushes with reproachful little eyes. As she watched, they formed into the shape of an arrow and began to creep along the path.

"Found it," Greg's voice called from a distance. "Follow the mome raths."

"Coming," Mary said. " 'Bye, Cat."

"Beware the Jabberwock." The Cat yawned, and disappeared again.

"Oh, no." Mary's hand went to her sword, but she

wasn't wearing it. "Greg! There isn't a Jabberwock in this thing, is there?"

"Well, yes," Greg said, as his light came darting between the trees to meet her, "but it won't attack you or anything. It just whiffles by along the path. Come on, I've found the way out, among other things. The way this guy has it set up, the door from *The Golden Road* into here dumps him back in his home directory, just in case he has to get out and look busy in a hurry. But the door *in* is concealed way down the filestructure, disguised as something else, in the hopes the sysadmin won't find it. But I know his pathname, and I know his real name, and I'm gonna tell Professor Markheim on him."

"Greg, is *this* place legal? Aren't these images under copyright?"

"The Tulgey Wood images? Of course they are. The difference between this and *The Golden Road* is that this is licensed. The software company negotiated a deal with the owners—look, there goes your Jabberwock—"

The Jabberwock stalked by, planting its big bird feet delicately on the path like a heron, whiffling and burbling as it went. It was a fine sight, shading through tints of purple from almost white on the belly to almost black on the spines. Its expressionless squid's eye glanced at Mary for an instant and looked away.

"—they'd been doing cartoon screensavers since the old days. And they got a license, they pay a fee, and everything's legal. Here's the door."

It floated in the air before them, about three feet high. The face on the doorplate glared at them and muttered, "Go away, there's nothing here." Greg's light slipped through the keyhold and the door opened onto darkness.

Mary glanced behind her. A family of auto horns ran along the path, honking in irritation. The spectacle bird had returned and perched, bobbing patiently, in the nearest tree. Mary sighed and turned away; it probably cost a bundle and wouldn't run on her little system anyway. She thought she would have to clamber through the little door one leg at a time, but as soon as she put her hand to the jamb it dumped her out into the dark space behind the tapestry.

"This one must have been added later," Greg said, looking thoughtfully at nothing. "The other ones are all together down the hall." They slipped from behind the tapestry and walked down the smooth-walled hall to a round room with a vaulted ceiling. On its walls were four tapestries and three bare doors. "No, they're not," Greg contradicted himself. "Seven here, one back there, one way down in a dungeon somewhere."

"Do you want to skip that one?"

"Mmmm, no, we'd better collect everything we can. We can get into it through here." He led the way back to where the vault branched and took the passage to the right. This tunnel was walled and vaulted with coarser stone, as if it were older, and the mortar was black as if the moss on it had grown old and died. It took a sharp turn and ended at a stone staircase that spiraled upward and downward into darkness. Greg looked up and down it and began to descend. The stairs spiraled tightly downward, with room for only about one-and-a-half people to go abreast. They came to a landing with another tunnel vault going by outside. Greg took his bearings, and they continued downward.

"This stair's built wrong," Greg commented. "It curves the wrong way."

Mary glanced down the spiral and extended it in her mind. "Yes, it goes widdershins, opposite the sun. (At least, if you're heading this way.) Wouldn't that be appropriate, here?"

"Yes, but the reason a castle stair spirals clockwise is to make it harder to attack, easier to defend. Look." He turned back toward her. "Now, if you were attacking this stair, and I were defending it, I'd be swinging my sword up at you." He brought his right arm overhead, as if striking—awkwardly, because the curving wall that hid the central core of the staircase got in his way. "See? In a clockwise spiral I'd have more room to swing on my right side, and you'd have less. But it's the other way around." He turned back and continued to descend. "Maybe this stair is supposed to be defended by left-handed NPCs. Or maybe they just didn't think of it. Though this castle has been very well designed, so far." They came to a second landing. "Or maybe the stair's designed to impede people who are trying to fight their way *up* from the depths. Hmmm. The gateway's over here somewhere." He followed the corridor to the right.

"Are we walking into a trap? Is that the idea?"

"We could be. All these rooms, you understand"—he indicated the thick oak-plank doors that lined the hallway on both sides—"are full of monsters, ready to provide an encounter (and, probably, treasure) to those who care to fight them. You set them off by opening the door. But there are other triggers too. Some of them will attack if any lawful-good PC crosses their path—if he manages to get this far at all, which takes some doing."

"So why haven't they all attacked us?"

"Because we look like elf-karls. They haven't the intelligence to look inside the book's cover. But most of them have another trigger condition: 'If RT is true', and I don't know what RT is. It's defined somewhere else that I haven't found."

"If RT is true, then what?"

"Then attack. I'd like to know what it is, obviously; so I can not do it, for one thing. This door, however"—he tapped the wood with his forefinger, and the tiny sound echoed up and down the silent hallway—"this door contains no monsters. This is the gateway. Hmmm, what's this?"

"I can barely see it. X marks the spot?" She traced it with her fingers. "Keys? Yeah, it's a pair of crossed keys. Wards upwards, that's the default position, if I remember my heraldry."

"St. Peter's keys? *Here*? What's a saint's emblem doing in this castle?"

"Well, but it's a door to elsewhere. Maybe a place for the good guys to sneak in behind enemy lines? Maybe we'll open the door and walk into Rome?"

"There isn't a system doing Rome, so far as I've heard," Greg said. "There's certainly no system playing *Chivalry* in Rome; they would've had to apply to us for a license and source code. Well, let's see." He tugged on the door's heavy latch and pulled it open.

It led onto the top floor of a round tower, a large

one, no mere sheath for a staircase but a major part of a castle's defenses. A conical timber roof topped it, and its narrow windows were shuttered; without their elf-sight it would have been hard to see anything at all. Greg threaded his way between stacks of weapons and bales of supplies to the nearest window and opened the shutter.

It was near midnight here, and the moon near the full; it shed a cold light over a medieval city huddled within stone walls, a river curving around it not far from where they stood. The houses were small and huddled together, not much different from those of Alfheim, and not a light showed anywhere. But away to the north a Gothic cathedral lifted tall towers to the stars.

"That explains the keys," Greg said. "This is York, another city dedicated to St. Peter. That's the Ouse at our feet, and York Minster over there. So the Philadelphia and New York systems are both gated into this. I wonder who else—" He broke off. Something was howling under the moon, somewhere in the darkened streets below.

"That's a wolf. How picturesque can they get?"

"Nothing wrong with a wolf out there," Greg said. He was frowning as he peered out the window. "Remember, I told you, the forest begins right outside Bootham Bar—which you can't see from here, but it's just to the left of the Minster. But I could've sworn that howl came from *inside*." He leaned out the window. "Look."

In the street below three figures moved, two men and a wolf (or very large dog). They stopped, looked around as if to get their bearings, and disappeared into shadows.

"They're out after curfew, so by definition they're up to no good," Greg commented. "And there are some funny bits of code here. I can't stop to investigate now, but it looks as if someone's set up a dungeon crawl here too. I've heard funny things about the York system; it's owned by a consortium, and they aren't players."

They stepped back into Alfheim. The door, Mary noted, was disguised on the York side as part of the castle wall. It would be hard to find unless you knew where to look; even in daylight this tower would be fairly dark.

They returned to the stairs and Greg sighed. "Lead us not into temptation," he said. "You know what's at the bottom of this dungeon?"

"What?"

"Theodoric."

"Oh, my. Sitting down there in the snakepit, waiting for Hildebrandt and Widia to come and rescue him?"

"And guarded by a couple of elves—I think they're elves. They're NPCs of truly impressive stats."

He put out a foot to start up the stairs, drew it back. "Wups. Somebody's coming." They retreated to the hallway, and after a moment Greg gestured them invisible. The party coming down the stairs was carrying some real light.

Three armed men and one in a Benedictine habit; it was he who carried the light, a horn-paneled lantern with a flickering candleflame inside it. (Now, wait. In this still air, and with the lantern to shield it, why should the light flicker?)

The party had reached the landing; they stopped for a moment for the monk to examine his light, shake his cowled head, and point downward. The party went on down the stairs.

So these must be the good guys: Christian knights and a monk of not inconsiderable piety, with a blessed and enchanted light to show them the way. And there they went to try to rescue King Theodoric.

Markheim's Theodoric: a strange character, meaning well but subject to violent rages for no particular reason. One of Mary's friends had called him the second chaotic-good character he'd ever encountered. It was as if Markheim had been building up to explain some of his later acts as King of the Goths and Italians by his long captivity among the elves. She tugged at Greg's sleeve. "Can we go down and watch?"

Greg hesitated, as if consulting an unseen clock. "For a little while. If it turns into a long battle, we'll have to leave it." They crept down the stairs till they were only a few steps above the party of adventurers.

The landing below—Mary craned her neck—opened through a blunt pre-Gothic archway not onto another hallway but onto a single room. Its ceiling and its far walls were lost in shadows, and its floor moved uneasily. Now and then a flat reptilian head rose on its long neck above the slithering mass, hissed disdainfully, and fell back again.

In the center of the room a round platform rose, man-height and big enough for an elephant to bed down on. Here a long bench stood, and a small table with a cup standing on it, crystal footed with silver. A man sat on the bench, one leg drawn up, arms clasped over his shin, head bowed on his knee. He was big and had reddish hair: That was all they could see of him. The archway was blocked not with an ordinary door but with an ornate grillwork that looked like wrought iron but was probably something else—tarnished silver, maybe. On the outside of it hung a naked sword.

To either side of the grille stood a guard, sword at his side, spear in hand. These were surely elves: their faces deadly calm, their eyes bright, their long black hair pulled back from their faces into a neat braid that fell in front of the left shoulder. There were silver rings in their ears, and their hauberks seemed to be made of silver. They stood still; if they could see the party on the stairs (and they should, from where they stood), they gave no sign of it. Perhaps there were more enchantments at work.

The lantern was enchanted, of course, or blessed, which came to the same thing. Having led the rescue party to the site, bending its flame this way and that, it would now blind the defenders' eyesight by so many percent and improve the attackers' aim by so many more. That was the kind of improvement in verisimilitude VR had made in fantasy- and role-playing games in general. If you came into a dark corridor, it was *dark,* and you couldn't see your hand (let alone your opponent's) in front of your face unless somebody had brought a light. (And, unless somebody had brought a bag of holding, that loot you collected was too heavy to carry.)

The monk glanced from side to side at his companions. Mary could see them better now: one big and red-bearded, one fair-haired and looking scarcely old enough to fight, one short and broad and dark. The monk looked at each of them, saw that all were ready; he crossed himself and began to speak. *"In principio creavit Deus caelum et terram. Terra autem erat inanis et vacua—"*

Well, even Mary had the Latin to understand that. It was Genesis I; and if he could get to the end of the paragraph, he would achieve a serious advantage over the enemy. But at the first word the elf-guards had gone alert, seeming to see the party for the first time. They lowered their spears and attacked, and the human warriors raised their shields and struck out with their swords—not very accurately.

"Dixitque Deus, 'Fiat lux'—" and the red-bearded knight took a spear in the gut and stumbled backward onto the monk. The two of them fell in a heap on the landing. The elf's beautiful cruel face smiled, and he raised his spear again.

"Et facta est lux!" Greg shouted. Well, it must have been Greg; the voice was his, but she couldn't see him. It didn't matter. He had completed the spell, and the landing lit up with a soft pearly light. The elves staggered and cried out, throwing their arms over their eyes. The monk got himself out from under Redbeard and began to recite a blessing to cure the wounded man. The other two moved in on the shrieking elves.

But even under the assault of light, the elf-guards were no pushovers. Dropping their spears, they had drawn their swords and were swinging wildly, as much to beat off the knights' strokes as to land any blows of their own. The human fighters' blows did strike them betimes, but their armor was tough and their injuries healed fast.

Blackhair seemed to have decided the only way to kill his opponent was to wear him down. Shield close to his body, fending off the elf's flailing blows, he got in perhaps one stroke in ten; but some of those were hitting home. Slowly he beat him back across the landing toward the stairs.

Perhaps he meant to drive the elf backward till the stairstep behind him tripped him up? Or gave him a chance to run away? If so, he wasn't very bright; the elf could sound the alarm. More to the point, he was about to knock the elf straight into Mary, whom he couldn't see, standing there one step above the landing.

There was really nowhere for her to go; she couldn't retreat back up the stairs without stepping on Redbeard, and she had no idea where Greg was. She raised her shield in haste to fend off the elf's wild backhand stroke; it rang against the steel of the shield rim. Well, now she was engaged with the elf whether he'd intended it or not. She drew her sword and struck, aiming for the elf's heart and catching him somewhere amidships.

There was an eye-searing flash: Lord, yes, those enhancements on her sword, the dragonslayer. The elf moaned and collapsed in an untidy heap on the floor. Blackhair struck him once more on the helm, out of momentum or to make sure he stayed down, but there was really no need: The elf was dying, crumpling like an old balloon as the air slowly leaks away.

The human turned back to help his fair-haired companion, who was finding a half-blinded elf still very rough going. The elf had one hand over his eyes, a narrow gap between the fingers providing limited vision, and was fighting with the other hand. Even with his eyes protected, the blessed light was doing him no good. The pale skin was darkening into a muddy purple, and raw patches that looked like burns were breaking out on his hands and face. Mary wondered vaguely what the spectrum of the light was and put the thought to one side. This was a matter of the light of Heaven lighting up the darkness of evil and could not be measured in Angstrom units.

Redbeard, his wound healed, came down the steps and joined in. Ill, blinded, and one against three, the elf didn't stand a chance, but it still took them many blows to beat him down, a cascade of hit points. Mary looked away. Still no clue where Greg was, but he could find *her* whenever he chose just by casting a spell. Or rather, by looking at the code. One tended to forget this wasn't real; well, that was what made VR fun. She didn't care much for this kind of adventure, sneaking and hacking and no place for the rules of honor, but there were many who did. These three had at least chosen to side with the good, though you might not guess it from looking at them just now. They left the dead elf in an oozing heap and looked around to see what was next; and a voice called out, "Who's there?"

Theodoric had risen from his bench and was standing there, his hands clasped behind him, watching from the rim of the stone platform.

"We are Christian knights, vassals of the Emperor. We've come to set you free."

"To set me free! Ah! My thanks to you. Can you beat down the door? I could make short work of these serpents, if I had my sword."

"That's my task," said the monk. He made his way between the fighters, his lantern in his hand, and came up to examine the grille.

"Careful, don't touch it," Theodoric said. "It bites."

"We found that out last time," Blackhair said. "Here, Rolf, you've the lightest fingers among us; see if you can get Nagelring off that damned door." Fairhair reached up cautiously, touching the sword only at the pommel, and lifted it gingerly away from the wall.

"That's mine," Theodoric growled.

"Waiting for you, milord," Fairhair assured him, "as soon as we can get you out."

"Hush," said the monk, raising his hand. "*Aperite mihi portas justitiae,*" he began, and Mary smiled. But the security here was tougher than in Greg's building, and the monk had to recite the entire psalm, complete with *Gloria Patri.* As he pronounced the final "Amen," the grille shivered and fell away into dust.

"Here, m'lord! Catch!" Fairhair cried, and flung the sword Nagelring in a high arc across the moat of snakes. Slowly it turned end-for-end as it flew. Theodoric marked it with his eye, and stretched out his hand to seize it by the hilt.

"*Deus, qui mare rubrum ante Moÿsen aperuisti,*" the monk was chanting. Something about the Red Sea opening and the snakes of Pharaoh's magicians getting swallowed, but it didn't seem strictly necessary. Theodoric had leapt into the pit, sword swinging, drops of cold blood flying left and right. The snakes were getting rapidly out of the way, as if they knew what was good for them. Theodoric crushed with his heel the last flat head in his path and bounded across the floor and over the threshold, grinning like a tiger. He was tall and broad shouldered, with gray eyes and black eyebrows, startling beneath the curly red hair. He brandished his sword in the air, and the knights took a step backward. And somewhere near Mary's ear Greg murmured, "Uh-oh."

"Save your blows, Theodoric," the monk said. "There will be plenty of time for fighting later, but now is the time for stealth. We need to get out of here without calling the whole castle down on our heads." The pearly light was fading, and soon the only real light left in the room came from the monk's lantern.

"Very well," Theodoric said. "Lead, and I follow. How did you find me in all this dark pile?"

"Later," the monk said. "Hush." And surprisingly (or was it? He had been raised as a warrior, and must have some notion of following orders), Theodoric obediently hushed. The party went up the stairs (Mary squeezed up against the wall to let them pass) and were gone. And Greg reappeared, and Mary's own shape around her.

"Okay," she said. "What for 'uh-oh'?"

"Well," he said, "it's just that as of the moment he stepped through the door, 'Condition RT' is now true."

Chapter 8

Confused Noises and Garments Rolled in Blood

"Uh-oh," Mary repeated. "And now everything's going to attack. Those guys are going to have an interesting adventure. Maybe we should get out while the getting's good?"

They now had the two circles of the spiral stairs to climb again, and Mary could see what Greg had meant about the left-handed spiral: If something attacked them on these stairs, it would be damnably hard to fight; every time she raised her sword arm it would clash against the wall. In an ordinary castle you'd have such a staircase in a tower above ground level, to hinder attackers trying to fight their way up and in. Here—well, yes, it made sense: This tower was designed to hinder rescue parties trying to fight their way up and *out*.

Never mind; she'd fought often enough under SCA rules, whereby if your sword arm was taken you dropped your shield and fought with your off arm, that she was reasonably adept at fighting left-handed. The enchanted sword and shield would have to make up the gap—and the Carolingian roundshield, with its central handgrip, would work for either hand.

Above, something screamed. Not a human something, she thought: too many high frequencies in the sound. She switched her shield to her right hand and loosened her sword in the scabbard, making sure she could draw it with her left.

But nothing attacked them on the stairs. As they passed the first landing, something darted out of the hallway and up the stairs ahead of them, moving so quickly they could not guess what it was. But since it was headed away from them, it didn't matter much—unless they caught up with it.

They had reached the next landing when they heard the screams again, ahead of them in the branching tunnel vault. Mary switched her shield back to her left hand and drew her sword. The screams, loud enough now to cool the blood, were mixed with the clash of metal against metal and duller sounds like an ax against a tree.

"Undead of some kind," Greg said, and drew his own sword—which had better be a disguised lightning thrower or something, since he'd had no practice with the real thing.

They rounded a bend in the tunnel and found the battle raging: Theodoric and his party versus half a dozen—well, as Greg had said, undead of some kind. They might have been human once; now the flesh hung in rags and tatters from their bones, and their armor was thick with rust. But that didn't prevent them from putting up a good fight. Fairhair was down, the monk bending over him, while the others fought off the dead warriors.

All this was going on in the middle of the path that led, if Greg's bearings were right, to the rest of the gateways; and it didn't look as if either side would honor a request to play through.

Mary raised her shield and waded in, glad she'd had a chance to reverse hands again. One of the skeletal warriors was raising its sword to behead the unprotected monk; Mary cut its arm off. The sword fell with a clatter, the bony arm with a rattle, and Mary's next stroke took off its head. The skeleton crumpled in a heap and fell into dust—and another skeleton stepped in and struck down the monk anyway.

"Damn! Greg?" But Greg was busy; his shield raised to eye level, his shortsword resting on the rim, he was sighting along the blade like a rifle and sending off bolts of what looked like neon but was probably Dispel Undead, Plus Five. As she watched, he took out the last skeleton—and three more came down the corridor (or, possibly, out of the wall). Theodoric hacked the first to pieces; Mary took out the second; Greg fried the third.

"Come on," Redbeard cried, "let's get out of here—oh, Christ, which way is out?"

"*That* way," Greg said, pointing him toward the wall where the fungus hung, little fringes fluttering in the air. "Godspeed and good luck. Go with him, Theodoric, don't linger here."

"What about Rolf and Clement?" Blackhair looked around, confused. "We can't leave them—"

"They're dead," Greg said, pointing to the empty floor where they had lain. "Get Theodoric out of here. If you can get him into the West, you'll change the whole course of the war. Get moving."

But now three trolls were pounding in from the smooth-walled corridor, and from behind the fungus came an ominous dark-robed shape, nine feet tall, that stank of sulfur. "Theodoric, you take that one," Greg said. "The rest of us will take the trolls."

"Can he handle that thing alone?" Redbeard asked.

"Trust me," said Greg, "he can," and then the trolls closed in and there was no chance to speak. Four against three should have been hard to beat, with Mary's skills and enhancements and Greg's wizardry; but the trolls were surprisingly tough, and by the time Greg and Mary had taken out two, the third had struck down Blackhair and Redbeard.

"Blast," Blackhair muttered, coughing. Greg knelt beside him, leaving the third troll to Mary. "It was a good fight, though. See you in the next life. Get Theodoric out of here, if you can." Blackhair died and vanished. Redbeard was already gone. They turned back to find Theodoric wiping his sword; there was no sign of his black-robed opponent, but the swordblade was stained a burned ivory-black that would not come off, no matter how industriously Theodoric scrubbed with the hem of his tunic.

Something white came drifting in along the smooth-walled corridor. Filaments floated about it like tattered graveclothes in a light wind or the tentacles of a jellyfish. Its feet, if it had any, did not touch the floor. It was almost on Theodoric before he felt something—a chill, perhaps—and turned to meet it. His sword seemed to go through the thing without encountering resistance, but when a drifting tentacle touched him, it sizzled like a drop of water on hot iron.

"This is messy," Greg said. "There are monsters headed in from all over the castle, converging on this spot, and more being generated all the time."

"But the rescue party's dead."

"Doesn't matter; they'll keep coming as long as Theodoric is out. They won't kill him—that's why I knew he could take the hulker—but they'll push him back to his cell by sheer force of numbers if necessary."

There was a pop like a burst balloon and a faint scream; Theodoric had found the one tangible spot in the wraith's misty body and, as the gamers said, criticaled it. It collapsed in a heap and melted away like frost.

Greg glanced toward the fungus; something heavy-footed was coming this way, its tread making the stone floor vibrate under their feet and the fungus on the wall pull in its tendrils and shrink up out of the way. Mary flexed her fingers and shifted the grip on her sword. But Theodoric began to amble down the corridor as if he were going to go pick dandelions.

"Not that way," Greg said.

"I can take them."

"I know you can, but there are more where they came from. Back this way."

"I'll not go back into that stinking pit!" Theodoric rumbled.

"You don't have to; there's another way, one only the Elf King knows, and myself."

"Then lead the way," Theodoric said. He touched

his cheekbone, where a tentacle-touch had left a raw patch like a freezer burn. "Mother of God, that stings."

"Oh, sorry. I can fix that," Greg said. He said nothing, did nothing obvious, but the blemish disappeared. "Thanks to you," the Goth said, and went ahead of them to take on three ugly little rock-dwarves that looked as if they had missed the rehearsal for *Das Rheingold*.

"You're sure that's an NPC?" Mary whispered to Greg.

"Absolutely. He's good, isn't he? I wish I could take his code home with me in a box. I've downloaded a few nice features, but the channel isn't wide enough to maintain our personae, *and* nine or ten traces, and download him too."

Theodoric dispatched the last of the rock-dwarves and they joined him on the landing. "Down two flights," Greg said. Theodoric gave him a suspicious look; but they could hear feet clattering on the stairs from the floor above, so he followed them without comment.

Greg paused on the landing to listen. There was nothing to be seen from where they stood, but the hall was not quiet; the air was full of little scrapes and giggles and whispers, a monstrous game of hide-and-seek.

"This is going to be—" Greg began, in a low voice, and then, "No, I'll tell him! Theodoric! This is going to be the hardest part. We have to go down this hall, around the bend, and halfway down the next. Up till now our path had been easy, because we've been going the way they want us to go: back and downward, as they think, toward your cell. But now we're going another way, and they're going to rise up to force us back; we shall be like salmon swimming upstream."

Theodoric grinned. "Let them come," he said.

"But mind: Whatever we find here, if it doesn't get in our way, let it go. Anything that tries to impede us, kill it; but if it's only standing by gibbering at us, let it be."

They stepped off the landing into the hall, and there was a sound as if everything drew breath together. The doors were rattling against their latches, impatient to open. But the first sending came out of none of the doors, but dropped from the ceiling.

It was a giant spider. Not a big furry friendly tarantula, such as most Californian children have held and petted at the science center: Its legs were thin and its body smooth, and it looked mean. Theodoric began taking its legs off, joint by joint; this took a while. When the creature managed to put a coil of silk round Theodoric's body, Greg said, "Oh, blast," and made the silk disappear. "Speed's what we need at the moment, not verisimilitude."

Theodoric lunged and split the spider's cephalothorax in half. The rear part staggered and began to wander back the way it had come. It might take a while to die, but without eyes or jaws it was no longer a threat. They stepped over twitching bits of leg to clear ground. "What's verisimilitude?" said Theodoric.

"It's when something happens as it would in the natural course of things," Greg said. "Such as you being driven down to the snakepit again, which I don't intend to let happen."

Theodoric looked at him with respect. "Neither do I."

But now a door was slowly opening, and they had to stop and fight three goblins and a werepig. After that they realized that if they could only get upstream of a door before its creatures came out, they would not attack. Thus they had only two more battles before they reached the door marked with St. Peter's keys.

They opened the door and stepped through. Theodoric seemed dazed, and they had to take him by the wrists and pull him across the threshold. "What place is this?" the Goth asked, blinking and looking around.

"This is a tower in a fortress," Greg said, opening the nearest shutter and letting the moonlight in. "And outside is the city the Romans called Eboracum, but the Saxons call it Eoforwic. There is something evil loose in the city; I don't know what it is, but when wolves roam the streets of a city at night, there's something very wrong in it."

"Then I shall find it and kill it," Theodoric said, and before they could speak he plunged down the stairs, sword in hand, without waiting to see if they were following.

"You're going to turn Theodoric loose in York?"

"Why not?"

"When we go back out and close the door, won't he disappear?"

"Of course not. Our software is based in St. Alban's; we're remote through—how many?—four domains. Doesn't matter. The channel is still open, even when the door is closed. What it will do, though—" He put a hand to the door. It opened only a crack and stopped. "Oh, come now." Something hit the floor outside with a loud thud, and Greg opened the door. A dozen yards away a huge troll was sitting on the stone floor; it got to its feet, rubbing its backside, and lumbered toward the door again. Greg drew Mary to one side, and the troll passed by without looking at them. It sniffed at the door to York, fingered the latch, and settled down against it as if prepared to wait. A little spindly, spiky creature in tattered green came up to wait beside it. Two lizardmen joined them, and a winged pig with three-inch fangs was close behind. There would soon be quite a crowd at the door, but none of them tried to go through it.

"They're all programmed to go after Theodoric," Greg explained as they made their way back to the stairs, "but they don't know about domain boundaries. Neither does Theodoric; you saw how we had to drag him through. They know he went through that door, but they don't see it as a door they can go through. Wups." A pony-sized beetle was bearing down on them. It seemed willing to abandon a Theodoric in the bush for a skirmish in the hand; there must be a bug in it. Greg blasted it and they went on.

"They'll keep piling up there indefinitely, possibly till somebody reboots the system or generates another Theodoric back in his cell. The former would be a problem for us; we'd wake up with a headache and no traces. So let's move it." And they hurried back upstairs, flattening themselves against the walls as eager monsters descended, and went back along the smooth-walled corridor past the Prometheus tapestry.

They took a quick look over the round room; it seemed quite empty. "Why have they got tapestries on these other doors and not on those three?"

"Why tapestries is easy: verisimilitude. To keep light from leaking through. Remember how photophobic Markheim's elves are. Tolkien's elves love the starlight; Markheim's are downright allergic to the sun. You saw how the light affected those guards. I don't know if anybody's actually playing an elf as a character—I wouldn't let 'em if it were my system; elves are just too powerful, aside from their photophobia. Now, let's see. Taking them in installation order—" He selected a tapestry and ducked behind it. There was a moment's silence and then the sound of gunfire. Mary flung the tapestry aside and drew her sword as she fumbled for the door with her left hand.

She stood in what was left of an adobe building; parts of two walls and the roof had been blown out, and the remaining bricks were slowly crumbling away. It was hot, and the air smelled of dust and—where she stood, in the darkest corner—stale wine and urine. Greg, wearing GI fatigues and helmet, crouched behind one of the remaining walls and peered out of a window with a broken shutter. Mary was wearing the same gear, with—she glanced sideways—captain's bars on her shoulder and a large .45 in her hand instead of her sword.

"You can put that away; you won't need it," Greg

said. His dusty Eisenhower jacket had an American flag patch on the sleeve and no rank insignia at all. (What would that make him? A war correspondent? Maybe.)

"Where are we?"

"This is *ETO*—a World War II game. This is Sicily, I think. Look, there they go." Mary looked between two slats of the broken shutter and saw a row of jeeps drive by over a bumpy road. After them came a long column of foot soldiers, dust covered and carrying heavy fieldpacks. The sound of cheerful curses drifted by. Mary saw a glass bottle pass from hand to hand: Coca-Cola, maybe, or the local wine.

"Good luck, guys," Greg said. "They'll march and fight all day and get hot and tired and sweaty, and when they go home, their wives will say, 'My gosh, Harry, this is worse than soccer.' "

"Are all these soldiers real? I mean, are they players?"

"Some of the doggies are NPCs. A lot of the players want to be officers, but there aren't enough commands to go around. So you wait in line a while, or pay extra."

There was a droning, buzzing noise somewhere in the distance, like a big greenbottle fly beating out against a windowpane the brains it hadn't got. It was growing louder. About the time Mary realized it must be a plane, or planes, a whistling sound was added to the engine drone. Then something exploded, as it seemed, in their laps, the noise was deafening, and the blast kicked a spray of sand through the empty window frames. For several seconds Mary could neither see or hear. She brushed sand out of her eyes. The engines had faded to a soft drone again, and its bomb blasts seemed no more than burst balloons on a thundery summer day.

"It's all right, lady," Greg said. He patted her shoulder. "It's just a plane, and they're just bombs. Anybody who gets killed has to buy a round of beer outside; that's all the harm it does. We can go now. I've got an ID on this link."

Back in the round room, Greg glanced around again at some set of labels Mary couldn't see, and chose another tapestry. The door opened onto a nineteenth-century parlor full of shadows and silence; sunlight filtered in from a pair of windows at the other end of the room. From somewhere a thread of sound drifted in, a man's tenor voice singing, "I am a poor . . . wayfaring stranger. . . ." The singer had had, perhaps, one or two beers more than he needed.

Outside the windows was a wooden sidewalk shaded by a wooden porch roof. An unpaved street, and the morning sun, and across the street another shaded wooden sidewalk in front of buildings with false fronts, trying to look two stories high. "Old West?"

"Right. Cowpersons and Native Americans. It's *Dodge City*: shoot-'em-ups at high noon, two-thirty, and four o'clock. It's morning now and quiet; want to look around?"

"1880s? I'd have to put on a hoopskirt, wouldn't I? I thought so. No, thanks. I'd rather you finished your survey so we can get out of here."

The doorway behind the next tapestry opened into a library: quiet, indirectly lighted, with soft carpeting underfoot. The library seemed to specialize in bound collections of journals, for the books came in blocks: two shelvesful of crayon-blue bindings, a dozen shelves of garnet red. Far down the aisle between two walls of books, someone was browsing among the shelves. "Ah," Greg said. "Don't move; I'll have to hit the front desk to get the ID. I'll be right back," and disappeared.

Mary waited. The person at the other end of the stacks was moving toward her, but not quickly. A person? Oh, probably. She could see light between the legs, and the shape of an arm lifted to the shelves. She looked at the books on the shelf nearest her; the spines read "Invoices Feb 2015," "Invoices Mar 2015," and so on through December and into 2016. Not much meat there. Then Greg was at her elbow again. "Let's go."

"Another business system?" she asked, pushing the tapestry aside.

"Right. That's what most commercial VRs looked like before Prometheus. It illustrates the old saying: Power and user-friendliness vary inversely. This one's next."

"This one" was one of the uncurtained doors, and as soon as Greg opened it, they could see why: The place was dark enough to keep any elf happy. A Dashiell Hammett VR, maybe, the foggy, shadowed side streets of San Francisco after dark? And the brief glint of light from that street corner, a period match and cigarette?

Migod, no. Those were *eyes*.

Greg tugged at her sleeve, and they stepped silently backward and shut the door. "What was that?"

"*Blood Path*. You're not interested, I hope."

"Vampires? Yuck. No, I'm not. What's next?"

The next door, a tapestried one, opened into the shell of a burned-out barn, with a tall scorched tree barely clinging to life beside it. Again the door had led into a corner right in the thick of things but concealed from the casual glance. A player could slip behind a tree and sneak uphill and into *Golden Road,* and no one else would be any the wiser.

Across a valley the sounds of distant rifles popped like popcorn. Two armies struggled over a ridge, in blue and in gray: the American Civil War.

"The interesting thing about this one," Greg murmured—most of his attention was on tracing the system's pathname and establishing its ID—"those are all PCs. One of the Civil War societies got a cheap group rate on plug surgery, and hundreds of them bought in." He was wearing faded denims and a red calico shirt.

Mary looked down and saw a tight-fitting bodice in a green leafy print, with—she reached behind to touch her back—dozens of little buttons fastening it, a style that proclaimed, "I'm a fine lady and I have a maid; otherwise I could never get into this dress." Shucks! Why couldn't she have been an ordinary farmwife in a loose calico work dress? The skirt was very full, and under it hung a huge bell-shaped hoop, much wider than the bustled styles of the 1880s. Damn verisimilitude anyway. Mary had never worn one of these things before, but she knew from hearsay that one had to take tiny steps or send it swinging for yards in every direction.

There was the sound of another explosion—a cannon, nearer and sharper than the aerial bombing in

Sicily—and a chorus of rifle shots. They peered through the gap where the door had once been.

In the valley below them, the air was hazy with smoke. Mary couldn't see clearly who was doing what to whom, and she doubted the participants could either; their generals must be going by Braille and the history books.

(And people did this voluntarily, for fun. Well, look at what she herself did for fun: put on twenty-five kilos of virtual steel and ride out to knock her friends off their horses. If she cared about honor on the field, this lot cared just as much about authenticity.)

"Where are we?"

"Gettysburg, I think. Hush for a minute, this is complicated. They've put three systems together for this encounter and I'm not sure which . . ." His voice trailed off.

Mary hushed and watched the battle, what little she could see. All the blood and gore was lost at this distance, all the massing and trooping and killing and dying reduced to moves in a game of blindfold chess. Uh-oh. Three men were coming up the hill, two of them supporting the third. "Greg," she ventured, "company."

"Bother," Greg said. "What are they? Blue or gray?"

"Looks black under the dirt," Mary said. "Navy blue, I guess. Union."

"All right," said Greg, as navy-blue uniforms took shape around them. "Lie down in that corner; you're a dead soldier." Mary lay down, feeling something awkward binding under her clothes. Right. She was a Northern lady who had bound down her modest bosom and gone to the ward disguised as a man. History brought to life. Greg knelt beside her, as if in prayer.

Mary closed her eyes and held her breath. You could do that indefinitely in VR; it was an inaccuracy she was willing to keep. The men had arrived with a clatter of boots and the moaning of the wounded man.

"Oh, Lord, here's another one," somebody said. "How is your friend?"

"He's dead," Greg said.

"Lay me down beside him, boys. I'm going too, soon." The man's breath caught in his throat. A heavy shape settled down at Mary's side, grunting as his friends lowered him into place. She could smell burned gunpowder and fresh blood. (Heavens! You could carry authenticity too far!)

"Lie easy, Johnny. We'll find a doctor—"

"No use. Don't you mourn for me, friends, when I'm gone; for I'm going to a better world than this. Tell my mother I thought of her, as I lay a-dying, and God protect the Union—"

There was cannon fire again, distant in the valley, and a cry of "Charge—!"

"We better get back."

"I don't like to leave Johnny."

"I'll stay with him," Greg said. "Lost my rifle anyhow."

"Thank you, friend," the soldier said. "And may some kind friend do as much for us when it comes our time."

"Amen."

"Amen."

The boots stumbled away and were gone.

"You can breathe now," Greg said presently. "Johnny's dead, his friends have left, and I've got my trace."

Mary sat up and got to her feet hastily; Johnny, lying there beside her, had made his dying speeches with most of his guts shot away.

"Take it easy. It's only a VR."

"I know it. It's ghastly anyway. I wouldn't want to be the kind of person who could take that in her stride, whether it was in VR or an illuminated manuscript."

"The Civil War groups always were big on authenticity," Greg said. "You couldn't go to an 1863 reenactment wearing boots that didn't come out till 1864. Now they can have authentic virtual typhus and food poisoning and gangrene, and get wounded and bleed to death without getting into trouble with the mundane authorities."

"And the bodies don't go away when they die? Is that authenticity again?"

"Of course. They'll collect the dead when the battle's over and bury them, and Lincoln will come to speak; he's a very good NPC. This is Gettysburg, you see. Let's get out while the getting is good."

Before the next door Greg stood for a while, rubbing his chin with a fingertip and murmuring, "Well, well."

"Well, what?"

"Does this door look any different to you?"

"Well." She took a quick look around. "It's a naked door instead of a tapestried door. That puts it in the minority. And I note it's directly opposite the archway into the rest of the castle. Does that mean anything?"

"It might. Makes it easier to find. Now, when I look at this door, I see it as a very wide one. If the other doors are garden hoses, this one's a one-meter water main. Or to vary the form, you could send an army through this door. No, of course you can't see it. If the players could see all the nuts and bolts, they couldn't enjoy the game. Take my word for it, this is a very wide door."

It was wide enough, at any rate, to take the two of them side by side. It opened out onto another long dark corridor, lined on both sides with unlabeled doors. "Ha," Greg said. "Thought so. We've got 'em now; this is the Backbone."

"It's up, then?" The long-promised interconnector among VRs had been vaporware since last year, as eagerly awaited as the Second Coming and so far with as little result.

"Last month, for beta testing only. They had a couple of spectacular drops this summer, and they didn't want to try it out on the general public yet. But it doesn't matter; any court will recognize access from the Backbone as 'publication' whether anyone has actually taken the route or not. I suspect a few have. Look, the door's marked." Mary had to look closely: Faintly outlined on the door was the cross-and-cinquefoil that appeared on the bindings of several editions of *The Golden Road.* You had to be looking for it to see it. "And down at the other end"—Greg pointed to a distant cluster of lights far down the corridor—"there's Apex and Norbert Systems and InterReality and whoever else is beta-testing this thing. Nobody's going to be connecting out this far for years yet. No, wait a minute. There's one other door live—"

"I was going to say," Mary said, "that there's a label on this one." The door was across the hall and two doors up from the *Golden Road* door. "It just says 'Open—' " and at the sound of her voice the door swung open and she fell inside.

Chapter 9

The Dark King

Stars, thousands of stars, and all of them in motion, like a swarm of glowing bees. It was like the Prometheus system gone negative: She hung bodiless in a space filled with complex detail, but dark patterned with light. There was no immediate clue as to what the moving lights represented, but the system was keeping track of thousands of them, all in motion. Remembering how the Prometheus directories had opened when she looked at them, she tried to look at nothing. It made her faintly dizzy.

But she could look at the ground; this system had an up and down and a floor to it. Occasionally one of the drifting lights settled to the floor, turned green, and went out. Forgetting herself, she watched one of these as it descended and touched down, watched long enough that it sprouted a glowing green label: *UA5402 LANDED.*

Oh, *shit*.

Again she tried to look at nothing, but again she didn't have the option; no eyelids to close. It must be hell to work here. Look at the ground, she could do a lot less damage on the ground. Oh, God and seven thousand Technicolor saints, how did you get out of here?

But suddenly she *was* out again, Greg's hand gripping her swordbelt, watching the door close on a dome of twinkling lights. In the wan light of the outlined doors Greg looked very pale. "Let's go outside; we have to talk."

Greg's face and hair were dripping with sweat; he picked up a small terry towel from a stack by the console and began toweling himself dry. His snakeskin-patterned T-shirt was soaked through. Mary felt as though she might be sick, and she fled to the bathroom; but by the time she reached it, her viscera had settled down again. She leaned against the doorjamb until a wave of dizziness went away, then washed her face and the back of her neck in cold water.

When she came back, Greg had put out crackers and cheese and was brewing coffee. His T-shirt now was black, with the outlines of a dinner jacket and a starched white shirtfront on it. The shirt studs had been touched up in gold. "I think we've earned a little break," he said, "and we have to figure out what to do next. Do you know what that system was?"

"Air traffic control?"

"Yes. For the whole state of California, plus Nevada and the major corridors to Hawaii. The normal way to get out, incidentally, is to descend to the ground and head for the green EXIT sign. You get in on the ground too, after going through a whole battery of security routines. Only somebody put in a back door. Mary, we have a serious problem here."

"I should think it is! Air traffic controllers sneaking off the job to play *Golden Road*? Is that why my plane nearly crashed Sunday night?"

"Not exactly. There'll have to be an investigation later on, but I can't see an ATC sneaking off the system when he's supposed to be on it. More likely the reverse. It takes a certain kind of mind to work in that system, and those who can stand it at all tend to love it a lot. Especially those who've been around long enough to remember the old pre-VR systems, where you stared into a screen for hours on end, hoping the computer would have enough judgment to show you all the important stuff.

"No, the problem they have sometimes is getting them to come out. You can see how someone might get a sensation of godhead, of omnipotence, after a few hours in that thing. In fact, they had a case last year at JFK: Two ATCs got illegal plugs, without cut-offs, so they could stay in indefinitely, living on caffeine pills and black-market Ultrajolt. But they got caught before any harm was done. To the system, that is—one of them had a heart attack and the other had kidney failure."

"How long were their legal plugs rated for? The standard ten hours?"

"Probably. But remember, the sensors don't measure time; they test for fatigue poisons and low blood sugar and dehydration and so on. Ten hours is about how long the average healthy adult can stay in—assuming the connect activity isn't particularly stressful. I bet you've never tried to joust for ten hours straight."

"No."

"But I also bet your plugs would've timed out before that, if you'd tried. I got bumped out once, when I was writing my doctoral thesis, after about seven and a half hours. Low body mass, that's why. It's not a painful exit; you find yourself drifting off on a cloud while the system plays lullabyes." From the kitchen came an agonized choking, sputtering sound, like Bugs Bunny catching sight of a visiting Martian. "The coffee's ready."

"I'll get it."

"What probably caused your plane crash," Greg went on, "is that somebody got into the system from the Backbone by accident, like you, and unlike you didn't have the sense to hold still and refrain from playing with all the pretty blinkenlights. We're lucky it wasn't worse."

"Why would they want to connect the ATC system to the Backbone anyway? You'd think they'd want to protect their security. Yes, sugar, please."

"Eat some cheese too; otherwise your blood sugar'll go straight up and straight down again. My guess is that somewhere else on the Backbone there's a door into another ATC system—Vancouver-Portland, maybe, or Phoenix-Santa Fe, and anyone who knows about it could switch from one to the other without the bother of descending to the ground. Remember, I told you, they start feeling like gods in there. Why should they mingle with mere mortals and submit to their petty security checks?

"We now have a much more serious responsibility

than I thought. Or I have, anyway. This isn't just a case of copyright infringement any more; this is a hack that could kill somebody. Has killed somebody, four somebodies to be precise; and once the Backbone comes into general use, there'll be any number of bored or curious users wandering up and down it trying all the doors.

"This thing has to be shut down, and whoever set up that back door has to be identified and taken off the system. We now have the data to do just that. I have a documented and continuous set of pathnames from *Golden Road* to the Backbone, to York and the other systems, and through St. Chad's stable and Winchester, back to here." He tapped his console with one long forefinger. "I could call up Markheim right now and give him the evidence. (Only I'm not going to; I'm going to wait till a reasonable hour.) And we could pack our plugs away and go get some sleep. You can, if you like."

"You're going to stay up?"

"For a while. What we've got now, you see, is a line on the system that's violating Markheim's copyright. Maybe on some of the people running it. This doesn't mean it'll lead to the people who've been attacking you, but it easily might if we followed it long enough. I'd like to find them—and toast them like marshmallows inside, and kick their little butts into jail outside! If I spend some more time on this system, I may get some clues. It's a point of honor. They can't treat a lady like that and get away with it."

Mary chuckled and sat up straight in her chair to bow from the waist. "Thanks for your courtesy, good Brother. I'd like to see you do it."

Greg flushed and looked at the floor. "In addition to which—you don't play these kinds of games, so you may not understand—I don't want to just unplug and vanish in a puff of smoke *ad libitum*. I want to get back out the way I got in, in spite of all efforts to stop me. I want to finish what I started."

"Another point of honor," Mary supplied. "Let's get started, then. Oh, yes, I'm with you—even if all I can do is to bash the Balrog while you climb the tree."

Back on the Backbone for the last moment while Greg made sure of his data, Mary peered down the length of the corridor to where the few lights of the beta-testers shone bravely, like the fires of the first settlers in the wilderness. One day, assuming the tests went all right, this whole corridor would blaze with light, a glowing sign on every door, like a prosperous mall. The Backbone itself would turn into a huge meeting group, where personae in various degrees of disguise strolled up and down playing Who are you? Who am I?

Science and science fiction writers had mined the topic for decades, from late-twentieth-century punk through turn-of-the-century earnestness into the current wave of retrorealism and phantasmata. Now somebody was heading around toward punkishness again, probably without intending to. There wasn't much point in speculating who these guys might be who had loved *The Golden Road*—or money—or both—not wisely but too well. In a few hours, maybe, Greg would find out.

They stepped through the door and stopped. From the hallway opposite came the sound of voices.

"Calm down, will you?"

"I am calm. I am as calm as I need to be. I'm just letting you know"—the voice was rising out of the baritone into the tenor range—"that if the sysop sees that entry log, there's going to be serious trouble."

"That part is *your* problem. Maybe you should just go back there and start cleaning up. *My* job is finding that intruder and pinning him down long enough to get a trace. Then somebody can go after him outside; then—"

"Why do you keep saying 'him'? There're at least two of them: one naïve enough to bumble around opening up directories and needing to run Tulgey Wood, and the other expert enough to—"

"Will you shut up!"

"There are five of them," Greg whispered. "Give me your hand." She held it out, and as he took it he disappeared. So did her arm a moment later. They stepped cautiously across the round room. She could see the men in the hallway, five elf-karls in armor that glittered in the dark, clustered in front of the Prometheus tapestry. With a little bit of luck they could sneak right past them. There was still one gateway unexplored, but surely eight out of nine would be enough—

"—And I've phoned the King; he was asleep outside, so it's going to take him a few minutes."

"He better get here quick."

"He will. He's got a lot invested in this place. In fact, if you wanna know, he's in over his head. And his *system*"—the elf-karl spoke the word with strange scorn—"isn't working worth sour owl crap. So it's worth everything he's got to hunt these guys down."

"You could call the Queen."

"Oh, sure. Sure, I could call the Queen. Have *you* got her number? But in the meantime I've got an Eye—"

So much for luck. The Eye in the elf-karl's hand, a glowing ember the size of a blood-orange, flared brighter as he lifted it, and he said with surprise, "Oh! They're here!" Mary felt a tug at her hand and followed it to the nearest door. She was trying to remember which one it was, and the elf-karl with the Eye was shouting, "There they go! Stop—" when the closing door cut him off.

Again she floated in darkness, surrounded by points of light. Stay out of trouble, look at the ground—but there wasn't any ground, and they hadn't come into the ATC system from the round room anyway; it opened off the Backbone. And the lights were fixed, not moving. And no matter how hard you looked at one, it never sprouted a label. They must be stars.

No, there was one moving, a single bright reddish point that must be a planet. It grew brighter, became a disk, and now there was a down to this place because Mary was falling rapidly toward the planet's surface. She swallowed, told herself that it was only VR, and resisted the impulse to shut her eyes and curl into a ball.

Then something sketched rapid lines in the air, a cabin or compartment around her, a contoured chair that she was lying in, a control panel in front of her. And a great wealth of overlapping, confusing lines beneath her that she had no chance to puzzle out before the cabin solidified around her, claustrophobically small and full of dangling cables. She didn't think much of the engineering. There were viewscreens (maybe just windows) all around and overhead; the control panel featured incredibly high-tech controls with lots of blinking lights and levers. Some kind of spacewars game, she guessed, the kind little boys generally loved and little girls traditionally disdained. "Uh, Greg?" Mary might not have disdained the game at the proper age, but she never could have afforded it. "Greg, are you there?" Greg, on the other hand, being both male and well-heeled, must know something about it, and where was he anyway? Coming through the door at the same time, they ought to have been dropped into the game together. Unless it had some kind of goddamned randomizer in it. "Greg!"

"Here I am," said a speaker on her control panel. A heavy door slid open before her, revealing a bleak landscape: a desert plain, a few rocks, a wintry sky. "Right over here. Can't you see me?" And a shape moved into her rightmost window, a gigantic man-like shape encased in armor the Middle Ages never dreamed of. Then it went transparent and vanished, but at eye level a little air- or spacecraft, a one-man shuttle of some kind, began a leisurely circuit of Mary's control room.

"Greg, I assume this is some kind of spacewar game, right? Photon torpedoes, battle robots, all that stuff?"

"Suits, not robots. It's a Mecha game; there are dozens of them. Haven't you ever played one?"

"Of course not. Are these the controls here? I can't find either a steering wheel or a joystick."

"There isn't any, not in this version. Direct neural connection. You pull down the neural impulse helmet onto your head and it makes the connection—like plugging into the suit, only the transition's not as smooth. You'll see. And you'd better hurry."

No need to ask why: A kilometer away from her, among rust-colored bluffs, another warrior machine was taking shape. Only one? Only one so far. She'd better assume the others were on their way. She pulled the helm down out of a nest of tangled cables and put it on her head.

For a moment, nothing. Then a rush of colored shapes across her vision, like the illusions of migraine, the controls dimly visible behind them. Her head swam, and she felt queasy and wondered whether verisimilitude would support her getting sick all over the tiny cockpit. But the circuitry seemed to tune itself: The vertigo faded, and the test pattern dissolved to let her see clearly. And now she could feel the armor.

Interesting. Like a medieval king, she had two bodies. She could feel the armor's heavy limbs as if they were her own, planted on the barren ground and swaying slightly in a gust of wind. But her own body was there too, curled up in the pilot's seat in the cockpit inside the armor's helm. Like a child's idea of his soul, lurking in his brain, peering out of his eyes. There was a small lever under her left hand, a trigger grip in her right; she slipped her fingers around them. Experimentally she took a step and found it like walking underwater with lead weights on her feet. "Greg? They do this for *fun*?"

"Well, yes," Greg said. "Does it matter? Start walking toward the other Mecha and the armor will take up the pace itself, so you don't have to concentrate on it. That's right. If you want to stop or turn, grab the control override under your left hand. Your primary weapon's in your right."

"What is it, a laser?" Mary eyed the armor's massive fist with distaste. "Greg, I have just about zero experience in missile combat."

"That's okay. It's tuned short enough that you can use it like a sword—a sort of one-handed claymore with all its mass in its hilt."

Mass in the hilt. She moved her right arm about and verified this: The laser was a glorified fencing foil, good for thrusting and lousy for slashing. She hadn't fenced since she was an undergraduate. Damn. "Anything I can use for a shield?" She raised her left hand, its forearm as swollen as Popeye's, its forefinger a hollow gunbarrel. "This is massive enough, I guess. Not as big as I'd like."

"Well-l—if you've got to block a head blow, okay, but don't do it very often. That's not just dead mass, that's a launcher and twenty small rockets. Don't think of it as a shield; think of it as a *main gauche*."

All this time Mary's armored envelope had been stalking toward the other Mecha. It felt like a snail's pace until she saw at the side of her control panel a display reading "60 kph," with a gauge indicating that she might be able to get up to a hundred. Well—those were fairly long legs she was walking on.

The other Mecha was not as humanoid as hers,

squat and hunched like a crab on giant's legs. There was a device painted on its chest: a coiled dragon. Peering down out of her side viewport, Mary caught a glimpse of a sun-in-splendor painted on her Mecha's ankle. "Should I be wearing my own arms? Do we *want* these guys to know it's me?"

"Actually, you're bearing the sword-and-sun of House Montano; this is their territory, so far as I can tell, and it seemed appropriate."

The crablike Mecha was raising and lowering itself on its bent legs, moving its arms back and forth. Maybe the elf-karl inside it was new to the game too. "Are Montano the good guys?"

"To the extent this system has any. I recognize this game now; it's *Shards of Empire*. It's five major and lots of minor warrior Houses playing dog-eat-dog in the ruins of a fallen empire, the sort of thing that makes for lots of fighting. This game's been around for ten or twelve years, but the genre is older than computers. The first VR I ever did was a place where you sat in a plywood pod with a television screen and a joystick. They had to lift me into the pod; but it was my first step into a larger world."

"Then why aren't you fighting this thing instead of me?"

"Because I'm not a trained fighter, and you are. Your opponent is bearing House Asaro, incidentally, which is as close to the bad guys as you'll care to get. But you're going to have to fight him anyway; no matter what he's bearing, he's the one who followed us in here."

Now the two Mechas were only a few hundred meters apart. Mary stood on a scarp three or four meters in height, and the red plain directly beneath it looked very far away. Elephants, massing a whole lot less than a Mecha, cannot jump and can be confined by any ditch too deep to sound with their trunks. Mary could see herself stumbling down the scarp and landing with an impact that would shear her shins off. But the machine didn't share her caution, and she had forgotten to hit the override; it paused on the edge for a moment and jumped two-footed to the plain. The noise of its impact nearly deafened her, and the physical shock rattled her like a peanut in its shell; but when the vibration died down, both she and the Mecha appeared to be undamaged.

The other Mecha was closing steadily. Very well, she'd attack. She bent her armor's mass into its walk and hastened it as much as she could—which wasn't much. Seven-league boots in slow motion, it stalked across the shuddering plain. "Greg, has he got any vulnerable spots? Have I?"

"Mostly on the back; try a snap or something."

"You can't do a snap with a weapon with no mass in the tip!"

"Oh. Well, do what you can. His armor's pretty good, but yours is even better; I've given you a few points' improvement. Your mass is greater, meaning your armor is thicker, than it's supposed to be, and I've boosted your power to compensate. Listen, there's a structure on his back that contains the jets, among other things. If you take that out, he can't fly."

"Fly?"

"And the joints are less heavily armored than the

limbs. Get him a good one on the back of the knee and you can probably bring him down—and if you can cripple him without killing him, it'll take him a lot longer to get back into *The Golden Road* and come after us."

" 'Leg him and leave him.' Got it."

The Asaro Mecha raised its right arm and fired. The beam hit Mary's shell in its head, lighting up the cockpit for a moment and raising its temperature from chilly to lukewarm. Exhaust fans whined as they tried to dissipate the heat. "Is that the best he can do?"

"That's enough to eat through your armor in time. I don't expect you to give him that much time."

Her Mecha lengthened its stride a little and stepped over a fissure in the plain, not big enough to fall into but big enough to trip over. Then she was closing on the Dragon, saw it growing larger in her viewscreen. She tried to think of it as just a big heavy fighter, a sort of heavy javelineer (and a hunchback at that) with not nearly as much striking power as he thought he had, and herself as another big heavy fighter with a few tricks learned through long experience. "Come on, Scalybuns," she murmured. It didn't matter if he could hear her or not.

She raised her Mecha's left arm to guard. A rocket launcher, Greg had said? But for her purposes it was simply bulk and mass. She had seen fighters win the Crown of the West fighting Florentine, with a sword in each hand, but it had never been her style and she wasn't going to attempt it now. The Dragon fired, and fired again, filling her cockpit with a wash of heat. She closed in, raised her laser, and touched the trigger.

A thread-thin light burst from the tip of her laser, pale green, a mere guidelight for the laser's coherent beam, with a focus almost as long as the Mecha was tall. She brought it up before her face in salute—she didn't want to strike it against her shield-forearm, and the Mecha had neither a nose nor thumbs. Then she reached out and touched him with her sword-blade.

It was as easy as a demo for the Cub Scouts, where everyone took plastic boffers and gave the little kids a chance to fight. You let them whack at your shield three times, and then you reached out and touched them and gave some other kid a chance to play. The kids had no defense whatever, and neither had Scalybuns, but where her sword struck his carapace, there was a shower of sparks but no apparent damage. *He's got very, very good armor,* she reminded herself, *but mine is better. Let's see if we can wear him down before he parboils us.* For the ambient temperature in her cockpit was still rising, and beads of sweat were beginning to crawl down her back. She took a moment to unzip her jumpsuit to the waist—there was no one to see, anyway.

Her Mecha had stopped walking, perhaps sensing that it was within striking range. Mary hit the override and made it take a step forward, and another. Scaly took a step back and fired again; she caught most of it on her shieldarm. For a moment the heat was intolerable; then it fell away. (People went to saunas on purpose for just such a sensation.) A red light flared on her control panel: some kind of damage. It didn't affect her sword arm so she ignored it. She struck again at the base of Scaly's cannon, raising another mighty shower of sparks. And the cannon slumped a little, just a little to the right, nodding on its damaged neck. At the least she'd spoiled his aim—but she must have done better than that, for the cannon never fired again.

Scaly raised its fists—well, its boxy weapon mounts at the end of its arms—and fired again, two handed. Mary's leftmost viewscreen went blank, and she muttered, "Oh, shit." But she still had better visibility than in the sharp-faced bascinet she wore for SCA combat, let alone the tiny eyeslits of a tilting helm. "Okay, Scalybuns," she said, "let's *you* fight Florentine."

She feinted high and then struck low, an ankle shot that raised sparks and did no apparent damage. Scaly stepped backward again, trying to get out of range. She pursued it, feet thudding across the rusty ground, sword arm cocked back across her shoulder. She closed in again and struck at the back of Scaly's carapace. Something went off like a fireworks display, and Scaly turned and ran. Ha! She'd hope that was the jets Greg had mentioned. She took off after him; she didn't want the bastard flying away—or running away—back to *The Golden Road* and telling the King—

Good God, in the haste and busyness of the last few minutes it hadn't struck her till now. Somebody was playing the Elf King as a PC? That would be someone awfully hard to beat. Better to kill off this turkey, or rather leg him and leave him, and see how quickly she and Greg could get away.

Scalybuns had turned, fists raised, and now red spikes of guide light extended from each; he had decided to try her with her own weapon style. "Good luck, Lizardface." She closed in again, hedging the Dragon on its left, turning it in slow stages till it was facing the red bluffs, its back turned to the way they had come. She had thought of something.

Scalybuns was striking wildly at her now, two handed. Her shieldarm took most of it, and the armor was soaking up the rest. Another trouble light appeared on Mary's control panel, more damage to the weaponry in the left arm. No matter. No doubt you paid the system heavily for damage repair, but so long as she got out in one piece Mary didn't care if she left a pile of half-melted junk behind. She wasn't coming back. From time to time her sword flicked out and hit the Dragon on the side of his left knee. The joints were *supposed* to be weaker than the rest of him. She kept him on the defensive, and retreating.

Then a third of her lights went red, and Greg's speaker on the dashboard said, "Oh, Lord." And before her eyes a little sparkling cloud began to grow—and froze—and shrank away to nothing.

"What was that?"

"That was the rocket launcher in your arm starting to explode, milady," Greg said. There was, if that was possible, an edge to his gentle voice. "Only I rewrote it so it didn't go."

"Oh. Thank you, milord. Sorry about that; I told you I don't do missiles," and she reached for Scaly's knee again.

The pieces of the endgame came together all at once. Three huge Mechas, all marked with the Asaro dragon, loomed up behind their comrade: one squat like Scalybuns, one humanoid like Mary's, one blocky and gigantic. "Greg!"

"I see 'em. Don't worry, you've got reinforcements too; look to your left."

"Can't," and she struck at Scaly's knee one more time, and saw him falter. He took one more step backward, and stepped into the crevasse toward which Mary had been herding him. Bit enough to hide a man, it took up Scaly's heavily armored heel, and he fell. Once the impact vibration died down, Mary stepped back to avoid the dust. Maybe that was the wrong move: The other Dragons could now see her plainly. What was it Greg had said about reinforcements to her left? She turned her whole body and looked. Three other Mechas were standing where her blind screen had hidden them from her sight, one small one and two big chunky ones, all bearing the sword and sun. And a voice was sounding, tinny and distorted, in the earphones of her helmet:

"Unidentified Montano Mecha! Captain Dango here, Ravaging Ravens, House Montano. Do you require assistance?"

"Why, thank you, sir," Mary purred. "I've been coping up to now, but I'd appreciate a chance to fall back and cool off. I see three of them and three of you; I think you've got them outnumbered." It was like rallying a small pickup unit in an SCA war; not knowing whether this culture bought death-or-glory, she left that part out. "Greg," she said in a conversational tone.

"I'm here," the dashboard said. "Turn around and walk away—turn a little more to your left."

But her left was her blind side, and as she began to turn there was a flash of light and her left leg crumpled under her. She fell, bouncing hard against her seat's straps, and now she was looking at everything turned ninety degrees, and she couldn't move at all. "Greg? Mayday."

"Be right with you; don't worry." Very well, she wouldn't. A little scout boat might not be much use against three of those lumbering great lizards, but if necessary Greg would turn into a battleship the size of a planet to get her out of this.

From her tilted viewpoint the encounter of Montano and Asaro looked like the last battle between the gods and the Titans, and the Titans were losing as usual. The first Ravaging Raven took the first Dragon unprepared and blew its head off (and, she assumed, its pilot too). After that it did nothing but wander about the field like a headless mantis on its wedding night, blundering into its own allies more often than not, until it got into the same crevasse that had tripped up Scalybuns, fell, and never moved again.

After that it was nothing but a bloodbath. The Ravens hurled flaming mass and energy at the Dragons as if to melt them down on the spot. The Dragons were firing back with everything they had, but their range seemed to fall short of the Montano fighters' limits by a few meters. The two big Ravens quickly realized this and fell back to the appropriate distance, taunting the Asaro fighters over their radios and bludgeoning them from just outside their reach.

Under cover of its allies' fire, the small Raven darted in for the kill. Any of the big Asaro Mechas could have squashed it, given time, but they were not to be given time.

The little Raven hopped from target to target, jabbing with bolts of laser light, pecking with small sharp missiles. As Mary watched, it hit some crucial part of the biggest Asaro Mecha, sending its reactor into an uncontrolled critical state. The colossus began to glow red, melting down from its own internal heat.

The third Asaro Mecha, the weaponry shot away from its arms, turned to run. It was headed toward Mary, centered in her screen, its feet aimed directly at her head.

Then her view shifted and she felt a surge of acceleration as something scooped her up into the sky. She could see two fingers of the hand that held her; the whole hand must be the size of her Mecha's head, the entire fighter large enough to dwarf even the gargantuan Dragon.

She got a last glimpse of the Ravaging Ravens firing steadily at the last Dragon, which stood knee-deep in a puddle of its own slag. Through a burst of static she heard Captain Dango say, "Did you see that? Where in the hell did that come from?" and Greg, "Mary? We're out of range and out of sight. You can unarmor."

"I can't move."

"Sure you can. The Mecha's dead but there's nothing wrong with *you*. Just take off your helm." She did, and the whole physical envelope of the Mecha, unthinkably heavy, fell away from her, and she rose like a bubble in beer. Stars, and cool air, and darkness, and she hastily rezipped her jumpsuit.

The round room was empty but for themselves, and quiet and delightfully cool. Cool enough that she was glad of the padded tunic under her hauberk. "Greg, there were five of them out here," she whispered. "Only four in there. Where's the other?"

"With luck, he did as he was told, went back into Prometheus to cover his tracks—and ours—from his sysop," Greg said. "But I've still got the trace on his system." He gestured, and threads of golden light stretched through the air, one to every door, two up the corridor to Prometheus and York, all running into a ball in Greg's left hand. Then they vanished again. "Let's see if we can get out of here without any more alarms." Greg vanished, and so did Mary's hand as he took it to lead her away.

There was no motion, no sound behind the Prometheus tapestry as they went past it. At the branching of the tunnels Greg stopped for a moment, perhaps to inspect the fungus on the wall; but if it covered yet another gateway, he didn't stop to explore it. Here was the archway into the Great Hall, not empty now but glowing with the deep-sea light of those who stood in ranks and files and clusters, waiting for them.

She tugged on Greg's unseen arm and drew him close to her, felt along his shoulder and under his helm for his ear. "What time is it here?" she whispered.

His hand on her jaw drew her head forward till he could whisper back. "Midafternoon. Yes, if we can get out into the sunlight, most of this bunch can't follow us. I don't see anybody else with an Eye, so let's try it."

He let her go to arm's length, tucked her hand into the crook of his elbow so that she could follow in his unseen footsteps, and led the way through the hall. They passed to the left of a troop of what looked like humanized toads, lumpy and bulging-eyed, shifting uneasily from one flat foot to the other as they leaned on their heavy clubs. They wore a single tattered tunic apiece. Recruits from the eastern provinces? They passed to the right of a squadron of near-humans with fox faces, neatly drawn up in ranks, sharp ears raised, sharp noses sniffing the air. But they passed them unperceived.

Halfway across the hall. Something like bats flew overhead, fanning the air into uneasy currents against their faces. But Greg's spell was still proof against their echolocation, if that was what they were using. Five-eighths. They said that when Achilles set out to catch up with the tortoise he never made it, since first he had to cover half the distance, then half the remainder, then half of *that*, never arriving; no, but Greg would never let that happen to them, being master of the code and wizard among the hidden parameters.

Only a stone's throw now, less than that, to where one leaf of the great door stood half-open in a pool of dull gold. A pair of fox guards stood just outside its edges; the toads and bats dared not come this close to the sunlight. Here was the crucial moment: Would they cast a shadow, and so be discovered? Greg halted for a moment, to call up some useful subroutine perhaps.

But they never got to put it to the test. From behind them a cold voice said, "Now," and a huge shape moved into place before them to block the door and the sun.

Perhaps it had been bred for this purpose; it had a thick shell on its back, broad as a turtle's, that might be proof against the sunlight. The shell peaked like a cowl behind its head and ended in a thick skirtlike tail behind its booted ankles. Its face was round, its expression appropriately stupid. It was carrying a heavier club than the toads had, and it would make a better door than a window.

Mary drew her sword. "Wait a minute," Greg murmured. But the thing had raised its bludgeon high over her head, and there wasn't time for discussion. Mary plunged the blade up to its narrow hilt where she hoped the thing kept its heart.

The creature settled onto its haunches, its expression unchanging, and died with its back to the door. Little shivers ran over the dead flesh. They heard the shell crack in a dozen places, and the corpse yielded to the sunlight and turned to stone.

It blocked the door very effectively. (Bred for the purpose.) Unless they could climb over it, or get the other half of the door open.

"Now," said the cold voice again, and their invisibility fell from them. Turning, they saw the elf-troops part and fall back to let the Elf King pass.

He was tall, but not grotesquely large like some of his followers. An inky cloak fell from his shoulders, and his armor was a fine-textured scale, as if made of thousands of blackbeetles' wings; it glittered as he moved. He was bareheaded, his dark hair cropped short against the fashion, and his narrow face was pale. It was a face Mary had never seen in life but might have come across on a book cover somewhere. She didn't bother to ask if this was a Player Character; the elf-karl had gone outside and phoned him, and here he was.

"Well," the King said. "For two such doughty warriors, you've done strangely little harm. One would think you were not warriors at all, but spies. Take them alive; I'll find out how much they know."

"Stall him," Greg muttered. "I need a few minutes to solve this."

Mary swung her sword in a lazy arc around them; a platoon of pig-troops fell back, almost trampling each other in their eagerness to get away. "Well," Mary answered, "I too am surprised, that the King of the Elves thinks he needs an army to take two Christian knights. But then, there are two of us, so perhaps that's right. Would single combat shorten the odds? I don't want to make it too hard on you."

The King's pale eyes narrowed, and he swept the troops aside with a wave of his arm. Some fell back against the walls; many simply disappeared. Out of the shadows he drew his helm and set it on his head. From the blackened steel grew a pair of antlers, writhen and sharp-tined; give him a point for style.

She stood her ground and made him come to her. Behind her, she assumed, Greg was solving the code of the door, or of the fallen turtle-man, or of something else to their benefit. She wouldn't be drawn away from the door. If need be, she'd fight to the death and go outside, to be recalled when Greg was ready for her. Her sword, her shield, her armor were all enhanced, and she was a Knight of the West. Perhaps she could fight the King to a draw.

After his first few steps, taken to threaten, not to cover distance, he moved in quickly. He was fast and taller than she, and his swift overhead stroke came down on her shield rim with a force that should have jarred her back teeth; but the shield absorbed it. It felt light on her arm, as light as the small early-period buckler it was supposed to be, but it absorbed energy as if it were made of concrete. Greg's enhancements were in force.

It was no Sunday walk, just the same; the man was good and fast and made her move at top speed. She swung low and then high, but the King's shield dipped and rose to block both blows.

It was like a dance, a quadrille of seeming cooperation, meant to betray: a dialogue spoken with body and sword. The cold knot under Mary's hauberk began to melt. The guy was good, but not that good, a competent fighter, but no better than many she'd met on the field and bested when her luck was in. Gleefully she struck again, got through his guard and struck his helm a glancing blow, zing! No damage, not even an antler cropped, but Mary grinned. The King fell back a pace. "Do you yield?" she asked politely. The King bared his teeth and growled like a wolf, then stepped in again.

A step back, and another, and the King followed; and she strode forward into range again and struck, and struck again without waiting for him to recover. ("If I have a choice of hitting or being hit," her instructor had always said, "I'm going to hit.") *Dilly, dilly,* said the dance, *come and be killed.*

You're wasting your time, the King said with feet and sword. *You can't escape; I shall have you in the end. Bide, lady, bide.*

What's your hurry? Mary said, drifting a little to the left. (There was something standing in the archway behind the King, dark and featureless even to elf-sight. Scaly, escaped from his ravine? He was the tallest near-human she'd seen here.) *We have all the time in the world,* and gave him a backhanded stroke that went in under his guard and scored a line across his midriff, a shower of sparks. Still no damage; this fight was getting nowhere fast, which suited her fine. How long had it been? How many blows? A minute or so? She couldn't spare a glance for Greg behind her.

The King's next blow caught her helm and shield rim together, and the helm rang like a glorious bell. She drifted a little to the right. Out of the corner of her eye she saw Greg, apparently doing nothing. He had drawn his own sword and was holding it, the cross-hilt over his heart like a Crusader on a tomb. He was doing his work in a realm she couldn't see. But what about the King? She leaped forward, striking at his body and head: He mustn't have the leisure to take a good look at Greg.

Dilly, dilly, if you were King, who'd be your Queen? Ha! She got him a good one just above his knee. Still no breach in his armor, but he had felt it; the leg would've gone numb for a moment. The King fell back a few steps, almost hopping. No doubt he had good healing spells. No doubt she did too.

Now he rushed in again, striking furiously at her head and body, a fast double blow that she blocked automatically. He had struck twice, rapidly, not going back to rest between blows. A fast, effective shot, one she had encountered before and knew how to block. Yes, she had seen that stroke before.

Maybe Greg was doing something to virtual space or time. Maybe it was only her attempt to fight and think at the same time. The world was drawing in around her, walls and watching creatures forgotten, all closing in to a space of a dozen paces around her and the King. And she had ample time to watch each of his strokes take form and descend, time to recognize each of them, if only she could get her wits together.

You're wasting time. You're running out of time. Come and be killed.

Old, weary, wicked King, I've got more time than you have, and she danced a little sideways capriole and let him strike at nothing. He had a characteristic style, and he had been disguising it until she got in that leg blow and made him lose his temper. Head blow, body blow. Who was it? She had seen it, strike and strike again, under the bright skies of London. And she had her own style, too, and could be recognized behind this Carolingian mask. What if she changed now? Worth the risk? Who had a signature greatly unlike her own? Well. . . .

—and sprang forward with a rain of little blows, tap-tap-tap-tap-THWACK, the renowned blitzkrieg attack of Sir David of Truro. Whether it deceived the King or not, it certainly took him by surprise, and the final blow went through his guard and struck him between neck and shoulder. Indigo blood welled up, and the King fell to his knees. Behind him the dark shape in the archway winked out, leaving a white afterimage that slowly dissolved in the blue elf-sight. The observer had observed, and left.

Around them, the ranks of troops (yes, she could see them again) muttered and rumbled. Mary swung her sword in a wide arc, warning them back. And behind her Greg cried, "Now! Back this way!"

The King was getting to his feet. He had dropped his shield and taken his sword in his left hand. Mary risked a glance behind her: The turtle-man was gone, not even gravel left behind, and Greg stood in a shaft of sunlight, beckoning. Now the King was on his feet, striding toward her. She backed toward the door. Greg's hand took her swordbelt and pulled, and she backed faster, out the door and into the street. The sky was overcast, but there was enough sun to discourage most of the local folk. Two fox-troopers were backed against the wall. Another dozen paces and they could run for it—

But the King stabbed his swordpoint into the air, as if cueing an unseen trumpet section, and a violet light began to flicker over him. Sunscreen, no doubt, and here he came out the door with a wordless shriek of rage. Greg pulled Mary to one side and met the King with his own sword, point foremost, straight into his heart.

—And lifted him on the swordblade like a chicken on a roasting fork and flung him into the sky.

Mary was still trying to see where he had gone when Greg seized her hand. "This way! Run!" and they turned northward and ran, ten yards, twenty, till the pavement ran out and they plunged headfirst into the river.

Chapter 10

I Have Been a Salmon in the Stream

They plunged into the water and didn't come out, and nothing seemed to be pursuing them. After a dozen moments they reached the opposite bank and Mary had time to catch her breath—no, not to breathe, but to take stock. She felt very strange. Her arms had gone away, and her back was as supple as an eel's. No, not an eel; but some kind of fish: She could see her tail flashing behind her out of the corner of each eye in turn as she swam. But a stone wall was in front of her, lining the riverbank, and where was Greg?

She had seen a documentary once on the "phantom limbs" experienced by amputees. Sometimes when the sensation went away it did so piecemeal, leaving a handful of fingers to waggle disconsolately from a shoulder point. So she was now. Her fingers were fins that sprouted directly from her sides. With a little delicate sculling on one side and the other she could back away from the wall and turn around. Let's see, as a fish she should have color vision, but there was nothing here to test it on, only grayish wall and murky water.

The water was neither warm nor cold; she felt it only with her hand-and tailfins and when a passing current traced a long line down her side. And the river was full of smells, most unidentifiable, none too disgusting, many even appetizing. *Cherry-tart, custard, pineapple, roast turkey, toffee, and hot buttered toast. . . .* Somebody had written a masterwork in this fish. Greg's own? Stock software off the shelf? She hoped the Elf King didn't have a platoon of pike.

Here came another fish, fading in out of blank water as it approached, and she looked at it carefully. Trout or salmon? She couldn't tell, but it had little red and brown freckles and a green line running all the way along its back. Was it Greg? It came near and turned away sharply, its tail flinging out a current that ran along her lateral lines like a warm breath in the dark. It swam away a little, turned back, turned away again. *Follow me.* She flicked her tail and followed before it could disappear.

They swam only a little further downstream before the Greg-fish stopped and backed toward the bottom. Then, tail flashing, he swam quickly upward and through the glistening surface, out of sight. Mary followed . . .

. . . and landed on the bank with all four feet. A footpath ran along the riverbank, and on the other side of it was a pile of trash, timber or firewood and a couple of old bones, stacked roughly against the wall of a house. Half-hidden under the pile crouched a little dog. Mary joined him.

She settled in beside him under the shelter of a plank and wrapped her tail neatly around her body. Well. They weren't even wet. She took a look at her forepaws and decided she wasn't a dog, like Greg; she was a cat. She ran a paw over her face to confirm this, but she didn't try to lick it and wash. The smells around here were intense and authentic.

"Look there," the dog whispered. "To your left, up on that tall spire." She looked. High up, where a shaft rose like a needle from the tallest tower of the castle, something was impaled like an insect on a scientist's pin. It changed shape. It was moving.

"Cripes, Greg. Is that the King?"

"Yes," said the dog. "Mind you, whoever was playing him went outside as soon as he found he was stuck. But I've gimmicked his persona; it won't wink out when he goes outside. Up there the King is writhing in agony—only there's nobody there to feel it, you understand—with a six-inch shaft through his gut. But he's an Elf; they're remarkably hard to kill. Like a wounded snake, he'll go on twitching till sundown, distressing the hell out of his loyal followers, who are now trying to figure out how to get him down, which leaves fewer of them to hunt for us."

The ground began to shiver under them, rhythmic vibrations that tickled their paws and their bellies. "Somebody's crossed the river. Okay, you're going to run and I'm going to chase you. Go for it."

Mary sprang out of hiding and dashed away. Greg followed, going "Yip, yip, yip." Their path wound between buildings, over low walls and through kitchen gardens, under the feet of a slow-moving line of changelings carrying sacks. The world was all in black-and-white. Something smelled funny: ranker than the usual bouquet of a preindustrial city, rank as all hell—and they dashed past a search party of fox-men. And damn, there were a pair of mounted elf-karls up ahead, but they didn't do anything, only paused to watch and laugh as the frantic cat and furious dog raced by.

She was slowing down; so, presumably, was the dog. Their carnivore bodies were designed for short sprints, not for long-distance running. There was the city wall in any case, and they would have to figure out how to get through it; and here was an arched stone bridge that spanned the river, with some dark underneath spaces where it left the bank. She scuttled underneath and found there was plenty of room. A rat with a scaly tail took one pop-eyed look at her and jumped into the river and swam away. The Greg-dog joined her under the bridge.

"All right, we've gained some ground," he said. "We need to get to the north bank at some point; it might as well be here where we've got a bridge."

"Sounds good, but let's not run, okay? Look, I'll walk across, a respectable cat minding her own business. I'll hide under the other end. Then in a minute or two you can come after."

"Okay, but don't hide under the bridge; walk on down the bank to the city wall. Wait for me there. I'll be another cat, so nobody needs to run."

There wasn't much traffic on the bridge—it was still daylight, after all. A human-looking man smiled at her and said, "Hey, puss, puss," and she rubbed against his leg as she went by. This was kind of fun.

A hand reached down, gloved in thin black leather, and thumb and finger neatly circled her neck. A gentle grip, but it stopped her. She glanced upward: A black-cloaked humanoid towered over her, its face hidden in its hood. The fabric was scattered with crystal beads, like dim stars.

"Pretty kitty," a voice murmured. Tenor, or contralto? "*Miese-miese-kätzchen.* You shouldn't be out here, cat; this is a dangerous place. Too dangerous for such a pretty cat." The hand released her neck and made one long smooth stroke down her back, leaving the fur bristling. When she could move, she ran. She reached the wall without further incident and curled up on a warm stone where the river gurgled and foamed through the slots of a heavy timber water gate.

Presently a tomcat wandered up, a fine-looking feline with a broad face, black-furred with white blazes at forehead and throat, and eyes as green as olives. (From what she could see, she herself was a plain tabby with white toe-socks.) He settled down on his haunches beside her and yawned, displaying a fine mouthful of sharp teeth. Then he took a second look at her. "What's the matter?"

"I met the Black Knight on the bridge, or somebody remarkably like him. Or her. Whoever it was took me by the neck, petted me, told me I was messing with things too dangerous for me—something like that—and let me go and walked away. Greg, who in the hell *was* that?"

"Who it is outside, I haven't a clue. As to who

it is in here—you remember the elf-karls mentioned the Queen."

"The Queen of Air and Darkness? That's *her*? Greg, that's scary."

"I know. Even in the book you never get a good look at her—except maybe in the scene where she and the King are playing chess with live pieces—so whoever is playing her can design her persona with a very free hand."

"I think I saw her in the Great Hall too, during the fight: just standing there watching. But when she saw the King was about to lose, she disappeared."

"If it's really bothering you, you can go outside."

"And let you have all the fun? Certainly not. I can hear myself already, 'No shit, there I was, face to muzzle with the Queen of Air and Darkness—' "

"I can hardly wait. Now, here's my plan," he said. "No more running for a while. Relax; we're going to be rotten logs drifting downstream. Just stretch out into that shadow over there—"

She stretched, enjoying the play of muscles along her back, a long line from forepaws to tailtip. It was dark in the shadows but not cold; in fact, she couldn't feel a thing but the slow rocking motion as the ripples went by. Slow rocking ripples. Better not go to sleep. Find something to think about. The changelings in the bean garden. The woodwose—no, not the woodwose shriveling on the point of her lance. Nor those moments of panic in Prometheus and Airtrafficland.

But the impaled image of the woodwose called up that of the King, and all the moves of that single-combat came crowding in, like cats, demanding to be paid attention to. And now at least she had time.

Okay, so the player who played the King had been disguising his style. Why? Had he expected to be recognized if he didn't? If he expected Mary to know him, he must know *her*. (Oh, dear.)

Not surprising, though. When Greg changed her armor to the Carolingian style, he hadn't changed her persona (as far as she knew). In these open helms you could see enough of a person's face to know it again. Did that mean, then, that he was someone *she* knew? Or only someone who had seen her from the gallery or on the tube? The price of fame in a whole new sense. She put that tangle aside for the cats to play with. He had been disguising his style for her; therefore, she must know him, or at least must have fought him. She visualized that fast double blow again, head and body without returning to rest. Yes, she knew it, knew it well enough to have countered it without thinking. Under the bright skies of virtual London, the stands full of spectators, garlanded with flowers. Head-and-body, and she had blocked. And far off in San José some sluggish brain cell woke up and plugged into the network, and it all fell into place. Head-and-body, block-and-block; she had done it a hundred times. It was one of his characteristic moves; she must have been very rushed indeed not to know it at once. But what a complication! And what were they going to do about it—?

"Wake up," Greg said. They were sitting on the riverbank near the edge of town, and they were cats again.

"Was I asleep? I thought I was thinking. Greg, I've figured out who the Elf King is."

"Hmmm. By his fighting style, like the Grey Knight? Is it the Grey Knight again?"

"That puppy? Not a chance. Greg, he's Nick Carter."

"Ah," Greg said. "I was beginning to think so myself."

"You didn't mention it."

"No, and I'll tell you why." The black-and-white stretched and yawned and began to wash his face with one paw, to hide his speaking mouth. "I got a pathname when the golden knight attacked you; I checked with the Network Information Center, and it said the machine he was logged in on belonged to Nick."

"Oh."

"But I thought . . . *I don't know for certain; maybe he sold the system and the Center doesn't know yet*. Because Nick has been selling off a lot of other stuff recently."

"What for? The man's got piles of money."

"Maybe. How much is 'enough' varies from one person to the next anyway. St. Francis was content to own nothing whatever. Diogenes went to the fair and said, 'How many things there are of which Diogenes hath no need!' Many people will settle for enough to live on. Many won't. Nick talks like a prosperous man—though that may be a front. But he must need more money than he's got for *some*thing. In the past eighteen months he's sold off his five-eighths of London. I know because I own the other three-eighths, and he had to notify me."

"*Why*? Who'd he sell it to?"

"Corporations with bland uninformative names. I don't know why he needs money, or thinks he does. I don't think it's drugs. Could be gambling, which is a drug to those who take it that way."

"Fast women and slow horses?"

"Maybe. What Lord Peter called the amateur professional. Or maybe he's just losing it, developing an irrational fear of poverty. Maybe they'll find him someday, starved to death with twenty million in cash hidden in his mattress."

"Maybe. Remember what Richard I said? He wanted to go on Crusade and he said, 'I would sell London if I could find a buyer.' Nick found one."

"Several of them. In any case, we'd better keep moving; you can bet they're still searching for us."

"How long will it take him to fix his persona?"

"To get the old one down off the spire, quite a while. To do a redundancy override and bring up a new copy, seeing it's Nick, not very long. That's one of the reasons we can't waste time. Come on."

He got up and touched noses, as cats will in greeting. He smelled of cat, and sunlight, and a hint of sandalwood. He trotted off, and she followed.

"Seeing it's Nick, a Lord of the Lists and all, can't he find us just by looking at the code? The way you found the gateways?"

"Oh, I've changed our process ids every time I changed our shapes. He can't *track* us in that sense. If I were he, I'd start pattern matching to take a look at everything moving west. But I know we're moving west, and maybe Nick doesn't. Are you tired of being a cat? Would you like to be something else?"

"I kind of like being a cat, but wouldn't we travel faster on horseback? Or as horses?"

"Yes, we would. We'd also attract more attention. All right, we'll be a pair of elf-karls; I'll borrow a couple of real ones who aren't playing at the moment. We'll have a gallop through the Wosewood."

Mary's point of view shifted suddenly upward, fast enough to make her dizzy for a moment. She was now a tall man in burnished armor, with reddish fur on his hands and arms and—a glance upward—five black dots on a golden banner. (A leopard's spot, and she had changed to it.) She spurred her black horse and galloped after Greg.

They rode at top speed through the wood, hoof-beats muffled on the soft leafmold, while little things like rats scuttled out of their way. There were still no woses. They burst out of the forest at the western end and slowed to a trot.

"Aldo! Hey, Aldo!"

Damn, oh, damn. Here came two more elf-karls, riding to meet them along the road from the river. And one of them knew one of their borrowed personae. She glanced at Greg, now a big black-a-vised scoundrel with a wolf's head on his pennon. "Run for it?" she murmured.

"Fake it."

"So, Aldo," the elf-karl said when the two groups were a dozen yards apart, "you find anything?"

"Not a damn thing," Greg said in a basso growl.

"Yeah, but I asked Aldo, not you."

"We saw a couple of rats," Mary said. (Strange to be speaking in a baritone voice; it buzzed in her throat and tickled her whole chest cavity.) "You think they want us to bring in rats?"

"Don't be funny. Aldo? You all right? What happened to your accent?"

Greg said not a word, lifted not a finger, but suddenly both their horses leaped forward and took off as if a gun had gone off behind their tails. The wind whistled past Mary's helm and stung her eyes. They were passing the field of knotgrain where the wose had taken shelter. "Get ready to jump," Greg said.

And the horses were gone, and they were flying through the air, falling into a sea of green, running and scrambling through a forest of stems. They must be very small. Here was a rough-textured wall rising high over their heads; no, it was a rough-hewn plank, part of a pig's trough, and here was a burrow leading under it. They scrambled down into darkness. Here was something warm and furry, and she was warm and furry herself. ("Greg? That you?") ("Yeah. Shhh.")

"Damn," said a voice high overhead. "Where'd they go? Who is this Aldo guy anyway?"

"That wasn't Aldo, you dumb shit. That was *them*. Aldo's got an accent"—the man's voice put on an exaggerated hillbilly drawl—"like a trucker talkin' on the CB, good buddy. That wasn't him, and I don't know *where* they went. But we better find them, 'cause if they get away they can shut this whole system down. Look, there's somebody. You! You there!"

Mary ran small delicate hands over her face. Long muzzle, bulging eyes, chisel teeth. "We're rats, right?"

"Right. The King might find us, but those two never will. I'm sorry, is that my foot in your eye? Come, curl up here."

They lay curled together, Greg's warm breath on her neck and his whiskers tickling her ear. Overhead a voice said something like "Ahhhng?"

"Yes, you. Did you see two knights ride by? Two men on horses? Did you see two of *anybody*?"

"Odo, I don't think those things can talk."

"They can point, can't they? Point which way they went." A pause. "Back that way? Right."

"Odo, that's a crock of shit. If they'd gone back that way, we would've seen them."

"You got any better ideas? Come on!" And the sound of hoofbeats gradually faded away.

"My goodness," Mary said when the last sound had died. "Does that changeling have enough sense to remember that I saved her life and to lie to protect us?"

"Not a chance," Greg said. "But it's fairly easy to make one raise an arm in the wrong direction. I'm going to take some time now to let those two get further away, and to read some code. Relax, my lady; you're a rat; you'll outlive civilization."

Mary wriggled, wrapped her tail round her flanks and got comfortable. Her mind drifted back to the night of the burglary, when she had gone to sleep imagining herself lying in the arms of a great hero, name unspecified. Now she lay in the arms of a rat. A heroic rat, who had braved the evil things in the east to bring out not the great Theodoric but a thread of secret knowledge that would save lives if he brought it home intact. It was good to lie warm and comfortable, even as a rat, good to lie in the arms of a hero. You could do safely as a rat what might lead to something dangerous outside.

Or had they written marital software into this system? Succubi that came out at night for the entertainment of the elf-karls? Professor Markheim had been chastely silent on the topic. Even if they had, surely they hadn't written any for rats.

"Greg?"

"Mmmm?"

"What happens if he catches up with us?"

"Oh, well. Then I see what I've got in my software collection. I've got a few spitballs, overripe tomatoes, and rotten eggs in my repertoire; and so does he, I bet."

"So it would be a wizards' duel."

"I suppose so. But do I want to fight a wizards' duel? No, Socrates, I do not. I'd rather get home with the evidence after a short, dull ride through boring scenery. Would you pull in your left hindfoot a little? Thanks. We'll wait a little longer. Don't go to sleep—you might fall outside without meaning to."

He was right. They'd had a long day inside, and it wasn't over yet. She tried to reckon how long it had been, but what with three disparate time zones her reckoner threw up its hands and quit.

"All right," Greg said presently. "When we start moving again, we're going to climb the nearest tree and turn into birds. There are a lot of them out already; I'm afraid Nick is back on board, either as the King or as somebody else. He's got a hundred or so ravens out, searching for us. But they're only subroutines; they shouldn't be able to tell that two of their number aren't what they seem. And they do have an excuse to fly west. I'm going to hope we can get as far as St. Felix's. Ordinarily, the farther we got into

Christian lands, the weaker the elvish forces would get, but that doesn't hold true so much for birds. All right; up we go."

They scuttled out of the burrow, across the garden patch to the base of a tree. The rough bark was as good as a ladder, and presently they were perched on the highest branch, swaying uneasily in the wind. "Have you ever flown before?" Greg asked. "As a pilot, I mean. Any hang gliding?"

"No."

"Oh, well, you'll pick it up," Greg said cheerfully. "Here we go." And there they were, high aloft, the roads fine ribbons and the Wosewood a parsley patch far below.

It wasn't as frightening as it might have been. The air bore up Mary's wings as solidly as pillars, and she seemed to weigh next to nothing. Her raven's eyes could see for miles. There at ten o'clock was another raven who had damn well better be Greg.

Without her willing it, her wings began to beat, and the earth slipped backward beneath her. Greg must be running her flying for her: a good idea. They were over a larger forest now, perhaps the one they had ridden through this morning. The parsley garden had spawned several different varieties and gone out to conquer the world: Patches of different shades of green butted up against each other in an endless patchwork. Occasionally she caught a glimpse of the road beneath. Greg must be following it—he could see the code right through the trees, of course—and it must be the right road, because it was leading them straight into the westering sun.

A cleared patch glimmered on the horizon and

slowly came into sight. Somebody had carved farmlands and buildings out of the forest, yes, and a church with a cross on the roof-peak over the door. This must be St. . . . St. . . . St. Paulinus, that was it, or she could hope it was. Because that would mean St. Felix was only twenty miles further west. And the stable where the gate was, not so far beyond that.

The clearing drifted eastward beneath them. After a while another came into sight. She couldn't tell if it was St. Felix or not. Never mind, they would get there sometime—

"Gruk!" something croaked behind her, and she glanced back. Her bird's vision covered nearly the full circle from horizon to horizon, but her human visual centers couldn't take it all in at once. Three other ravens were coming up fast on her tail. "Greg!" she cried, but it came out "Gruk!" and now her wings seemed to be under her own control. She flapped and banked, turned to meet the attackers. Fight in midair? Well, birds did. She'd seen two mockingbirds duking it out at treetop level in the spring. What had she to fight with? Beak and claws—quite a massive beak to peck with, and medium-grade claws. And these were only subroutines, unless somebody was piloting *them*. She sailed in to meet the first one, beakfirst. She got it a good one in the throat, she thought, but not enough to kill it; it pecked at her head and blanked out her vision for a moment. She clutched with her claws and got its wing; wing buffeting wing, they plummeted together, beak against beak. They had fallen almost to the treetops when Mary landed one more good peck and the other raven went limp and winked out with a faint pop. One down. How was Greg doing? Far overhead they wheeled and clashed, several against one. *Oh, no you don't.* She beat her wings and rose through the air.

Greg was holding his own so far; there were feathers drifting in the air, including a primary spiraling lazily downward, but they didn't seem to be his. One bird was attacking, the other merely keeping station. Maybe there was only one player running them all. Nick, like as not. She'd show him. She got some altitude and dive-bombed the attacker, piercing its eye with her beak. It fell ten feet and disappeared. Another woke up and moved in.

And there were six, eight, ten more moving up from the east. The Greg-bird saw them and croaked, "Oh, blast it all!" and the whole flock disappeared at once. "Now our cover's blown. Come on." He grew and changed, grew long red-and-gold pinions and a cruel beak, banked steeply into the west. Mary followed, seeing the same colors on her own wings and wondering what she was. No real European bird: a roc or Garuda bird or something out of a non-Newtonian mythology, something that flew very fast. The landscape blurred beneath them. St. Felix vanished, settlements flickered by—that must be the stable.

There was something behind them, something huge; she didn't try to look behind her but swooped down behind Greg. Their human feet hit the ground running. Greg snatched open the stable door, yanked Mary inside, slammed it shut. Something hit the wall outside with a great crash and began to hammer at the door. Greg held out his hand, fingers spread. The blows against the door grew fainter, and stopped resonating, as if the door were growing more massive. Then they stopped altogether.

There was a fissure in the bottom wall by the door, like a mousehole. Something like a long finger, nailless and double-jointed, came probing through the hole; Greg pointed his own forefinger and a spark arced between them, blue and dazzling. The air stank of ozone. "There we are," Greg said. "I've shut down all the channels into *The Golden Road,* and the network control channel too. There is no way on earth anything can get in from that side. Let's go."

The stable stood dark and quiet, full of the warm scent of horses and the sound of flat teeth munching hay. A single horn-paneled lantern cast a smidgen of yellow light. There stood Virtue and Ignatius, placid and at ease, as if they had never left the place. All they needed was to be saddled.

"Okay, he knows who I am," Mary said, casting the saddleblanket over Virtue's back. "Does he know who *you* are?"

"If he's had a chance to check the system log here at St. Chad's, he might," Greg said. "I didn't give my name to the steward, but I didn't disguise my persona, either. That could make life interesting"—he tightened Ignatius's cinch and took hold of the reins—"because Nick knows where I live."

"Oh. Let's move it, then." They turned toward the door on the Winchester side, and it opened.

"Wups," Greg said, and pointed a finger. The door closed again. Something roared outside, and the door opened again, torn off its hinges, and landed with a clatter in the yard outside.

It was dark inside and darker outside, and it was hard to tell what it was that stood in the doorway, except that it was big. It had to duck its head to clear the doorframe and ease its broad shoulders through one at a time, like a midwife delivering an infant football player. It lowered and it growled, and Greg said, "Oh, come now," and raised a finger, and the whole stable lit up.

As if an out-of-period incandescent bulb hung from every rafter, every corner was revealed and the creature in the doorway made plain. It groaned and covered its eyes with one clawed hand, and with the other reached behind it and pulled out a wooden visor with carved eyeslits: in-period Inuit sunglasses. Ingenious. It was awfully big, and it meant them no good. Mary put her hand to her sword.

"Troll," Greg remarked. "Typical dungeon denizen. Big and strong; a bit slow. The biggest problem is that they regenerate. If you carve pieces off it, I'll burn 'em."

"Where's my shield?" It vanished from Virtue's back and appeared on her arm. Greg was kneeling in the straw behind her, setting out a row of iconic props—a book, a crystal ball, an hourglass, a bowl of water. Mary drew her sword and went to meet the troll.

The blade in its hand was a nasty shape, as if intended for an instrument of torture rather than for a fair fight. It came whistling down from overhead, and Mary raised her shield to block. The crash shook the whole stable, but the shield held. Mary ducked under and slashed at the green arm. The hand came away, bleeding thick dark blood, and Mary kicked it away, sword and all. The troll hissed and moaned, and from Greg's finger shot your basic magical laser beam, burning the hand to ashes.

"I thought you said those things couldn't get inside this domain?"

"Did I say that? Most of them can't, but this one seems to have some enhancements." The troll, sniffling and muttering to itself, was holding up the stump of its arm and watching it. A lump was swelling at the end of the wrist: the size of a melon, the size of a pumpkin. It opened clawed fingers and flexed them experimentally. "Most trolls can't do that. Hmmm."

"Greg, that can't be Nick. He's got better taste."

"No, and he would've had to go the long way around. No, I think he went outside and phoned somebody: 'Hey, Fred, I want you to go to St. Chad's, waste whoever you find there, and go get that door open.' Look, he's got a scroll tucked in his loincloth. That's the routines for opening the channels."

"You know too much," the troll growled. He reached behind him and brought out a large rock, hurled it at them. It flew over their heads and crashed against the door.

"Yes, that's the whole point, isn't it?" Greg agreed. "I know enough to shut down both St. Chad's and *The Golden Road*, and Nick Carter's going to be up for copyright violation, endangerment, attempted murder, conspiracy, and whatever else. When the cops raid the computer, will they find your name in it? If I were you, I'd cut and run."

"Little man," the troll growled. "Big mouth." He brought out another rock and threw it. It bounced against an unseen wall in the air, fell to the straw and vanished.

"Bigger than you think," Greg said. "*Absarka.*" Nothing happened. "Well, hmm. Mary, is this the Grey Knight again?"

"I dunno. I'll find out." She raised her sword and charged forward. The troll reached rapidly into thin air and brought out a gigantic shield covered in scaly hide and a sword that seemed borrowed from a smaller monster, dainty in his massive hand. Mary struck out at his thigh, up to his arm, and the troll blocked and blocked and didn't try to strike at all. After a minute of this Mary fell back again. "Well, I think it is. But he's fighting pure defense, so it's hard to tell."

"It's always nice to run into old friends," Greg remarked as he threw a fireball. Most of it splattered harmlessly against the shield, but a few drops clung and fumed on the green skin. The troll howled and beat them out with the heel of his swordhand. "Hmm, yes, fire's the thing," Greg said, and threw another.

Suddenly his long face split open in a prodigious yawn. " 'Scuse me," he said, putting his hand to his mouth, and yawned again. "Uh-oh. Let's see if we can wind this up." He threw two more fireballs and a bottle of something that shattered on impact, staining the shield's hide a dingy purple. None of it reached the troll.

Mary went forward, striking low, trying to cut the troll's feet out from under him. But the damn thing regenerated too fast; by the time she had the second off the first was putting out toes again. And even on his knees he was too big to ride over. Mary got in a lucky stroke under his guard and sliced open his belly. Pallid guts fell out—and crawled back inside like photophobic worms. Mary fell back again.

Something was ticking like a clock, and chiming, and playing a melody in a minor key. Prokofiev's Cinderella: It was coming from Greg's hourglass. "What's that?"

"That is a complication," Greg said. "That's a five-minute warning that my plugs are going to time out. I'm going to have to go outside, get some coffee and/ or a short nap."

"Go ahead; I'll hold the fort. I don't suppose that thing can tell me how long *I've* got? How about the troll?"

"You've got at least an hour. As to the troll, well, he's a problem, you see. Either that's an NPC—which is absurd, as the geometers say—or he's got illegal plugs that won't time out on him."

"Oh, great."

"Can you hold things down till I get back? Maybe an hour." He looked thoughtful. "Maybe less."

"I can do anything I have to."

"Good." He took her hand, sketched a little bow, and kissed it. "I'll leave you everything I can. His rocks can't touch you, and—see that candle? It'll generate a new fireball for you every forty seconds. See you later." And instead of winking out, he went over to the stall where Ignatius stood and lay down in the straw behind him. Looking down at the small dormant body, Mary could not tell when its owner went outside.

"Getting tired, are you?"

"Who, me? I'm fine. Brother checked me over; I can hold out as long as necessary. What about you, that's the question." She reached tentatively toward the candle. An inch or two from the flame, the fireball appeared in her hand, warm as a muffin. It startled her and she threw it convulsively, missing the troll altogether and hitting the doorframe. The fireball exploded into a shower of sparks, peppering the troll and raising blisters like lima beans. On his shoulder, six of them ran together into a welt the size of fried egg. "Those Mogadishu plugs of yours'll let you stay up later—later than is good for you, by definition—but how long is that? You have no way of knowing. It'll be interesting to find out.

"But you won't find out, will you? You'll just fall asleep. We'll let you know, though; we'll visit you in jail with a plate of cookies and tell you all about it."

With a howl of rage the troll bounded up from his haunches and cracked his head against the ceiling. Hardly pausing, he charged, sword hurtling downward. Oh, my children, if ever you take up fighting, don't try a straight overhand swing on a fighter smaller than you; she will carve you to pieces before you know where you are. Mary severed the troll's calf muscle, sliced his gut again, and pinked him in the thigh where his femoral artery ought to be. The troll clutched at himself and fell backward, rolling mostly outside the door. His swordarm was still within reach and Mary cut it off again and kicked it away. She retreated enough to collect a fireball and burn the hand, lest it sneak up on her. She was making an interesting collection of bad guys' swords. Unfortunately, there appeared to be an infinite supply outside the door. She went back to the door and took up station just inside it.

Out in the stable yard a waning moon was falling toward the west. Its light showed the troll sitting on the packed earth, watching one hand grow back while the other fumbled inside his loincloth. Mary didn't care to wonder what he found there—or hoped to find there, or feared not to find. (She'd been aiming for his femoral artery, but there was only a few inches' difference.) Marital software for a troll? Yucch! Who'd have him? Unless he was designed to carry out somebody's really nasty rape-fantasies, now there was an unpleasant thought! No, it was all right, he was just trying to find his door-opening scroll, which had fallen inside. He laid it on the ground beside him. "Lose something?" Mary asked cheerily.

"Oh, shut up." The troll glared at her and rotated his sword arm, which still hadn't any fingers.

Behind the troll, crouched in the shadow of the great hall, three or four creatures huddled together. Standard-issue dungeon orcs? She couldn't really see. One of them was holding a sword rather too large for him; maybe he was fetching it for the troll. Yes, here he came, trotting across the stable yard, wincing in the moonlight, a ripped-off Tim Kirk orc with little fangs in his lower jaw. He gave the sword into the troll's new hand and made a hasty retreat.

Mary's position was much improved now, with the stable doorway between them, an opening rather smaller than the troll himself. He thrust his new sword arm inside and she dodged easily and hacked at it. He drew it back, hanging from a flap of hide.

While he waited for it to reattach, Mary risked a glance behind her. Greg was still asleep.

And meanwhile, time was passing. Was Greg's hourglass keeping track of anything useful? Not that she could see. When this was all over, she was going to have to learn enough code to be able to read the system clock at least. . . .

The troll sat scowling at her. He had finally realized he couldn't get through the doorway too. "You want to play the Riddle Game?" she said. (It was a traditional ploy for human vs. troll, and the sunrise couldn't be too many hours off. If she couldn't hold him till Greg got back, maybe she could hold him till he turned to stone.)

"No, thanks," the troll said. "I refuse to have a battle of wits with an unarmed opponent."

"Oh, shucks. If it doesn't bother me, it shouldn't bother you. Come on, I'll spot you two puns and an Undistributed Middle."

"Stuff it," said the troll, and turned his attention back to his arm. They were silent for a while.

"You make me sick," the troll said.

"That's what I was going to say," Mary said sweetly, and the troll snarled.

"You and your sanctimonious friend are a couple of sheep. You've bought into this world, and you don't even realize how dark it is. The EMC telling everyone where to live and how to live and what to drive and how many children to have, and the mask laws, which are a life sentence to be nothing but yourself. This is the only escape we've got"—he gestured at the dark, whispering night outside—"and the plug regulations kick you out when somebody else thinks it isn't safe. And you and Hampton want to shut it down because of some damned law."

"*The Golden Road* is Dr. Markheim's to use as he sees fit," Mary said. "The software's stolen from half a dozen people." (Oh, shit, he knew Greg's name? Nick must have told him.) "If siding with Law against Chaos makes me a sheep, well, I'm in the company of the finest sheep going, and the Lord is my shepherd, I should worry. Ba-a-a," she added to drive the point home. The troll spat.

"Sing ba-a-a to him, ha, ha, to him, and that is what I'll say," Mary hummed under her breath; but singing wasn't one of her strong points, and she couldn't remember the rest of it anyway.

Was the sky growing a trifle pale behind the troll's blunt head? Was the dawn at hand? Maybe it was only the moonlight. Certainly the critters that populated St. Chad's night phase weren't acting as though the sun might be about to rise on them. By ones and twos they had drifted into the stable yard, squeaking and gibbering between the midden and the horse trough. Standard dungeon fodder, orcs and ogres and a couple of undead, shivering in their tattered rags of flesh.

With her enhanced stats Mary could probably take them all, but she didn't want to. What fun was there in chopping to pieces creatures that had little skill and no honor? What point in hauling off tons of virtual gold that wasn't worth a dime outside? The one time she'd gone through a dungeon VR, she'd persuaded her host to write her a special persona, no weaponry but infinite defenses, so that she could wander around and see the sights while the guy hacked and slashed their way through mountains of orcs. Maybe it was something about the difference between men and women—

But no, you couldn't generalize that far, or if you did you had to admit exceptions. Because look at Greg. He was definitely male, and he could have, like many another wheelchair rider, gone power-tripping through the virtual universe; he had the money and the leisure to do it, too, but he didn't. He had taken the persona of a man of peace and had worn himself to exhaustion to protect a copyright, the integrity of a Backbone that wasn't even up yet, and the lives of any number of frequent flyers.

Why a monk? He wasn't in holy orders outside, or it appeared not, so it wouldn't be a real vocation to religious life. Maybe he liked Gregorian chants. Certainly he spoke beautiful Latin, a talent he must not have much use for outside. Maybe he found the loose-fitting habit comfortable, or the ready-made persona of one devoted to peace. He could have been a mighty fighter, like Nick, like his other colleagues, and had declined to. That in itself made him a valuable exception to the common run of men—

Something moved. Good God, she was nodding off, sitting there in the straw, and the troll was leaning forward. Hastily she raised her shield and caught his blow face-on, *thwack*. This wouldn't do. She got to her feet.

"Getting tired, are we?" the troll jeered. "Had a long day?"

"Oh, a splendid day. So educational. I learned so many interesting things." There, that wiped the grin off his ugly face. "I have been a salmon in the stream, a cat among cats, a raven in the air. What about you? How long has your day been? Lots of activity? Were you an elf-karl, rushing about in the defense of your King? Or were you just the big turtle I killed by the door?

"Were you a GI with a bottle of warm Coca-Cola? Were you Johnny, who died with his guts falling out and a string of platitudes on his lips? Were you—oh, shit, I know who you were. You were Scalybuns, weren't you? The Asaro Mecha that kept falling over its feet? I should've known." The troll growled; she had struck home. " 'This circular gamut brings you again, damn it. How long has this got to go on?' " And deliberately she yawned.

The troll sniggered. Mary smiled sweetly and yawned again. Yawns were contagious, everybody knew that, and if this lad had been up as long as she had, illegal plugs or no, he must be getting tired—

Suddenly the troll sucked in breath and clambered to his feet. He raised his swordarm and struck so fast Mary scarcely had time to block. (Damn! she was getting slow.) The troll struck again, low and high; it was the best attack she'd seen out of him in a couple of days. Maybe he was getting desperate; maybe the dawn was closer than she thought. He was finally making her sweat, and she kept her shield busy and looked for an opening—

And a fireball whistled over her head and set the troll's face on fire. He fell back, howling and slapping at the flames, and Mary turned. Greg was up again. He was settling down on the straw behind his props, flexing his fingers. Mary hastily got out of the line of fire. Greg threw something at the troll, moving so fast she couldn't see what it was. But it struck the troll with a pink splash, and flowers began to sprout all over his skin, pastel-colored and shaped like crocuses. The troll howled again, his voice rising into the countertenor range. The blossoms didn't seem to impede his fighting, but as a morale buster they were hard to beat. "Nice," she said.

"Thanks. Go on outside and get some rest. There's coffee in the pot—but get some sleep first. I can hold out here as long as necessary."

"Okay." Was the air turning cloudy pink? Were unseen sprites playing sweet lullabyes? She couldn't be sure they weren't. Better to go willingly than to be dragged. She lay down in the warm place Greg had left in the straw, next to Ignatius' hooves. She pulled off her helm and laid it beside her. "Excuse me?" The mule moved aside a grudging few inches. She took a final glance at the combat: Greg must have picked up some extra subroutines somewhere. Half a dozen fiery-eyed ducks were circling the troll's head, trying to nibble him to death, and three Siamese cats were stalking his feet.

They pounced. They must have been vorpal kitties at the very least; they severed his hamstrings while the ducks went in for the kill. The troll howled, and his howls subsided into whimpers. The biggest cat, a monstrous tom with feet like furry galoshes, reached out and clocked him behind the ear, and the troll was down for the count. The cats curled up here and there on his slumbering body and began to wash. The ducks settled down into the straw. Mary smiled and went outside.

* * *

The futon was unfolded and there was a warm place there too. She didn't even dream.

Presently she was drifting upward again, through the crushing weight of fathoms of water, her drowned treasure clutched to her breast. The light was green, then golden; the surface glittered like a wrinkled mirror overhead, and she burst through, shattering it into fragments. "Good morning," Greg said. "We won."

"Oh? oh, good." It was remarkable, her head was actually beginning to clear. She found her hands and rubbed them together.

"Cold?"

"Yeah."

But instead of going to look for a blanket or something—she heard him take a deep breath—he lay down beside her and put his arms around her. And he was as warm as toast, and his arms as strong as those of a legendary Duke of the West.

Her face was up against his T-shirt, and she was inhaling a mixture of old, new, and midrange sweat. It was all surprisingly tolerable. And yes, there was just a hint of sandalwood, left over from when he had last shaved, a million years ago yesterday morning.

"Better?"

"Yes." And knowing that she still had a choice, that nothing further was going to happen unless she did something about it, she turned her face upward to his kiss.

After a while he said, "Well. This is going to complicate things."

"Not unless you're really a monk."

"Of course not. But a monkish persona comes in very handy if you're shy; it provides a perfectly respectable context for treating ladies with honor and deference, and at a distance."

Mary's mouth fell open, and she heard herself asking, "Greg, what did you get your degree in?"

"EECS, of course."

"Aw, Greg." Her fingertip traced the line of his cheekbone, down past his ear where the micron-length stubble was already trying to curl, and back along his jaw. "Are we talking about the stereotypical computer maven who's afraid to talk to those mysterious creatures, girls?"

"Classic, isn't it?" His mouth was such a pleasant shape, and he was smiling.

"And what made you come out of your shell?"

"I saw you."

"Really." She hooked her finger behind his ear and pulled his face down again.

"Greg, that's the nicest thing anybody ever said to me, not excluding what Sir Brusi said the first time I defeated him in combat."

"What'd he say?"

"He said, 'You son of a bitch, you're good.' "

"Well, you are." His breath was warm against her ear. "You see what I mean about complications? I know we've been through death and life together, but it's only been four days. I think I'm gonna have to change my persona, and I worked so hard on it, too." He didn't sound regretful. "We'll figure something out."

"We're good at figuring things out." (How pleasant, absurdly so, to say *we*.)

"Right. At the moment, however, we'd better get back inside."

"Pour me some of that coffee, will you? What are our personae doing all this time?"

"Oh, yours is still asleep. Mine's standing there looking grim. It wouldn't fool a human being for long, but there aren't any around at present."

The bathroom mirror showed Mary her face, and she winced. Her hair was sticking up in all directions and there was a red crease on her cheek. Thank goodness she had worn no makeup to smear. *Still,* said one brain cell to another, *if he likes you when you're like this, he'll still like you when you're old, or sick, or pregnant, or*—but that was getting ahead of things, and she turned on the cold water and started washing her face.

Putting her coffee cup in the sink, she found a plastic packet on the drainboard, torn open and empty. The label—well, there was no brand name on it, only an Armed Forces serial number, but from the accompanying warnings it was clearly Ultrajolt. "Uh, Greg? How often do you use this stuff?"

"First time. And I hope you didn't want any, because that's the only one I had. Present from a friend. I may say, it seems to've worked. If I have to sleep all day tomorrow, I can. We'd *better* be done with this by tomorrow."

Inside, she sat up in the straw and put her helm back on, though everything was quiet. Greg was packing his magical props away back into the air. The troll was just visible outside the doorway, slumped and motionless.

Greg took Ignatius' bridle and led him out the door. Mary followed with Virtue, and they mounted. The troll sat with his back to the stable door, sound asleep, shackled hand and foot, and tastefully draped with chains. The moon was low in the western sky. The orcs and things in the stable yard were silent, and they fell back as the horses stepped forward. It was so quiet she could hear the troll's low-pitched snores and another sound, distant hoofbeats on the Winchester road. "Greg! Somebody's coming!"

And the yard exploded with noise and violence, all the dungeon creatures suddenly attacking boldly. Brandishing axes, bludgeons, even claws and teeth, they milled about looking for a target. Ignatius kicked a large orc into the laps of three larger orcs, knocking them all down. Virtue reared and stamped, smashing with iron-shod hooves. Mary kept her seat, just, and drew her sword and harvested heads.

But Greg said loudly, "Oh-eight-hundred," and raised a finger to the sky. And there was light.

The sun was just over the roof of the church, striking sparks of gold from the cross over the west door. The night creatures shrieked, moaned, popped, shriveled, evaporated. The troll fell over sideways and turned to stone, blocking the stable door. A gargoyle on the manor roof shivered, sprouted a comb and feathers, and began to crow. Away on the Winchester road something screamed with rage. "Let's go," Greg said, and they ran for it.

Chapter 11

Wizards' Duel

The road out of the valley sloped uphill, but Virtue and Ignatius were climbing out of it as if their tails had been set on fire. Mary glanced back: No, they hadn't been. But there was a darkness over St. Chad's that couldn't be explained by the morning mist off the river. It was too local, for one thing, and changing shape too fast for another.

"Greg, I think it's following us."

"I bet it is." Greg didn't look back. They were just coming to the top of the hill. "You may get your wizards' duel after all"—he glanced from side to side—"but if I have my way it'll be at long distance."

"Still got all your traces?"

"Of course."

The rising sun cast long shadows from shrubs and grass tufts and an occasional tree. Somewhere a lark sang, half heard over their hoofbeats. The sky was cloudless and the turf an innocent green, still sparkling with dew. "Look," Greg said, "you watch the right side of the road. I'll watch the left. If you see anything strange, yell."

"What kind of strange?"

"Any kind." They were on the flat now, and their hoofbeats were so loud that Greg had to speak in short phrases to be heard. "Incongruous. Mutated from what it should be. Remember, there ought to be nothing here but trees and grass. And birds. The sheep are probably all right. But they are a hack. Not part of the plan. So if one does anything funny, yell and skewer it. In that order."

"Aye, aye." There was nothing on her side to scan but a single tree. She gave it her attention as they rode to it and past it, but it didn't do anything. "Greg? What did you do to make the sun rise so fast?"

"I reset the system clock. Instant eight a.m. I'll apologize to Concha later—the Duke's sysop. Make it up somehow. An extra-long day for fighting. Or a long night for reveling."

Mary glanced behind her again. St. Chad's was now out of sight, but the shadows still loomed in the western sky. "What is that thing?"

"Well, you know *who* it is. As to what, I don't know. He's making it up as he goes. Don't worry about it. Nobody's seen the bottom of my bag yet."

They were still heading eastward at a full gallop. The horse tribe are sprinters, not long-distance runners; Greg must have interfered seriously with their code. But the shadow was still growing behind them.

They were coming to a grove of trees; the road ran through it. Mary took her lance from its rest and lowered it; even if they met nothing inside, she could avoid striking branches overhead. There was nothing to be seen inside but a sleepy owl that hooted twice and was probably legitimate; but the grove was darker than Mary remembered from the journey west, and she was glad to get back into the light. But as they left the grove, a flutter of wings began, and behind them a flock of black shapes rose out of the nearest trees and followed them. "What are those, bats?"

"Yes. But not English bats. They're the kind that bite. Hold on a minute." He threw something over his shoulder that Mary couldn't see, and the bats disappeared in a chorus of pops.

They were coming now to the little stream that crossed the road three or four times. It ran broad and shallow here, and water drops splashing underfoot flew into the air as bright as diamonds. But something was holding them back; the animals were slowing to a walk, picking each hoof out of the water with a faint sucking sound. There was something dark green underneath. Algae? It was putting up dark green fingers to seize at Virtue's ankles. Greg had to point downward and zap it in half a dozen places before it let go. As they reached the bank and rode away, dozens of little green fingers waggled disconsolately behind them. They accelerated again.

When they reached the next crossing, Greg muttered something and spiked anklets appeared on the animals' feet. Not big blunt spikes like those on the collar of a bulldog (Mary had actually seen an old bulldog, mild as milk, that wore such a collar). These were set with rows of trim steely needles, a couple of inches long and looking very sharp. "What are those for?"

"What do you think?"

" 'To guard against the bites of sharks'?"

"Right."

"I don't think this water is deep enough for sharks."

"You never know."

And sure enough, as they splashed into the stream for the second time, something began to worry at their ankles, beating the water to a froth and staining it pink with blood. Since Virtue paid no attention and Ignatius' long face wore an expression of lofty disdain, Mary assumed the blood was all the attackers'. Something flew up from underfoot and landed in Mary's lap: a pretty little fish, the size of your hand and the shape of a leaf. Its sides were dull silver and flecked with bright gold on every scale; its toothy little jaws were opening and closing. A piranha; she had seen them in Steinhart Aquarium in the city. It was trying to bite through the mailshirt that covered her lap. She picked it up by the tail and threw it away. They left the shoals behind, and the water went calm again.

"What's next? Dragons?"

"I checked the table. No dragons at present. Doesn't mean there couldn't be one in a hurry. I'll give you all the warning I can."

The next bend in the stream was coming up, and here the road followed its bank for twenty or thirty yards before crossing it. Something was humming, a pleasant sound: bees, to pollinate the clover to feed the sheep to feed the dragons? No, it was singing, human or near-human voices singing in lush nineteenth-century harmony.

"Sirens?"

"Rhinemaidens, I think. That's their music, anyway. Look, the water's getting deeper."

The road ran under the water, coming out still dry on the other side. In midstream it came up to their saddlegirths. And now the Rhinemaidens appeared.

There were three of them, about human size. Their long weedy hair trailed in the water, and they were decidedly female, with wide hips, bobbing breasts, and what not. No chaste Arthur Rackham watercolors, these. They were dancing little quadrilles that would never have been allowed in Mary's high-school water ballet. They were also (by modern standards) decidedly overweight, which made them all the more distasteful to Mary's eyes. But she was not their target. There must be people on this planet to whom all that flesh would be a turn-on. She cast a glance sidewise at Greg; he seemed no more than amused.

"I suppose a real monk might be tempted?"

"A real monk would pay no attention, having his eye on better things. As have I," he said and smiled at her. As they rode out of the water, the last Rhinemaiden did something vulgar. "I guess Nick just doesn't know me as well as he thinks he does. If this water gets any deeper, I'll have to write a bridge."

Reminded of Nick, Mary glanced backward. The cloud behind them was looming higher overhead and nearer. His traps hadn't caught them, but they had slowed them down. "Let's run." And they ran for a mile or more, until the road began to rise and to switch back and forth across a steep slope. Here the stream, on their way in, had fallen in graceful cascades full of rainbows; now there was only a trickle over bare rock.

They climbed the last turn in the road and found out why. Something had dammed the stream with sticks and mud, and a good-sized lake had welled up behind it. The cause of the blockage was not hard to find: As they watched, two six-foot-tall beavers looked at them with placid eyes and lumbered away over the top of their dam to a place where they could slip into the water. "Oh, very good," Greg said. "Those are real beavers. I mean, their counterparts were real. But they're extinct. Now, let's see." A bridge sprung out from the end of the road and stretched over the water like a low causeway till it rejoined the road at the far side. It was smooth and modern-looking, apparently cast of concrete into which flakes of mica had been blended, and it glittered with a faint iridescence.

"Once again, you watch your side, I'll watch mine," Greg said as they started across. The bridge was steady underfoot, and they cautiously picked up speed.

"Surely those beavers aren't dangerous?"

"I don't think so. But I can't see him building a lake like this and not putting anything into it. So keep an eye out." The surface of the lake was calm and blue, ruffled only a little by the wind. They saw nothing, not even a fish, for several minutes.

When they were about halfway across, and the water presumably at its deepest, something moved far away downstream, near the dam. A little dark thing, the size of her fingertip, but Mary caught sight of it. "Bogey at three o'clock. What is it? Can you tell?"

"What would you expect in a lake?"

"Greg—no. The Loch Ness Monster?"

"Something along those lines. A virtual plesiosaur. And headed this way. May I suggest you get ready to fight the funniest Florentine in your career?"

"Florentine . . . ?"

"Lance in one hand, sword in the other as a backup. There's going to be very little time from the moment you can reach him to the moment he can reach us."

Mary took her lance in her right hand, her sword in her left. It felt funny, all right, but since she didn't have to use the weapons together, she thought she'd manage. The creature was coming closer.

"I hate to do this, Greg," she said. "It's probably the last survivor of the species."

"There never were any. Don't worry."

The creature came closer, and now she could see it hadn't the smooth plesiosaur head she'd been expecting. There was a frill behind the neck, and two horns—tentacles?—rising above it. (Eyestalks? Was it built on the giant-salamander model maybe?) The beast was dark green, mottled like a frog, and it smelled froggy.

She turned Virtue to meet the thing head-on, so that the impact would push her straight into the high-backed saddle. Virtue set his hooves and lowered his head.

She aimed the point of her lance at the base of the great neck as it moved in. Unheeding, its eyes on its prey, it skewered itself neatly on the outstretched lance. The wound hissed like a teakettle, like a fiery sword quenched in water, and the beast threw its head up on its long neck and whistled like an old steam locomotive. Then the head came lashing down again, and she raised her sword to strike.

The Nessie's hide, slick and fragile looking, was surprisingly tough. The sword made only a shallow wound, a few fingers deep, and the momentum of the descending head knocked from her hand. It fell to the bridge with a clatter.

Shield. Where was it? In its usual place on Virtue's flank. She snatched for it while the monster's head swung backward, preparing to return in force. She got it up before her just in time; she had it only by the handgrip, no time now to get her forearm inside its strap. But the spells (well, the enhancements) seemed to hold. The Nessie's head clouted her at an angle, as if trying to knock her from the saddle. But Mary had a good seat (she'd paid a bundle for it over the years), and she stayed on.

What now? Hang on absorbing blows until the heat of the lance cooked through the beast's vitals? That might be Nick's whole plan, to delay them with barely killable monsters until he could catch up with them.

But out of the corner of her eye, she saw her sword, bathed in ultraviolet sparkling light, rising from the floor like a dazed elf-karl. While Nessie's head reared again on its long neck, she snatched the sword into her right hand.

Maybe she could make the beast's own strength do some of her work for her. Its movements were fairly slow; she had time to look at the frilly head and look again, estimate its path, and at the last moment bring up the sword at just the right angle.

The point of the sword nicked the creature's skin, and then the edge opened up the wound as the great neck pressed in on the bias. It cut quite halfway through before the neck stopped moving; the head, almost at the level of her knee, gave her a brief look of pure disgust, before the beast slid backward into the water. With another handful of purple light Greg retrieved her lance.

The half-severed head flopped sideways. Here was a flaw in the design: The blood pressure in that neck should have been much higher, as high as a giraffe's, so it would spout blood in great fountains and not these measly little drops. Inside the neck, spilling into the water—"Oh, come now, Nick. Be serious. Clockwork gears?"

"I told you they weren't real. Come on, we're losing time."

Mary set her weaponry in place as they galloped toward the end of the bridge. There was a cow grazing among the sheep, a big black-and-white Holstein with untrimmed horns and a bell around her neck. She raised her head and looked at them with suspicion as they approached; she watched them as they went by but made no attempt to interfere with them. Just as well. No doubt Greg would have had some way of countering the attack of a suspicious cow, but Mary was willing to live her life without seeing it.

Mary risked a look backward. The shadow was blocking out a third part of the sky now, and within it was a shape half seen, half guessed at, something bipedal riding something quadrupedal, the details mercifully dim. "This isn't going to work," Greg said. "Stand by."

A ripple went through the air around them, a mirage up close and without heat, and suddenly they were no longer in the saddle.

The chariot they rode in was gilded, and garnets flashed from its wheels. Portraits of classical demigods covered its sides, their features made bland by their coat of gold leaf. The beasts that pulled the chariot had golden bodies and creamy white wings, heads of eagles and lashing lions' tails, hooves that spurned the earth: hippogriffs, in fact, and yet were still recognizably Virtue and Ignatius. "Oh, this is neat."

"Like it?" Greg grinned. The hippogriffs leaped into the air, and the chariot spread golden wings of its own and followed. "Set design for *Orlando*, my last year in grad school." With the road noises left behind, they could speak at normal levels. "Now, if you will be charioteer—just hold the reins, the hippogriffs know where they're going—I can turn around and get some work done."

The hippogriffs did know where they were going—they had only to follow the road from a height of ten or fifteen feet—so Mary could turn to watch. Greg had a little silver ball in one hand. With the other he pointed a finger at a tiny model of a catapult, plastic-action-figure-sized, as it wound itself up. He placed the ball gently in the spoon of the catapult and touched the release with a fingertip. The catapult went off with a little *ping* and a tremor that went all through the chariot, and the silver ball shot into the sky.

In the heart of the cloud it exploded, hurling out ten or twelve fireballs, and they exploded too, sending out cascading showers of silvery sparks all through the upper part of the cloud. It was better than the fireworks on the Fourth of July. The cloud roiled and condensed on itself and let down a shadowy trailing curtain all the way to the ground. A sudden gust of wind brought them the sweet smell of rain.

"That's pretty."

"Thanks. It was virtual silver iodide, you see. The major effect here is to cut him down to size, remove any psychological advantage he may have thought he had—and to let him know that I can reach him at that distance and it's not in his interest to come any closer."

"I'm surprised you didn't use virtual metallic sodium on the Rhinemaidens, set them on fire."

"I could've. I didn't need to."

Behind them, the rain seemed to be slacking off, and the cloud was much diminished. A flash of lightning lit it up for a moment, and after a suitable interval thunder rumbled. Mary found herself counting, six seconds, two kilometers, and wondered if the formula worked in VR.

The lightning flashed again, rather nearer, and a reddish light appeared on the horizon. It was a tongue of flame, and it was growing.

"Well," Greg said. "A real grass fire we could outrun handily. But this one isn't very realistic."

It seemed real enough. Already the stink of burning grass was reaching them, and Mary could feel as much heat on her skin from the west as from the east, where the sun was still climbing in the happy fields of the sky. There should have been birds and beasts running frantically ahead, trying to escape the blaze, but there were none. Perhaps someone had forgotten to write that kind of behavior into them—or else this fire was moving too fast for them.

It was closing in on them, a wall of flame reaching high overhead that roared like an enormous beast, a bellow of rage and hunger. The sound made her bones shiver. The fire was spreading out on either side as fast as it came forward, so there was no chance to escape by leaving the road. The heat was intense now, and little flakes of ash on the back of a scorching wind batted her in the face.

Greg raised his right hand as if to forbid the fire to come any closer. The hot wind was cut off, just as the fire swept up and engulfed them. Suddenly it was cooler—no worse than warm and stuffy, while the fire roared and raged about them. They appeared to be inside a bubble of something transparent and very refractory, its size hard to estimate from the flames that flickered outside it but big enough to contain chariot, hippogriffs and all.

Now Greg opened his left hand, and from his palm rose a little swirl of sparkling white flecks that spiraled up around them and blotted out the sight of the flames. They were snowflakes, and the temperature had dropped to a pleasant ten degrees or so. Still it roared, but in a higher key: It was a proper blizzard, the kind you read about in Laura Ingalls Wilder. It shone with its own cold white light, and it swirled and it howled. Somewhere, farther than Mary could see, fire and snow were meeting in a mighty annihilation, and a cloud of steam must be rising far overhead.

Ahead of them, the snow was thinning, and green turf showed faintly through the white flakes. The land ahead hadn't burned. Then they were out of the blizzard, which retreated behind them, blank as a marble wall a mile high. Snow lay in drifts on the ground, but it was melting rapidly, revealing green grass that shone in the sun. Far behind them the snow melted away, leaving a virtually unchanged landscape. The roaring died away.

They flew on in welcome silence for some minutes. "This is dragon country," Greg said after a while.

"Is there a dragon in it?"

"Yes, but it's way over there"—Greg gestured with the back of his left hand—"so unless it gets suddenly mobilized, you won't have to fight it."

"Good. We must be getting close to the domain boundary, then. How far is it?"

"At our present speed, twelve minutes, if nothing interferes." He glanced back at earth and sky. Nothing seemed to be interfering yet.

Several more minutes went by before Mary looked into the sky and saw that ominous thing, a cloud no bigger than a man's hand. It swelled rapidly, took on a tinge of green, and fell on them with a rattling sound like hail. The chariot was littered with what looked like frozen green peas. Greg materialized a little whiskbroom, the color of flame, and began sweeping them out of the chariot as rapidly as he could. The peas were sprouting, extending themselves like little green worms, lengthening and putting out small leaves. Mary tried to kick some of them out, but they wrapped around her ankle and tried to climb her like a tree. She drew her sword, thinking to cut them away, but her swordhand was trapped before she had drawn a handsbreadth. She ran the vines on her left hand over the sword's edge, but it did no good. It was a Crusader-period sword, built to break armor and not all that sharp: a chisel rather than a razorblade. Greg had swept out all but half a dozen of the remaining vines, but the survivors had taken firm hold. Now he must put a fingertip to each and wait several seconds, finding and killing each separate subroutine. Just as well he hadn't had to ID and kill each separate flame. Now Mary's vines had climbed to her throat and began to squeeze.

Mary set her teeth. The things couldn't hurt her really. She was still breathing back in San José, where it counted. The pressure increased, and her face grew warm as Greg fingered the vines one by one away from her throat. Her vision was blacking out by the time he got the last tendril off her neck.

The vines had spread forward to the hippogriffs, tangled their wings and prevented them from flying. They glided on the chariot's own wings to the ground, and Greg jumped out to kill the rest of the vines. "Keep an eye out."

Mary looked around and upward. Nothing. Nothing. A little black dot in the sky. "Here he comes."

"Hold him a minute, can you? I've got to write a 'foreach' command; there are too many of these things."

The shape was falling rapidly, stooping like a great

eagle. Lance or sword? Lance, to begin with. She got it from its rest at the chariot's side and took her shield on her left arm. The attacking bird wasn't an eagle; it had a human face. It brushed the lance aside, hurtled downward to crash against her shield and bounce away, wings flapping to recover height.

Not really a human face: sable feathered, with pallid talons, it had an ape's face with fangs in the upper jaw—a monstrous he-harpy that did look rather a lot like Nick. She had her sword in hand now but had little opportunity to use it with the harpy moving so fast. She caught its impact on her shield and struck out as the harpy rose again; she severed half a tail feather.

The harpy flapped a few times, hovering in a way a real bird that heavy could never have done. It scowled at her and bared its teeth, but it did not speak.

Then it screamed and stooped again, and struck her shield, but instead of rebounding it clung to the shield rim and beat at her with its wings, craning its neck as if trying to bite. From its mouth crept a long snaky tongue, its tip glowing deep indigo. It darted toward her head, struck her shield, and went dark. Grimly Mary held the shield overhead. Now it was she who was fighting pure defense—but then Nick had decades of experience on whoever the Grey Knight was. Where was Greg? Was he all right? She couldn't turn to look. She hunched her shoulders against the beating wings. The glowing tongue flashed again and went dark: a spell cast and broken against a mightier counterspell—or maybe just an electrostatic charge building up and discharging. She swung her sword around the edge, slapped the shield as if in salute. Something shrieked, and feathers flew. With luck she might slice off a few rump steaks before Greg got his act together.

There was something fluttering between her face and her shield, something small and fragile: a little butterfly, lavender tinged and delicately spotted, probably an endangered species. It seemed to be trying to get past the shield; Mary obliged, raising her shield arm, harpy and all, and it fluttered upward and flew straight down the harpy's throat.

The monster let go of the shield rim and backed off, beating the air frantically, coughing and spitting. It was perhaps twenty yards overhead when there was a muffled bang and the harpy flew into pieces.

Mary's shield, still raised and with its enhanced bow-wave, kept the bits and pieces from falling into the chariot, but they spattered the grass all around. *Yucch,* she thought. *It's not real, it isn't real, it's only VR.*

Now she could look behind her; Greg stood there dusting off his hands as if to say, "That takes care of *that*."

"Gee," Mary said as he climbed back in, "I didn't know they made butterflies like that any more."

"Oh, well, that was the famous butterfly that flapped its wings in Tokyo and started a tornado in Kansas City. Uh-oh, look there."

On the grass behind them a severed talon, the color of dead skin, was twitching as if with residual life. It shivered and went pale brownish-pink, became a human finger. It began to crawl away like a caterpillar.

A few yards back along the road it met two other caterpillar fragments. They snuggled together and coalesced, became part of a hand, still lacking its thumb and ring finger. It dug its nails into the turf and crawled away in search of its other parts. "Stubborn, isn't he," Greg said. "We'd better fly."

Now they flew in every sense of the word, streaking above the ground at a speed that made the air whistle in Mary's helm. They went by too fast for the sheep to raise their heads to look, assuming they had enough intelligence to do so. Far ahead, but getting closer fast, a taller shape moved among the fleecy backs. "Greg, look. Somebody's written them a shepherd."

"I see. A shepherd with no comments, no features. No, a shepherdess. Prepare for boarding—"

But the shepherdess didn't attempt to board them. Wrapped in a cloak that looked like simple gray homespun, she smiled up at them as they flew past. When Mary looked behind them, she had vanished.

The sheep were getting awfully thick over the ground—well, they had had a couple of dragonless days to replenish their numbers. Mary had never seen any lambs among them, so she supposed they sprang full-grown from the brow of a subroutine. No, wait now, they were getting much too numerous, and so fluffy you could hardly see their necks or feet, and some of them—

They were passing by underfoot too fast. She fixed her eye on one cluster up ahead and watched it as it approached and flashed by and dwindled in the distance. Yes, they looked like a slideful of bacteria, featureless rod-shapes, growing and dividing at their narrow ends, fissioning and drawing apart as she watched. Real bacteria took maybe fifteen or twenty minutes to go through one complete division, but these had been speeded up; and now they were rising into the air.

"Greg! You see those things?"

"Yes! I'm trying to avoid them." He shifted the reins a little to the left. "Those things are some very complex code, thought you mightn't think it to look at them, and to solve them will take more time than I've got. But if we can get into the London domain, I won't have to."

One of the featureless white shapes had risen almost level with them and was drifting their way. The sky seemed paler in its wake. Mary raised her lance to impale the thing—and was left with nothing but the handgrip and a few splinters as the shape passed by unharmed.

"Careful!" Greg said. "Anything that touches those guys, you'll lose faster than I can restore just at present. There's the boundary." A thread of silver shone on the horizon, and beyond it the land seemed dark. (Well, yes, it was hours—how many?—earlier in the London domain.) "But the interface is only about ten meters high, so I've got to bring us down." They descended rapidly, dodging floating clots of bacteria. There were many bald patches now on the ground where the grass had been either eaten away or blotted out, replaced with more bacteria. They hurtled downward, their smooth trajectory mutating suddenly into a stomach-turning drop as Greg dodged bacteria dead ahead. "Duck!" They skimmed over the boundary stream like an old warplane on a strafing run, and rose again into the London side. But the hippogriffs were gone. The chariot was scalloped as if with gigantic toothmarks; it glided on its stubs of wings to the ground.

They turned to look back. The sheep-bacteria were just beginning to drift over the boundary stream. "Firewall," Greg said, raising a hand, and all that was left of the Winchester lands vanished. The starry dome of the sky came right down to the grass. But on the London side there were three bacteria, glistening under the moon. Then four. Then five.

Chapter 12

Mopping Up

"Greg! They got through."

"Yes, I see 'em. Don't worry. This is the home stretch, and there are only a few of them. Even with a replication rate of twenty-five seconds, it'll take a while for them to do a lot of damage. Give me a little time and I'll put all to rights. Mmmm."

The battered chariot changed beneath their feet to a Persian carpet that rose gently into the air. It was perfectly steady underfoot, but Mary thought it wise to sit down, and after a moment Greg did the same. It was a fine carpet, closely woven and silky to the touch, with a worn place in one corner and a spot in another, looking like a tea stain.

"Greg, you didn't just write this carpet on the fly, did you?"

"Oh, no, no. None of the stuff I've used, and none of Nick's either, I bet, was written in real time. They're subroutines we've written in odd moments over the years or that a friend has written and we've borrowed. This, now"—he indicated the bacteria—"is something altogether new to me. Does damage like a virus, crosses boundaries like a worm. Maybe we'll *call* them bacteria. But I'm going to have to solve 'em now in real time. It shouldn't take too long; they're not that complex." And he settled down on his corner of the carpet, tucking his feet under him neatly, and did (apparently) nothing.

Mary sat and watched him and the bacteria in turn. Steadily dividing, slowly jostling for space, occasionally rising into the air, they shone in the moonlight like pearls on black velvet. But the velvet was getting motheaten. The bacteria were turning everything around them into their own substance, leaving bare patches, neutral as a photographer's test card, as gray here as they had been copier-paper white in Winchester.

There were several dozens of them now, too many to keep count of. As they spread out, they got nearer to the carpet, but before Mary could sound the alarm the carpet drifted away on its own. It had some kind of proximity sensor, she supposed, another item in Greg's bag of tricks.

She went outside for a minute, just to check. Greg was sitting quietly in his chair. Mary rose and stretched, visited the bathroom, got a drink of water, and went back inside.

Greg was still sitting there, his expression as bland inside as outside, and the bacteria were spreading out to either side. Soon they would have the carpet surrounded, but again it responded to some vigilant section of code and rose high into the air, higher than the bacteria had yet risen, and drifted back over them at a safer distance.

"All right," Greg said presently, and seemed to wake up. "That wasn't too hard. I've figured out their structure and how to undo it. Now watch and you'll see a sight. I could use some more light." He pointed upward and a bright light appeared, bright enough to see the green color of the grass and the white patches the bacteria had eaten away. "Tycho's Star, the supernova of 1572; way out of period for *Chivalry*, but it doesn't matter. I'm going to have to restore the system from backups anyway. Now watch."

He opened his hand, and on his palm lay a little white sphere, smaller than his silver-iodide bomb but larger than a frozen pea. It rose into the air and put out legs, and Mary said, "Euggh."

The whole thing was about a meter high. Its head, the size of a man's, was a single crystal with six or eight long triangular faces around its midsection and as many smaller triangles at top and bottom. It was a pale bluish-white and translucent, like clouded quartz. From its lower end grew a ridged shaft, like the one that adjusts the height of an office chair, and from the bottom of this grew half a dozen thin legs like a mosquito's. That was all, but the sight of it sent shivers down the spine. It looked like a predator. It was drifting toward the nearest bacterium.

"What in Heaven's name is that?"

"That is a model of a critter called a T4 bacteriophage," said Greg, sounding smug. "You've probably got zillions of them in your gut. They live off *E. coli,* which you definitely have zillions of unless you're sick. Again, I'd already written the phage, years ago, thinking it might be a useful vehicle for something of this kind. So all I had to write in real time was the code to load into it."

The phage, thin legs delicately probing the air, settled onto the white membrane of the bacterium. One foot touched down, then the others, and they splayed out till the base of the shaft was not far from the membrane. There was an audible "sproing!" and the shaft contracted to half its length. Something pierced the membrane like the ovipositor of a wasp. And something was draining out of the phage; its crystalline head was going transparent and one could see that it was empty. It was beginning to crumple as it clung to the membrane, and the bacterium was growing mottled, its milky color curdling. Five seconds, ten seconds perhaps. Then the membrane split open and five, ten, twenty new phages spilled out of it and rose into the air in search of more bacteria.

"I see. They're multiplying faster than the bacteria."

"Much faster. And they're quite specific; they won't attack anything else. I'll still have to restore the system, but I can do so knowing it won't get reinfected." The light of moon and star went out, and they stood in near-darkness in an echoing room. At the far end, candles flickered on an altar, lighting up a golden crucifix. There were faint smells of incense and human bodies, both rather stale. Dark hooded shapes were silhouetted against the candlelight, and they were singing, *"Dominus regnat: tremunt populi; sedet super Cherubim: movetur terra."*

Beside her, Greg let out a long breath. "Here we are. This is St. Alban's, in my home system. We are now perfectly safe." He put his arm round her and her head found a place on his shoulder that seemed designed for it from the beginning of the world.

"I have a couple of chores to do outside," he said after a while." You can stay in and listen to the chant or go out into the cloister and listen to the nightingales."

"Okay. Wait a minute. I thought you said you couldn't recruit any brothers here."

"I haven't; these are all NPCs. They sing all the Hours, but that's about all they do. I'll see you in a little while." He went out into the porch and disappeared.

One of the brothers had gone up to the lectern and was intoning a long reading, mostly on one note. Mary went out through the porch into the abbey grounds. She must have taken a wrong turn, because she was plainly outside the cloister, not in it, but since the nightingales were singing in every tree without discrimination, it didn't matter. They sang well, like fountains flinging crystal drops up and down the air under the moon, like mockingbirds with a conservatory education. She listened for a while, feeling the virtual adrenaline drain away, until she remembered that she had a body outside that could use food, drink, and a shower. Maybe even sleep. She went outside.

She opened her eyes and unplugged, wincing; her temples and jaw muscles were sore. Greg had showered (his hair was still damp), shaved, and changed into fresh jeans and an emerald-green T-shirt that said "C: it's not just a good idea; it's the law." He smiled and waved, but he didn't stop talking into the phone.

"—but I can't name him till the cops get to him and make an arrest. Surely you can understand that. The point is, the bug is in your system now and I've got a fix for it." He covered the mouthpiece and said, "Concha. Winchester sysop."

He listened for a while and said, "No. No. Yes, the phage would go through the boundary if I brought the link up, but so might other things. Just ftp through the Net to Saint-dot-Albans, the file is g2-underscore-bacteriophage. Get it and install it, and then you can reboot and they'll never have a chance to reestablish themselves. Goodbye, Concha, I've got to call Tintagel and Oxford, in case this reached them too. 'Bye." He punched HANGUP and DIAL and started punching numbers. Mary retreated to the bathroom.

When she came out again, Greg had finished phoning and was making breakfast: toast and eggs and lots of orange juice against likely dehydration. It had been a long night.

"So when are you going to tell the cops about Nick?"

"Oh, I've sent them an e-mail already, but I don't suppose they'll read it till eight o'clock. It's only five-thirty. Unless it's been a quiet night and the desk sergeant has been killing time reading the Net."

"Whatever." She drank her juice and poured another glassful. "Incidentally, Greg, what about St. Chad's? Do I still own it? Or is it going to go away, since it was a hack? Can it be legitimized some way, if Concha and the Duke are agreeable?"

"Sure it can," Greg said. "All we need to do is ask. Do you really care. Why do you?"

"I'd like to keep it if I can," Mary said. "Minus the dungeon crawlers, of course. It ought to be worth a bundle."

"I've been meaning to talk to you about this," Greg said. He poked at his plate with one tine of his fork, chasing egg scraps about until they made a neat cinq-foil. "Your knightly rank gives you the obligation to show knightly *largesse*. When the Grey Knight could not pay ransom, you could have released him. Why didn't you?"

"If I had, none of this would've happened, and we might never have met."

"Oh, I bet we would've. I've been lurking a lot since I finished the Tri-Valley project and the St. Alban's routines. I would've found some way to meet you.

"But we're never told what *would have happened*. Maybe, if you had released him, the Grey Knight would have been so shamed by your generosity that he would've confessed the whole thing. Then they'd've shut down *The Golden Road* Sunday night, some wandering nitwit wouldn't have gotten into the ATC system, and four people might be alive who are dead. But we don't know, we never can know. And a good thing too. It prevents us either from getting an inflated idea of our own importance or from being crushed under the weight of responsibility. All that's necessary for us is to do what honor and virtue compel us to do, without wasting a thought on the consequences."

"*Fais ce que dois, avienne que pourra.*"

"Exactly. Exactly that. Mary, I don't want to belabor this too much. It's not that you accepted a 12,000-mark manor when it was offered to you. It's that you wouldn't forgive a piddling little 1500-mark ransom that your opponent couldn't pay. That's only about a thousand dollars in real money."

"I love the way you can say *only* and *thousand dollars* in the same breath. You've always had money, haven't you?"

He shrugged. "Enough. Not vast amounts."

" 'Enough' is a relative term. Remember? Look, everybody's got something they're afraid of. I don't know what yours is, but—"

"Other than girls? That's easy. That somebody might take my chair away."

"Of being helpless, in fact."

"Right. I nearly took it into VR with me, though on the whole I think I'm glad I took the risk."

"Uh-huh. Well, me too. I'm afraid of being defenseless, of having no resources left. Of being broke. Can I have some more juice? Thanks.

"I guess you and I are about the same age? Well, back when you were a little kid with 'enough' for video games and to grow up feeling that money didn't matter—back in the nineties, right?—my mother and I were living in our car. My father walked out, we never found him, and my mother and I had to decide between paying the rent and eating.

"We got WIC, and when that was canceled,

Mother got a job cleaning apartments. We were better off than a lot of people, really. We always ate. The car had good locks on it. We never had to camp out in People's Park. We never got raped. Mother went to school part-time, and she kept me in school. I got real clever at inventing reasons why the kids couldn't come to *my* place to play. And then Mother got her certificate and a data-entry job, and we got an apartment. And I stayed in school, all the way through the MBA. I was going to make sure we never had to go through that again."

"Your mother is a very great lady. I'd like to meet her."

"Well, you can't, because she died in the duck flu, in 2019. But before that I was winning enough tourneys that she could've retired if she'd wanted to. And we had a nicer apartment, and I bought her lots of presents."

"And now you own your house and land and a healthy bank account. You sell your surplus electricity to SV Power. And you still don't feel secure, do you?

"Even if things go as I hope, and you find yourself enjoying some very comfortable community property—Mary, you will never feel secure: never in this life."

"Probably not."

"So you might as well allow a desire that will never be satisfied anyway to be overridden by your duty to show—"

And the speaker on Greg's terminal gave tongue. "Security alert! Security alert!" Old *Star Trek* sirens began to sound. "Security alert. Building security has been compromised—"

"Show me," Greg said, and the racket died down and a closed-circuit image lit up the screen, pale blue and ghostly from inadequate light. It showed the back of a man doing something to the front door, no, to the panel beside it where the speaker was. The lettering on his jacket said PACIFIC SECURITY SYSTEMS. He had a dark knitted cap pulled low onto his head.

"Is that a real business?" Mary spoke softly, as if the man could hear.

"*It* is, but I don't think that guy's for real. Jackets can be stolen or fabricated. No, I assume it's Nick. He is acquiring a taste for the dramatic." Greg picked up the phone and began to punch numbers into it; halfway through he put it to his ear, said "Mmmm," and hung it up. "Phone's dead. Now, that took some doing. All the cables are buried; he must've hit the switch center."

The picture switched to another camera, inside the lobby, as the man pushed open the door. He was wearing not a cap but a ski mast that concealed his face. "Oh, come now," Mary said. "He's breaking the law right there."

"Just as well. When the police get here they can bust him for that on the spot. Now, the security system, which has its own phone line, called them when he first started cracking, two minutes ago. They acknowledged and they're on their way, see?" He tapped the screen where a line of code ran along the bottom of the picture. "Now he's heading for the elevator. No, he can't use the elevator"—Greg typed rapidly—"the elevator's down. There he goes, heading for the stairs. I don't suppose he's ever used 'em, but they're labeled."

"Is there anything you can do with the building systems, to stop him? I don't suppose you could electrify the floor—"

"Nothing at present, though after this I'm going to think about it if I get the chance. You know what I should've done? I should've let him get into the elevator and then shut it down, kept him between floors till the cops got here. Too late now, there he is on the stairs."

"Could you set off the fire sprinklers?"

"Yes, but I don't think it'd stop him, only annoy him. I could turn out the hall lights." He considered this, while the picture switched again to show Nick at the head of the stairs. "Yeah, why not." He typed again, and the screen went dark—and lit up again with a shaft of light that hunted back and forth through the darkness, lighting up bits of floor and wall, doors, door numbers. Like a prudent burglar, Nick had brought a flashlight.

"When he finds my door," Greg said, "he'll have to crack it, and then crack the door inside. This may take him longer than he thinks it will. The police *might* get here first, at least scare him off." He pushed himself back from the console and looked around the room. "He knows I'm here. He doesn't know for sure you're here. If you hide under your bed, or in the closet—"

"Nonsense," Mary said. She was looking around the room too. "I have a better idea." She was looking for something rod-shaped, and reasonably massive, and about a meter long. "Why don't *you* hide—" A chair leg? No. Some of the chairs here had central spines, like the bacteriophage, and all of them had wheels. Take a slat out of the futon frame? Not in the time available. Ha: Don Quixote standing among the houseplants, tall and thin and made of some kind of wood. He would probably do. Mary took him by the head, shifting her fingers to find a reasonable place to grip. Which way did the door open? *That* way.

"Okay," she said. "Let's you hide in the kitchen." Did that wide base come off? Yes, it did. "I'll be behind the door."

Greg hesitated for a moment. "All right. It looks like our best chance. Good luck, love."

He backed up and wheeled toward the kitchen, while Mary took the folded futon and turned it ninety degrees to the wall. Kneeling on it, she leaned over the back to reach Greg. They kissed gently for a moment. Then the system went off again: "Security alert! Security alert! Sported oak is under attack!"

"I know," Greg said. "Hush." The system hushed. Greg's hand tightened on Mary's arm for a moment and then let her go. He wheeled into the kitchen while Mary took her place at the right side of the door.

Let's see. When Nick got through the interior door, he would have the console right ahead of him, the futon on his left (blocking his way into the kitchen), on his right the open door with Mary behind it. Was there—yes, there was a security camera above the console, nestling just under the ceiling. If Nick looked in the screen, would he see her? She'd have to make sure he didn't.

The screen flashed, SPORTED OAK COMPROMISED, and the picture changed to show Nick opening the outer door and starting to work on the inner one. What in hell was a sported oak, anyway? The door, or the system that was supposed to protect it? The camera in the entry showed Nick, flashlight in one hand, punching at the keypad by the door. Whatever one mind could encode, another mind could solve, and Nick was Greg's equal in the hacking-and-entering line. Wasn't there a deadbolt to this door? Yes, but it too was connected to the security system, and she couldn't see any way of jamming it, not to open on command. Damn! Greg must've wanted to enable it to let help in if he was immobilized for any reason and all alone. ENTRY DOOR UNDER ATTACK, said the screen. Well, if they lived through all this, he wasn't going to be alone any more and she'd see to it that door got a real live deadbolt.

ENTRY DOOR DISABLED, the screen said. Instead of bursting through at once, he stopped to put his flashlight back in his pocket and to take something else from another pocket. Then he pushed the door open. The picture switched to the camera above the console, giving Nick a fine view of himself and Mary an adequate one. Oh, God, he was carrying a gun.

He looked at the terminal, looked up to the camera above it (the mask rimmed his eyes with circles of angry red). He raised the gun and shot it out. CAMERA 29 COMPROMISED, said the screen, and another image appeared, showing Nick from the left; it was the one over the kitchen door. Nick turned toward it, and Mary stepped from behind the door, Don Quixote poised beside her shoulder. Nick heard something and began to turn back; Mary brought the statue around into his head. It made a horrid crisp sound like a dropped melon. Nick's knees began to buckle as he fired; broken glass chimed. Nick fell in a heap. Mary started checking things out: No, the bullet hadn't hit the computer; no, it hadn't hit her anywhere that she could tell; look, it had gone through the window. The slats hung at a funny angle. The bullet had taken one of the tapes with it; the police would have to search the atrium for the damn thing.

Mary turned away from the window. Greg had come out of the kitchen and sat half-hidden by the futon. Mary gave him a shaky thumbs-up. They were still looking at Nick, wondering if they should move him, when the police arrived.

Then it was hours of pictures taken, questions answered, calls made (by PB cellular; Greg's phone was still not up) to other departments. Paramedics came in and took Nick away, saying he would live to stand trial and even to serve a nice long sentence if required. Then it was more questions, more photos, Don Quixote confiscated as evidence, along with Nick's gun and ski mask, and relevant data dumped to a datacell from Greg's system and the building's, until Greg and Mary were almost ready to wonder why they had been so glad to see the officers when they had first shown up. Greg found a moment (while they were all watching Nick shoot out the camera and Mary clock him with Don Quixote) to whisper in Mary's ear, "As soon as you can get away, go get your mini out of the Triple A. Bring it to the parking lot that this building backs onto."

Mary could only nod, not ask why, because there were questions again. "Do you think," a plainclothesman asked, "that you had any *good reason* for thinking that Mr. Carter intended to harm you?"

"Well," said Mary. (Where did they get these idiots, anyway?) "In the context of everything that's happened since Sunday night, yes, I think I had." And looking at the list in a companion's hand-held, the plainclothesman had to admit that there was maybe some supporting evidence. Eventually they all went away. Astonishing: It was still only seven a.m.

"Your mini," Greg said. "How early do those guys open?"

"Eight, I think. It'll take me a while to get there by bus anyway."

"Okay." His fingers were tapping on the edge of the keyboard. "Whatever you can do. Only drive carefully; the commute traffic's already moving in."

"Parking lot, right? Greg, do I still have to watch out for the Grey Knight?"

"I doubt it; he should sleep for hours yet." But Mary kept an eye out anyway. The people on the bus seemed the usual run of morning commuters; they looked at her with as much suspicion as she did them. (She must still look pretty scungy.) She got her mini out and drove it by back streets to the parking lot; it was full of minis now. She let a bus pull out of the stop by the back wall and pulled into it. "Greg?"

A hand appeared atop the wall, and Greg pulled himself up to a Kilroy-was-here position. "Hi. You'll have to pull me the rest of the way over. Then pull on this."

"No problem." She boosted him over the wall and

set him in the passenger's seat. "This" was a long electrical cord, draped over the wall, its other end knotted through an arm of Greg's chair. From there it ran to a small duffel bag that clattered when she lifted it. She folded the chair and put everything in the narrow storage compartment in the back. "Where are we going?"

"Nick's place."

"Won't we find the police already there?"

"They didn't ask me for his address and I didn't tell 'em. His phone number is aliased. They're going to have to look in the tax records, which will take a little while; we might make it."

She glanced at him while they waited for a traffic light. Greg was pulling on thin latex gloves. "Greg, are we about to do something illegal?"

He looked thoughtful. "We're not breaking and entering; I know the door codes. We're not going to steal anything."

"It's still unlawful entry."

"Probably. They might even make out a case for obstructing justice, even though we're not obstructing anything in the slightest. It's in a good cause. Just don't get a speeding ticket; that could get awkward."

Nick's house was in a neighborhood that had been an elegant suburb a generation ago, then urban; now the buildings were thinning out as arson took them out or earth-shielded dwellings replaced them, and the district was going rural again. There was a woodlot to one side, and the house on the other had all its shades drawn. Greg scooted up the walk and punched a code into the door; it opened and they slipped inside. "Don't touch anything. Oh, good, it's up." He typed for a few minutes, inserted a datacell from the collection in his bag, and made impatient cranking motions at the side of the screen while filenames scrolled over it.

"What are you getting?"

"Nick's bag of tricks. I fought him wizard-to-wizard and won them fair and square. And I'm not depriving him of their use—though he's not going to get much use out of them now."

The datacell filled, and Greg checked its filelist and took it out of the drive. "So Nick hasn't sold his machine after all," Mary commented, "and the Grey Knight was logged in from here."

"Uh-huh. He's sold off most of his processor boards, though. I don't think you could run a VR on this system anymore, only log through to another one. But let's see." He took his plugs in their little plastic pouch out of his bags and plugged in. After a long several seconds he sighed, unplugged, and said to Mary, "It's a sad sight. Here are your plugs; no, don't touch the console. Just take a look for a moment."

Mary plugged in and stepped inside. She stood in an atrium the size of a Victorian police-box, its single door standing open.

The room inside, windowless and the size of a modest motel room, was stacked and piled and heaped with virtual things, as if the furnishings of an entire castle had been gathered into a little cell. Nick's armor stood near the door, Nightgaunt's bridle hanging from one gauntlet. A book lay open on the tiny patch of visible floor; as Greg had said, he had not stolen it, only copied it. Tables and benches, piled high, fine garments and jewelry and bows and swords, golden plates and crystal bottles and a falcon that seemed asleep.

Another door appeared on the opposite wall and opened. A woman stood there, tall, blonde, broad shouldered. Her beautiful face was no composite, but Mary would have priced its enhancements at several thousand marks. She stood motionless in her black cloak, looking at the remnants of Nick's life; then she sighed and closed her door again. The shape of it faded into blankness against the wall.

Mary stepped outside again, unplugged, and shook her head. "And you still don't know why?"

"I got only the briefest glance at his finances," Greg said. "Not really my business. But there were an awful lot of airline tickets to Nevada. The police will figure it out; speaking of whom—" He detached Mary's plugs, coiled them and stowed them away. "Okay, I've diddled the security and the system log; we've never been here. Check the peephole."

"All clear."

They got into the mini still unseen and sped away. The next address was an office in a small industrial park south of town along Highway 101. There was no sign in front of the place, and the windows were all curtained. "This is where the *Golden Road* machine is?"

"Right."

"And why are we here? More wizards' trophies?"

"No, for an even stranger reason. *The Golden Road* is a beautiful system. It's using material of Markheim's that it has no right to, but the software is a work of art. When the police get here they'll confiscate the hardware as evidence and hold it till the trial is over, plus time for several appeals. By the time they put it up for sale, the system will have degenerated. I want an archive copy before that happens."

"But you can't use it."

"I can't use anything of Markheim's. I can use the rest of the code, part of which is mine anyway. Even if I couldn't, it would be worth it. Let's move."

Again Greg keyed the door open unchallenged. Inside was a small sage-green box, a tall extended-memory bank against one wall, and a console where a young man slept with his head pillowed on his arms. The red hair was just beginning to grow back on his temples. "Cripes," Mary whispered. "It's Charlie. I should have fingered him before this: that cocky style. And pretending to be a newcomer, and faking everything—"

"I had just about decided there must be somebody else in on this," Greg whispered back, "somebody in the salle. Nick couldn't have been stealing that car in Mountain View and throwing rocks at you in San José at the same time. I had no way of knowing exactly whom to suspect. But now here he is. We could just leave him asleep for the police to find. I can work over his shoulder, if you'll hand me the datacells. Or you could show him charity and wake him up and give him a chance to get away."

"Me?"

"You can do it, or not. It's a question of whether you can forgive him. I won't interfere."

"He tried to kill me."

"Yes, I know," he said, and waited.

"Oh, hell," Mary said after a moment. "You are being a very bad influence on me." And she reached down to shake Charlie's shoulders. "Wake up! Wake up, you little stinker."

The redhead grunted in his sleep and moved his head back and forth over his arms. Then he mumbled, "Oh, all right," and sat up. He got his eyes open and focused them on Mary. Slowly an expression of terror developed on his face.

"Hey, unplug," Mary said. "If you jump up and run you'll hurt yourself badly. Oh, here." The kid's hands were shaking. Mary unplugged him. "Now listen, the following is true. Nick's under arrest. The police are looking for this place. They haven't found it yet, but they will."

"They'll find it in the NIC," Greg said.

"You think he'll tell them? Is he even awake yet?"

"No, no. Network Information Center. They'll get the Internet address from the data I gave them and the geographical coordinates from the NIC. It'll depend on how long it takes them to think of it. I didn't give 'em any hints."

"So okay, the cops are on their way. It would probably be discreet of you to leave now, while you can." The youngster got to his feet and backed toward the door. "Oh, go on. Get out of my sight. And for Pete's sake go and sin no more." He turned, snatched the door open, and was gone. "Okay?"

"Very okay," Greg said, opening the bag he held in his lap. "Enter 'shutdown 5' on the console, please? It'll take longer than that but I want the users off the system. Gosh! I hope I brought enough datacells."

"I've got six or seven gig empty on my home system, if you want to send some of it out," Mary said. She typed in the command. The console screen said, "Attention: The system is going down in 5 minutes."

"Thanks. I may, though this stuff should compress fairly well. But it would give us an excuse to go to your place instead of mine, where people might come and ask us some more questions." He fed in the first datacell and watched it begin to fill. At this rate they might finish and escape to Gilroy before the rest of the students arrived at the salle—she'd have to run the whole show today. She kept an ear out for sirens, but there were none so far. Greg was humming under his breath; it took Mary a while to recognize the prisoners' song from *Fidelio*. He was busting Theodoric out of jail again.

Chapter 13

Coda

On Christmas Eve Mary let herself into Greg's apartment to find he had not gotten home yet. She set down some presents wrapped in bright paper as well as a disk full of virtual presents (the latter had been by far the more expensive), and went into the kitchen to mull cider. Cinnamon sticks, broken between the fingers; nutmeg crushed under the mallet; shredded ginger; whole cloves slightly abused by the same mallet: The place was fragrant with the aromatics even before the cider warmed. And Greg came in, incongruous in suit and tie. "So what's the news?"

"News. Well. Nick woke up."

"Did he! Is he going to be all right?"

"They think so. He's talking and making sense."

"Did he finger the Queen?"

"He *says* he never met her outside and doesn't know her real name. It may even be true."

"Well, it doesn't surprise me," Greg said. "She always was a shadowy figure, even in the book; you could never put a finger on her. Whoever she is in the real world, anyone who chose that persona, I'm not surprised that she's melted back into shadow and can't be found." He wheeled toward his bedroom, pulling the tie from his neck as he went. Mary followed with one of her packages.

"Here, this is an open-first. So what happened with your meeting? Were they really Mafia?"

"Do I know? They were three guys from New York. They *said* they were lawyers. Thank you, love. What is this?" It was yet another T-shirt, deep blue and batiked with veins of gold like lapis lazuli. "They were certainly related by blood, and I suspect they own a lot of property. Are they the guys who bought off Nick's share of London last year? I think so. If they are Mafiosi, they're not the men their great-grandfathers were. Cultures do change over time. This lot don't do machine-guns in garages, they do leveraged buyouts. They wanted to know if London was a *safe* investment after the scandal and the current downtrends. So I gave 'em all the economic cycle stuff you fed me, and I told them I thought London would weather all its present difficulties and survive to make a profit. But I looked very serious while I said it.

"So they said they're going to have to think about it, and could I give them the name of a local broker who handles VR property? Just to get a second opinion?"

"And you gave 'em Kamaguchi's number."

"I did. I think we'll get it all back, but it's too soon to tell. Any other news at your end?"

"News? They're still evacuating Miami, mostly by boat. People they interviewed were saying they're never coming back, which since the sea's still rising may be true. Oh, yes, and Charlie Graham turned himself in in Arcata."

"See? He was inspired by your example."

"Or else somebody pointed out he could get off easy by turning state's evidence. Oh, and I talked to Chandra; he says every seat at the salle is booked. It's going to be quite a turnout. Speaking of which—"

"Oh, Lord, look at the time. We're late." He scooted up to the console and plugged in. Mary put in her disk and followed.

The great hall of the guest house at St. Alban's—Greg had finished writing it only last week—was filling up with guests. Overhead long swags of evergreen branches hung down from the beams, ribboned with penitential purple, filling the air with the cold scent of resin. In the center a green wreath floated, parallel to the floor, its one pink and three purple candles burnt down to stubs. Advent was almost over.

At the far end of the hall a huge Yule log burned on the hearth, something you couldn't do in real life anymore. A chance air-current brought her a whiff of woodsmoke. Though she was too far away to see them, she knew the flames were full of dancing salamanders.

At this end, monks in linen aprons were setting up trestle tables and spreading them with cloths. Every time the kitchen door swung open, wonderful smells leaked out: cinnamon and ginger and roasting meat.

Because Christmas Eve was a fast day in the Middle Ages, none of it would appear until midnight: not long now.

Mary circulated for a while, greeting people, avoiding one or two, overhearing snatches of conversation.

"So where's Nick? I haven't seen him for weeks."

(A shrug.) "Oh, you know. He's got life."

(It would probably be more like ten years; but the trial wouldn't come up till he could get up and about.)

"For two days he raged through York like a paladin, righting wrongs and slaying monsters and generally lighting up the dark corners; and then he disappeared. I mean, *poof* like that, disappeared."

"Monsters? In York? Where'd they come from?"

"I dunno, but one of the guys he killed was a PC who turned out to be one of the owners."

(Mmmm. Maybe York would go on the market too; they'd have to put a consortium together if they wanted to buy it.)

She looked over the crowd for Greg. There he was, talking to Chandra and some of the others who had logged in from the San José salle d'armes. He looked very fine in his emerald-green cotte with the flowing leafy-edged sleeves: it was the first piece of coding Mary had done since college and she had sweated blood over it, but it had turned out rather well.

"Uh, excuse me, Ms. Craven—or should I say 'Sir Mary'?"

"Probably, since we're inside. What can I do for you?"

"I wanted to ask—" the man looked from side to

side, as if to deter eavesdroppers. He was tall, muscular, and heroic-looking to an extent that was downright boring; a dungeoncrawler, she would bet. "I wanted to ask you if St. Chad's is ever going to come back. I had a lot of fun there and I miss it."

"The short answer is, 'Maybe.' We can't find the name of the guy who hacked St. Chad's into the Winchester domain. If you wanted to go to the police with data on how you heard about it and who you sent your check to, why, they might find out. But nobody's going to make you. Meanwhile, the Duke of Winchester and the remaining owners of London have sort of arbitrarily decided St. Chad's belongs to me because I won it in honorable combat, and I've got it on a datacell. I have been considering bringing it up, running it as a small business. I'd have to get a bigger machine.

"Anyway, if I do, I'll advertise in *Dragon* and *Netrunner's Digest* and so on; you'll see it. Or—Brother!" A soft-footed monk appeared at her elbow. "You can give Brother your mundane name and address and we'll send you a notice. And if you hang around here till midnight, I think you'll see a little magic. Now, if you'll excuse me—"

It must be almost midnight now; the monks were coming out with the wine cups and the platters of virtual food that had taken up most of Greg's time during all of Advent. Mary had alpha-tested most of it. Yes, here came the chief cook, his face flushed with the heat of his cooking-fires, mopping at his sweating tonsure with a napkin.

And behind him two strong monks carried in a platter big enough to curl up and take a nap on, and on it, the baron of beef: something else you couldn't do in real life any more. The entire hindquarter and thigh of an ox that had never walked in Altamont Pass, its tissues carefully crafted from the results of two long test sessions with Greg's steaks, fifty virtual kilos of it. The guests murmured with astonishment and delight. Later, she'd ask everyone for critiques; obviously the smell was right. Where was Greg? There he was.

"All right," she said as she reached his side. "Why do you keep watching that door?"

"Why, because I hope to see some people coming through it; why else?" He took her hand and tucked it into the crook of his arm. (Chandra eyed them sharply, and politely looked away. Those of their friends who had expected Brother Gregory's laicization party to be an engagement party as well had been as disappointed as they were premature.) And somewhere overhead a bell began to ring.

On the second stroke the eastern door opened and several people came through it: a knight from Lyme Regis whom Mary knew slightly, his lady, and another couple she didn't know, (three!) and a tall old man in a scarlet robe. The fabric was a Byzantine silk and the gold embroidery was thick on the sleeves, but the cut was simple: the garment might have belonged to Charlemagne. And the face was familiar; she had seen it somewhere, a face like an elderly Abraham Lincoln, or a kempt George Bernard Shaw.

The bell sounded a fourth time. "Greg! Is that Professor Markheim?"

"I hoped he'd show up." (Five.)

"How on earth? He hates the idea of surgery, he never would've done it just to come to a party." (Six.)

"Ah," Greg said. "Last week InterCom got permission to start beta-testing the induction plugs." (Seven.) "I know a guy at InterCom who lent me several sets. And I know another guy in Lyme Regis who knows some people at Princeton who know the Professor." (Eight.) "He said he'd see what he could do. Obviously, he did."

"So are you going to give the Professor a guided tour through *The Golden Road*?" (Nine.)

"I'm going to let him know he can have one if he likes," Greg said. "But not till the end of the party. Look." (Ten.) The tall Professor was looking around the hall, smiling and nodding, stretching out his hand to the nearest candleflame and drawing it back from the heat. (Eleven.) "He's been playing with the SCA for nearly fifty years; he's going to enjoy this."

The great bell sounded the twelfth stroke, and a chorus of little bells started cascading downhill like raindrops. The ribbons on all the evergreens turned from purple to white; brothers with long poles moved from pillar to pillar lighting more candles. Overhead the Advent wreath had regenerated from its stubs four tall white candles tipped with gold. A little pinwheel was turning above them, sending out starry sparks that drifted along the beams and descended to the guests, sprinkling their hair and shoulders with stars of gold. And a sound cut through it all, the first cockcrow of midnight, saying plainly, "*Christus natus est*," for those who had the Latin.

Science Fiction Anthologies

☐ **FIRST CONTACT**
Martin H. Greenberg and Larry Segriff, editors UE2757—$5.99

In the tradition of the hit television show "The X-Files" comes a fascinating collection of original stories by some of the premier writers of the genre, such as Jody Lynn Nye, Kristine Kathryn Rusch, and Jack Haldeman.

☐ **RETURN OF THE DINOSAURS**
Mike Resnick and Martin H. Greenberg, editors UE2753—$5.99

Dinosaurs walk the Earth once again in these all-new tales that dig deep into the past and blaze trails into the possible future. Join Gene Wolfe, Melanie Rawn, David Gerrold, Mike Resnick, and others as they breathe new life into ancient bones.

☐ **BLACK MIST:** and Other Japanese Futures
Orson Scott Card and Keith Ferrell, editors UE2767—$5.99

Original novellas by Richard Lupoff, Patric Helmaan, Pat Cadigan, Paul Levinson, and Janeen Webb & Jack Dann envision how the wide-ranging influence of Japanese culture will change the world.

☐ **THE UFO FILES**
Martin H. Greenberg, editor UE2772—$5.99

Explore close encounters of a thrilling kind in these stories by Gregory Benford, Ed Gorman, Peter Crowther, Alan Dean Foster, and Kristine Kathryn Rusch.

Prices slightly higher in Canada. **DAW 104X**

Buy them at your local bookstore or use this convenient coupon for ordering.

PENGUIN USA P.O. Box 999—Dep. #17109, Bergenfield, New Jersey 07621

Please send me the DAW BOOKS I have checked above, for which I am enclosing $_______________ (please add $2.00 to cover postage and handling). Send check or money order (no cash or C.O.D.'s) or charge by Mastercard or VISA (with a $15.00 minimum). Prices and numbers are subject to change without notice.

Card #_______________ Exp. Date _______________
Signature_______________
Name_______________
Address_______________
City _______________ State _______________ Zip Code _______________

For faster service when ordering by credit card call **1-800-253-6476**

Allow a minimum of 4-6 weeks for delivery. This offer is subject to change without notice.

C.S. Friedman

☐ **IN CONQUEST BORN** UE2198—$6.99

☐ **THE MADNESS SEASON** UE2444—$5.99

The Coldfire Trilogy

☐ **BLACK SUN RISING (Book 1)** UE2527—$6.99
Hardcover Edition: UE2485—$18.95

Centuries after being stranded on the planet Ema, humans have achieved an uneasy stalemate with the *Fae*, a terrifying natural force with the power to prey upon people's minds. Now, as the hordes of the *fae* multiply, four people—Priest, Adept, Apprentice, and Sorcerer—are drawn inexorably together to confront an evil beyond imagining.

☐ **WHEN TRUE NIGHT FALLS (Book 2)** UE2615—$5.99
Hardcover Edition: UE2569—$22.00

Determined to seek out and destroy the source of the *fae*'s ever-strengthening evil, Damien Vryce, the warrior priest, and Gerald Tarrant, the undead sorcerer, dare the treacherous crossing of the planet's greatest ocean to confront a power that threatens the very essence of the human spirit.

☐ **CROWN OF SHADOWS (Book 3)** UD2717—$6.99
Hardcover Edition: UE2664—$21.95

The demon Calesta has declared war on all mankind. Only Damien Vryce, and his unlikely ally, the undead sorcerer Gerald Tarrant stand between Calesta and his triumph. Faced with an enemy who may prove invulnerable—pitted against not only Calesta, but the leaders of the Church and the Hunter's last descendent—Damien and Tarrant must risk everything in a battle which could cost them not only their lives, but the soul of all mankind.

Prices slightly higher in Canada. **DAW 140X**

Buy them at your local bookstore or use this convenient coupon for ordering.

PENGUIN USA P.O. Box 999—Dep. #17109, Bergenfield, New Jersey 07621

Please send me the DAW BOOKS I have checked above, for which I am enclosing $__________ (please add $2.00 to cover postage and handling). Send check or money order (no cash or C.O.D.'s) or charge by Mastercard or VISA (with a $15.00 minimum). Prices and numbers are subject to change without notice.

Card #__________ Exp. Date __________
Signature__________
Name__________
Address__________
City __________ State __________ Zip Code __________

For faster service when ordering by credit card call **1-800-253-6476**

Allow a minimum of 4-6 weeks for delivery. This offer is subject to change without notice.